For my unknown grandfather, Private John Edward Reed,
and my grandchildren.

Author's Note

Many thanks to Whitby Archives for allowing me access to much valuable material, particularly concerning the wreck of the *Rohilla*, and the bombardment of Whitby in December, 1914.

To Reason Why

By the same author

Angel's War
Mirror on the Wall
Mirror Images

To Reason Why

C.W. REED

ROBERT HALE · LONDON

© C.W. Reed 1998
First published in Great Britain 1998

ISBN 0 7090 6277 X

Robert Hale Limited
Clerkenwell House
Clerkenwell Green
London EC1R 0HT

2 4 6 8 10 9 7 5 3 1

Typeset in North Wales by
Derek Doyle & Associates, Mold, Flintshire.
Printed in Great Britain by
St Edmundsbury Press, Bury St Edmunds, Suffolk.
Bound by WBC Book Manufacturers Limited, Bridgend.

From bank and shop, from bench and mill,
From the schools, from the tail of the plow,
They hurried away at the call of the fray,
They could not linger a day, and now, –
                    They are making history.
                            In Church, 1916 John Oxenham

PART I – Yesterday

ONE

M AY AND HER friend, Nelly Dunn, had gone into St Thomas's to get out of the rain. They had expected to find the place deserted, on the Saturday afternoon of Newcastle's Race Week. They had come from the 'hoppings', the fair on the Town Moor, which had all but dissolved into a sea of mud, despite the fact that it was the third week in June.

'Ah feel like one o' them poor drownded souls on the *Titanic*,' Nelly grumbled.

'Don't make jokes about it,' May answered automatically.

May was not keen to enter the cold, sanctified stillness of the church, with its dark, massive stones and pillars, soaring pinnacles and arches, the lofty timbers of the high nave. It overwhelmed her. It was so different from the plain, whitewashed homeliness of the chapel she attended every Sunday, the unpretentiousness of its grimy, four-square solidity. Besides, their best boots were filthy, coated with mud.

But Nelly insisted she wanted to say a prayer for her Aunty Ginny, who was seriously ill, had never 'been right' since the birth of her eighth child. In a show of independence, May refused to join her kneeling in the pew, and remained in the shadows by the font, studying the polished plaques in the dim light. She jumped with genuine fright at the startling, cheerful voice addressing her from the darkness, and the dramatic appearance of the two young men in working clothes, from a narrow doorway that led up to the tower.

11

'Hey up, Jack! Looks like there are angels after all.' The speaker was Arthur Mackay – 'Arty to me friends.' – but it was his companion, the taller, shyer one, who immediately captured May's attention. It was a natural pairing, she thought later. Arty and the blonde, extrovert Nelly were made for each other. May was much more attuned to the other one – 'This young shaver's Jack Wright. You'll come to no harm with him, miss. A proper toff, he is.'

The more they talked, the more she became convinced that Arthur's joking remarks bore more than a grain of truth. He spoke so nicely, the local accent so muted, hardly noticeable at all. And the way he put his words together – he was clearly well educated. And living out at Low Fell. South of the river, on the southern edge of Gateshead, it was more like a village, way out of town. They'd only just extended the tramlines out that way. She was impressed, and a little disappointed. A cut above you, lass, she admonished herself.

It was a feeling which grew when he told her his father ran his own small printing business, along with his older brother, Daniel. 'I'm an apprentice – to Waller's. They do restoration work, on churches. Any old buildings. Stonework, woodwork, the lot. It's really interesting.' She saw his eyes light up, and was surprised at the strength of her own sympathetic liking for his enthusiasm. 'I want to learn all I can.'

'Doesn't your dad – ah mean – don't you want to work for him?'

He shook his head quickly. 'He's already got Dan with him. It's only a small firm, not enough to keep all of us. Anyway, it's not what I want. I like what I'm doing,' he ended simply, and flushed a little.

She nodded. 'That's good.'

May and Nelly sat on the open upper deck of the clanking, grinding tramcar. The slatted wooden seats were still speckled with raindrops and they'd had to wipe them with their hankies before they could sit, but they always preferred to ride upstairs whenever they could, and downstairs was packed, with people standing and treading on one another's toes. The breeze stirring about them

12

would help to complete the drying of their damp clothes, and they enjoyed the view from up above, sailing through the Saturday crowds, the wagons and carts, and the motors which were so much an everyday part of the busy city centre these days.

They rattled over the High Level Bridge and began the steep, labouring ascent of West Street, at the top of which they would alight. Secretly, May was more than a little disappointed that Jack Wright was not riding with them, for this was the car he would have taken, though he would have remained on board for a further couple of miles to the terminus itself. She hoped he had not merely been making excuses when he had said he had a few errands to do before returning home. She didn't think so. After all, he wouldn't have asked to see her again if that was the case. And he had made it plain that he was keen, falling in eagerly with Arthur's proposal that all four should meet up the following day.

'Why don't we meet at the monument? Bottom of Westgate Road? You can get off the tram there. We'll have a look round the shops and that. Mebbes go for a drink.' He saw the dawning look on May's face, and added quickly, 'Ah mean a cup of tea or summat. Not tryin' to lead you lasses astray.' He roared with laughter, and Nelly delightedly slapped at his arm.

'You are a one!'

He probably was, May surmised, though she had only a vague notion of what 'a one' was. Jack Wright wasn't, that was for sure. But she didn't mind. Not in the least. As she bade goodbye to Nelly on the street and headed up towards her own holystoned step and glinting front door, she was taken aback at the excitement coursing through her at the prospect of seeing him again so soon.

That first Sunday, the day after their initial meeting, May felt nervous and uncertain, half wondering if she should go at all. What on earth must he think of her, agreeing to go out with someone so easily, after a chance encounter like that? She voiced her doubts to Nelly, who overrode her with her usual scorn. 'Don't talk daft! He's a canny lad, isn't he? Even if he *does* talk swanky.' It was clear that

Nelly was eager to meet up again with Arty. 'Come on, May. It'll be a right laugh!'

She had never had a man friend before. And that was how she felt towards him, from their very first time out together. At home, everyone treated her very much as though she were a child. And that included her younger siblings. And with Nelly – well, she could hardly get a sensible word out of her these days. It was all lads, lads, lads. Or sniggering gossip about what her work-mates had told her. She was hard put to hide her blushes sometimes at the shocking things Nelly came out with. She had an uncomfortable feeling that half the time that's why Nelly came out with them, just to see how much she could shock her. It irritated May to the point where her fingers curled with the desire to slap her pretty face and wipe off that superior, worldly expression. Nelly lorded the fact that she was out in the wide world now, while May was still at home, tied to her mother's apron strings, an ignorant girl still. It was no comfort that May felt she might well have a point.

It was so different with Jack Wright As she strolled on his arm through the city streets which were free from the weekday chaos of commercial traffic, stopping to gaze into the impressive frontage of Fenwick's windows, stretching on and on, in Northumberland Street, she chattered away twenty to the dozen, until she pulled herself up, with an embarrassed little laugh, her cheeks pink. 'Tell me to shut up!' she murmured. 'Me tongue's running away with me!'

But he smiled, and it thrilled her, the way his face lit up, and those warm, gentle eyes. It caught her by surprise, that feeling. It was so strong, so sudden. She felt it many times after that. She didn't want the afternoon to end. He looked so good, and really smart in his soft felt hat, the dark striped lounge suit with its neat, cut away jacket, and the buttoned waistcoat beneath, with the silver loop of his watch chain.

There was nothing flashy about him. Not like Arty, with his rattan cane with silver tipped handle, and his straw boater, which he kept taking off and twirling about like a minstrel in a show. But she could tell from the style of his clothing, as well as his manners, and that lovely, deep speaking-voice of his, that Jack came from a good background, one – the thought troubled her already – above her own.

She wondered if that was the reason neither of them said anything at home about their meeting. Or was it because she was shaken by the depth of emotion he aroused in her, when he was still little better than a stranger?

But, after two weeks, they were walking up Windmill Hill, when he suddenly stopped. His fingers plucked at the tassles of her shawl.

'Listen. I want you to come home. On Sunday. Meet my folks.' He could feel the tension in her frame.

'Oh, I don't know. Do you not think—'

'I think it's time they knew about you,' he said firmly. 'I want them to. I want to go on seeing you. Walking out.' His arm squeezed her shoulder, drew her into him.

'Won't they mind? P'raps we should wait—'

'No, I don't think so. Not really. I like you an awful lot, May. I want us to be real friends. Close. I don't like keeping it a secret.'

She nodded. She glanced at him, sadly, and he leaned forward, pursed his lips and kissed her lightly on her cheek. 'It'll be all right. I'll be with you. Then I'll have to go through the same thing with your folks!'

'This first scene is of the biggest lake, Lake Windermere,' Mr Wright announced. The family dutifully ah-ed and ooh-ed, though they had seen the twelve slides of the Lake District series several times before. The tinted image flickered a little on the stretched sheet which had been pinned at one end of the lounge. The acetyline gas hissed softly from the burners beneath the instrument, which had taken such a long time to prepare, with Dan and Jack hovering about their father, and even the thirteen-year-old Joe offering advice on the fringes.

'Oh, they'll be ages!' Jack's sister, Cissy, said scornfully. She was two months younger than May, her eighteenth birthday coming up that October. She was studying at a Business School. 'Pa's going to take me on as his lady typist, aren't you, pa?' she laughed.

'He certainly is not,' Mrs Wright declared.

May ought to have been comforted somewhat, in view of Mrs Wright's disapproval of young ladies working, when, in answer to Cissy's lively question, 'What do you do, May?' she answered inadequately, 'Nothing', but she was not.

It wasn't Cissy's fault that May was feeling so leadenly miserable inside. She and her brothers were doing their best to appear friendly towards her. She didn't mind Dan's condescending, older brother's attitude, or his teasing, young blade's over-familiarity. Even Jack's father tried to jolly her along, make her relax a little. But against the icy politeness and withering superiority of the matriarch of the household, their efforts blew away like rattling dead leaves.

'Jack's invited some workman's lass for tea on Sunday!' she had told her husband earlier in the week. 'Her father works in the ship-yards, you said?' She turned to her second son, whose thin face flushed deeply.

'That's right, mam. Her father's a carpenter and joiner. At Swan Hunter's.'

Dan and Cissy seemed to think it 'a bit of a gas' that their quiet, introspective brother should have behaved so surprisingly, but their mother could see nothing to smile about.

'It's that stupid job he's taken up with. No better than a common navvy! You shouldn't have allowed it, Ted! You should have made him come into the workshop with you and Dan!'

'It's no good forcing the lad to do something he's no heart for,' he urged her patiently. 'Besides, you know there's not enough for him to do there.'

'And whose fault is that?' Sophia queried sharply. 'There's no reason why you can't get more business, is there? Find more work to do. Make it grow!'

'Now, Sophy, we do very well out of it. I've enough on my plate as it is.' A secret guilt that maybe she was right to hint that he was not ambitious enough made him almost equally sharp in his reply. She was a strong-minded woman, though, he'd give her that. He might never have plucked up the nerve to make the move to start the business off his own bat. He began to feel sorry for Jack. And the little lass his son had invited round for tea. 'Best not make too much fuss, Sophy,' he cautioned. 'He's a young man now, love. Finding his feet.' He chuckled encouragingly. 'There'll be plenty more young lasses, I expect, eh? Look at our Dan.'

'Really, Ted! I'm surprised at you. Some guttersnipe from the bottom end of Gateshead, and he has the cheek to invite her into our home.'

'We don't know anything about her. And she's not exactly a guttersnipe, is she? Her father's a carpenter. A skilled tradesman. I was only an apprentice myself—'

'It's not the same at all, Ted and you know it. We don't know her from Adam. Picked up off the street. He hasn't known her five minutes—'

'Well, you know our Jack. He's a sensible lad. He's not the type to go gallivanting now, is he?' He added warningly, 'He can be stubborn, too, when he makes his mind up. The more fuss you make, the more likely he is to get a bee in his bonnet about it. Best take no notice. It'll blow over.'

Under cover of the dimmed lights, while they watched the clanking procession of slides flicker up on the screen, Jack sought May's hand, to give it a surreptitiously supportive squeeze. Her palm was clammy with sweat, but she returned his grip fiercely. She breathed deeply against the tight restrictions of her corset. Why should she feel ashamed? He wasn't ashamed of her, that was obvious.

When the magic lantern had been cleared away, and the lights were turned up again, the younger members of the family gathered round the piano. 'Do you play, er – May?' She even managed to make her name sound laughable, May thought, writhing with secret chagrin.

'No. We haven't got a piano. We've got a gramophone, though,' she added, with a hint of challenge.

'I bet you play that beautifully!' Dan laughed, and May felt the muscles of her cheeks ache as she stretched them in a smile.

Cissy settled herself, after fishing piles of music sheets from the interior of the plush-covered stool. At Mrs Wright's insistence, they started off with some hymns, in deference to the Sabbath. 'We're chapel. Wesleyan,' May answered uncomfortably, in reply to Sophia's question.

'Good for you!' Ted cried, a shade too enthusiastically, earning a veiled glance of disapproval from his wife. 'So are we!' He ignored the black mark of that look, and led them through several of his favourites, in a sturdy baritone.

Cissy played some pieces by Mendelssohn and other popular classics, until Dan commanded, 'Out of the way, wench!' and bumped Cissy unceremoniously from her perch with his hip. He set up the large *Hundred Favourite Songs* on the stand. 'Now let's have a real singsong, eh?'

'We're in for a real treat now!' Cissy said mockingly, but he vamped the chords loudly, and soon they were all joining in, bellowing for all they were worth. 'A reg'lar, reg'lar, reg'lar reg'lar reg'lar royal queen!' they chorused, while, from the sofa, Mrs Wright shook her head with resigned indulgence.

'Something a bit more sparky,' Dan announced presently, shuffling through the sheet music scattered all about him. 'Ah! Here we are!' His dark eyebrows flickered as he gazed at May, and she blushed tellingly. 'Join in, everyone. With feeling.'

> If I could plant one tiny seed of love,
> In the garden of your heart,
> Would it grow to be a great big love some day,
> Or would it die and fade away. . . ?

TWO

MAY TOOK HER time walking back up the gentle but long hill that led back onto Durham Road. She had just left Jack after their Saturday stroll along the crowded paths of Saltwell Park. Despite the intense happiness she found in his company, she was in an unsettled, nervous mood. The implacable hostility of Mrs Wright had upset her deeply. And her own folks hadn't met him yet. That pleasure was due for them the following day. And she was far from certain of his reception.

She saw the crowd ahead of her, blocking the pavement beside the high green railings of the Labour Exchange, and heard the shrill tones of the women. A bit early for a drunken brawl, she thought. But it was a hot Saturday, and many of them, men and women, would have been drinking all afternoon, she guessed. She wondered if she should cross over before she reached them, pass by on the other side, but curiosity and excitement got the better of her, and she came up to the fringes of the small crowd.

She was surprised to see that the centre of the disturbance was a tall, well-dressed young woman, though her smart clothing was looking decidedly ruffled. Her bonnet was skew-whiff, and long strands of her deep chestnut hair had come loose and coiled about her face. There was a dirty smear on one cheek, through which the tears had runnelled.

A policeman had hold of her right arm, which he was raising quite roughly, clutched in both his red hands, as though about to drag her off. May noticed that he looked almost as flustered as the girl herself. She realized why when she heard a thin, scruffy-looking woman in ragged skirt and shawl call out, 'Howay, man! Give her ower to us! We'll soon teach her to gan hoyin' stones about! We'll put her in the horse trough an' give her a bit of a scrub up, eh, lasses?'

There were plenty who supported this suggestion, and who looked poised to carry out their plan, whether the constable approved or not.

'Aye, that's reet! Cool 'er off, the hoity-toity little madam!'

'I did it for you – us!' the girl amended hastily. Her voice, though strong, was unsteady, catchy with her sobs. The mob stirred, a spiky grass sod thudded in, struck the flinching girl on her shoulder, spattering dry earth and a cloud of dust over her neck, and the embroidered front of her light summer coat. The women closed in, egged on by a few red-faced men who were standing by waiting to see the fun, and whose breath rose fumily on the mellow air.

'That's enough now.' The policeman tried to make his voice resonant with the majesty of law, but did not succeed. 'If you'll just come along with me to the station, miss.' The girl may have been reluctant earlier, but now she looked as though she would like nothing better than to be allowed to accompany him anywhere.

The small. ferrety woman, a self-appointed ringleader, barred their way. 'Not afore we've showed 'er what we think of 'er votes for bloody women, eh, lasses?' Again, there was a jeering chorus of assent. The girl, who was half a head taller, cowered back as she reached out and swiped the stylish little bonnet off the head. The thick mane of hair fell in further disorder about the shoulders, tumbling in chestnut waves, and she gave a small cry of alarm, backing off against the wall.

Although her heart thudded, May pushed forward, thrusting herself between the girl and the bristling figure who was threatening further assault. She swivelled round, almost stumbling against the woman.

'Ah know this lass!' May asserted, trying to keep the tremor from her voice. 'She didn't mean any harm—'

'Harm?' There was a raucous screech of laughter from the harpie who was nose to nose with her. 'She comes round 'ere breakin' bloody winders an' screechin' and yellin'—'

'It's only the dole!' May answered roundly, and there were one or two hoots of agreement from the crowd. Her sudden intervention, and her physical barrier between the foremost of the crowd and the object of their aggression, made them pause. Now the constable was flanked by two young lasses. And that's all they were. And this other slip of a thing was no lah-di-dah agitator. She didn't even look like a Suffragette, nor did she sound like one.

'Look, let the bobby sort it out.' May grinned ingratiatingly. 'She'll get a good hiding off her pa when she gets home if nowt else!'

'They want lockin' up, the lot of them.'

'Daft beggars! The' want summat better to do.'

'Keep to your own sort, lass! We don't want no toffs round 'ere tellin' us what to do.'

But the real threat of physical violence had dissipated, and they moved aside. Not without reluctance on the part of the ferret-faced leader, who aimed a cuff at the back of the chestnut head as the trio made to move off, May clinging to the girl's other arm. She stooped and snatched up the bonnet, and they were safely out of the ring.

The girl was shaking, her breath still catching in sobs. May suddenly felt weak, trembling, too, her stomach churning. She scarcely knew what had possessed her to act so precipitately. Except the naked look of fear on the girl's flushed face, her helplessness before that baying pack.

'Thank you, thank you!' The girl's voice shook now with relief. She couldn't keep back the tears streaking her dirty face. 'I'm Iris Mayfield. I don't know you, do I?'

'No. That was a bit of a fib,' May smiled. She became aware that she was still holding on to the girl's arm, just as the policeman was still imprisoning her other arm, and she let go, with an apologetic little laugh.

'You're not one of them?' the constable enquired critically. His

21

long moustache twitched with distaste. May shook her head. He tugged at the tall girl's arm. 'Ah should have left you to them.' His helmeted head jerked back at the slowly dispersing group behind them. 'You don't know the trouble you cause, you lot. We don't need your sort in these parts.'

Iris Mayfield wiped at her grimy cheeks with her free hand. 'There's no need to hold onto me now, constable. I won't run away, I promise.' Her face was flushed. An interesting face, May thought. Handsome. Well bred. And her voice, with its impeccable accent, went with the looks, the general manner of her bearing. 'Are you going to arrest me?'

'I ought to, for sure. Give me your particulars.' He was unbuttoning his pocket, taking out pencil and notebook. 'Name, home address, etcetera. You'll be charged, I should think. Malicious damage. I expect you'll be fined.' He wrote down the name, then the address. There was no number of the house, just the name. Four Winds. Durham Road. They were all great houses along there, mansions, in their own vast gardens, overlooking the park where she had just been, and the valley beyond, where the River Team ran.

'Mayfield. Is your da Mr Nicholas Mayfield? The timber merchant?' The policeman looked a little shocked, then more so at the casual acknowledgement from Iris.

She pulled a face. 'He won't be very pleased.' She turned to May, with a warm, ingenuous grin. 'You're probably right. I will get a good hiding off my pa.'

They had turned the corner onto the busy main road. 'You want me to see you home, miss?' The policeman's manner had changed completely now. 'You'd best get off there right away.' He stared at her bedraggled appearance, the ruined hat May was still carrying. 'Or mebbes you'd better come to the station after all. Your pa could send somebody to fetch you.'

Iris put on an expression of winsome pleading. 'Oh no! Please! Let me break it to him first. I'll get home all right.'

'You can come and clean up at our place, if you like,' May inter-

22

jected impulsively. 'I live just near here,' she explained to the policeman. 'Sidney Terrace.'

He continued to look doubtful, but Iris turned to May and clutched at her arm. 'That's marvellous!' she said, with that wide grin again, now thoroughly restored 'You've been so kind to me. You saved my skin, didn't she, constable?' She linked her arm firmly through May's. 'I'll be all right, honestly I will,' she told him.

A sudden doubt assailed May at her impulsive generosity. 'We're not posh, you know. It's just a terrace. In off the street. I hope—'

'Don't be silly. I'd love to come. You've been so good to me.' May felt the pressure on her arm again as they moved off together. The dishevelled, red head bent in towards her confidingly. 'And I really do need to carry out repairs. More than you might think.' May could feel her shaking with laughter, a schoolgirlish giggle erupting which made her smile in sympathy. 'It's very embarrassing, really.' She could scarcely get her words out for her snorts of laughter, though she was blushing, too, even as she struggled to speak. 'I found out that I'm not the stuff of which heroines are made, I'm afraid. Swear to me most solemnly you won't ever tell a soul, but when those horrid women attacked me—' her violet eyes opened wide, then she snorted through her nose again, and hiccuped with laughter, 'I had the most awful accident. I wet my drawers with fright!'

THREE

THE UNEXPECTED VISIT of Iris Mayfield threw the entire household of 7, Sidney Terrace into such disarray that it threatened to eclipse the scheduled momentous occasion of the 'Sunday tea' for Jack Wright. 'She's a real nob!' May's brother, George, declared, in suitably hushed tones, after May had hurriedly led her guest up the narrow stairs to the bedroom, with only the briefest explanation. Iris's voice could still be heard uttering profuse apologies for her intrusion as May swept her out of sight.

May came charging down again alone, bearing the basin and flowered jug which normally stood in isolated splendour on the dresser in her parents' room. 'I hope there's some hot water in the copper!' She grabbed at a folded clean towel from the rack above the kitchen range and raced off again. 'Can you make a cup of tea, mam? Best cups!' she hissed unnecessarily, while Robina glared indignantly after her retreating form.

'Best cups!' she muttered. 'What does she think? Ah'm gonna give her your enamel mug?' She scowled at the puzzled face of her husband, whose fingers were rubbing thoughtfully at his collarless neck.

'Oh, I'm sorry!' May said, red faced, when she re-entered the bedroom, and hastily made to put down the basin and jug of hot water on the chest of drawers, before heading for the door again. She had caught a glimpse of white lace, and a generous portion of black-stockinged limbs, as Iris was in the process of divesting herself of her dampened undergarment.

'It's perfectly all right,' Iris laughed, sitting on the edge of the bed and dragging clear the clinging silk and ruffled lace from her boots. She dropped the garment on the rug with a fastidious wrinkle of her nose, and another giggle. 'There! Would you mind getting rid of those for me?'

'Why no. They'll wash out fine,' May exclaimed, shocked at such profligacy. 'I can do it for you if you like and send them on.'

Iris stared at her in genuine surprise, then her cheeks pinked a little. 'No, no, it's all right. I can take them with me.' She looked embarrassed at what she felt was a social gaffe, emphasizing the difference in their status.

'There's some hot water here,' May said, in the awkward little pause which followed. 'Listen, do you want a pair of drawers – to borrow, like?' She could feel her cheeks glowing. She could see at a glance that none of the undergarments she could offer matched up to the elegance of those this handsome girl had so easily discarded.

Again came that infectious giggle which made May's cheeks dimple in the beginnings of a responsive smile, in spite of her embarrassment. 'No, really. I'll manage quite well, thank you.' She shook out her skirts, gave a little twirl. 'It feels rather nice, actually. Cool, and free.' She grinned at May in complicity. 'A hundred years ago we wouldn't have been wearing them anyway!'

She quickly washed her face while May stood by with the towel, then she crouched slightly at the cloudy mirror and began to pull out the pins and grips from her hair, struggling to pin up the heavy mass of chestnut waves.

'Let me help,' May offered quickly. 'Here! There's a hairbrush – it's quite clean,' she added, blushing once more.

Iris turned, put out her hand impulsively, with a beaming smile. 'Of course it is! You're very kind. Thank you.' She stood while May attended to the rich coils, brushing them before lifting them to fit into the elaborate arrangement held at the crown.

May picked up another long brush and made some swift, brisk

strokes across the girl's shoulder and the skirt of her outer coat, to remove the stains of the clod which had been flung at her. 'Good as new – nearly,' May smiled. 'I'm afraid your hat's had a bit of a bashing though.' They both laughed as she held up the elegant but battered headpiece. 'What was it all about?' May asked shyly. 'The winders and that.'

'Are you a supporter? Of women's suffrage?'

May shrugged, a little uncomfortably. 'I suppose so. I've never really thought about it that much,' she confessed ashamedly. 'I mean –I agree with it. But I'm not ... I've never done anything. Like you, I mean.'

'There's an act going through parliament now that will give the right to every man – *every* man,' Iris emphasized, 'over the age of twenty-one to vote. While we still have absolutely no say at all over who governs us. How can they justify that?' She swept on without giving May the opportunity to answer her passionate question. 'They've got to be made to listen to us. I'm sure that if the question of women's suffrage itself could be put to the vote, the overwhelming majority of men would support us, too.'

May thought of the male representative of the household downstairs at this minute, and his oft expressed views on the subject. And of the group of harridans who had not many minutes ago threatened violence to this spirited young woman. She kept diplomatic silence.

Iris suddenly laughed again, pulling herself up short. 'I'll jump down off my soap box before you knock me down, eh?' The violet eyes sparkled with mischief. 'There's a campaign started down in London. And other places, too. More civil disobedience. We're smashing windows, in post offices and labour exchanges. I thought I'd get us started up here. Why should all the fun stay down south?' She glanced down at the crumpled clothing at her feet, then her eyes met May's once more, and held them with an engaging honesty as the grin faded briefly. 'It wasn't much fun back there, though, was it? I was truly frightened. If you hadn't come along, I don't know what would have happened. That bobby wouldn't have saved me. Only you did that.' She leaned forward with typical impulsiveness, caught hold of both May's wrists with her hands and kissed her on a reddened cheek. 'You're a very brave girl, May. I hope you'll be my friend. Will you?'

May was glowing. 'Don't be daft! It was nowt!'

Downstairs, in the cluttered state of the front room which had already received a thorough 'bottoming' in preparation for the ceremonial tea on the morrow, an almost goggling audience stared while Iris gave a laughing and highly dramatic account of May's intervention on her behalf, while sipping at the tea from the best flowered china. There was little need of May's eloquent, surreptitious glances towards her father, who had been hastily dismissed to put on collar and tie while their visitor was carrying out her own repairs in the girls' bedroom. Even the head of the household needed no urging to temper his forthright views in the presence of such an exotic guest.

However, May crossed her fingers and uttered a silent prayer when Iris, with an arch glance over her teacup, said sweetly, 'I gather you don't actually approve of our movement, Mr Rayner?'

'That I do not, miss!' George answered roundly. 'Ah think it's run by a bunch of women who have—' the combined lances of his wife and daughter's looks penetrated, and he swallowed his words in flushed retreat. 'Ah think meself it's a man's game is politics.'

Iris laughed cheerfully. 'You'd get on well with daddy. I expect what you really think is that I should have my b.t.m thoroughly slapped. But you're far too nice to say so!' There was a muffled gasp of half-shock, half-amusement, all round. 'Thank you so much for the tea, Mrs Rayner. I'd better be off.' She pulled a mock-rueful face. 'Face the music at home. Can I get a cab anywhere near?'

The family glanced at one another at a loss, then Robina said to her oldest son, 'George! Run round to Mason's. They should be able to send one round in a while. If you don't mind waiting a bit.'

The 'bit' turned out to be almost half an hour, and when the taxi came rumbling along the cobbles, half the street turned out to witness such an interesting departure from the norm. But Iris, once more her thoroughly composed self, smiled happily. Before she turned to step into the interior of the cab, she hugged May, in full view of the onlookers, and kissed her resoundingly on her cheek.

'Next Tuesday. Is that all right? I'll call for you about eleven. We can have lunch.' She noticed May's hesitation. 'Please!' she begged, squeezing her hand tight. 'I haven't had a chance to thank you properly. And you did save my life, after all.'

'This is absolutely intolerable!' Iris fumed. 'They can't keep me shut away up here like some medieval princess in a tower!' She stood at the window, glowering out at the fresh green of the cropped lawn, beyond which the pale blue and purple banks of lobelia, alive with hovering bees, marked the beginning of the herbacious border. Further still, the elms stirred gently in the morning breeze, and, already hazy in the distance, she looked across the undergrowth of the valley to the patchwork of gently rising fields on the far side, which led up to the horizon.

Margaret, the maid, tugged at the laces of the corset, drawing it in until Iris grunted. 'That's enough. You're not under orders to suffocate me, are you?' The maid knelt, fastened the black stockings to the suspenders which dangled down at front and back of the corset, then held out the elastic waist of the underskirt while Iris stepped into it. Margaret stood, hauling up the ruffled layers to the slim waist, then helped Iris into the day gown which she fastened at the back.

'I don't know why I bother to dress,' Iris grumbled. 'I might as well stay in bed if I'm to be a prisoner in my room all day.' She sat at the dressing table, while Margaret skilfully pinned up the chestnut hair which she had already brushed out before dressing her young mistress.

'The master will be sending for you some time this morning, miss,' Margaret said neutrally. 'Your mama told me to tell you to be ready. He's not going into the office until he's had a word.'

'I'm twenty, for goodness' sake! I refuse to be cooped up here much longer. No wonder women are rebelling. We're treated like slaves, Margaret. That's all we are.'

'Yes, miss. Anything else you need?' She picked up the breakfast tray and gave a little bob before crossing to the door. Slave is it? she thought, not without a wry little smile, as she made her way along the landing to the narrow stairs that led directly to the kitchen. Still, she was a canny enough sort, Miss Iris. She couldn't help feeling sorry for her at the latest scrape she'd got herself into. Then the smile broadened, with a shocking sense of delighted outrage. Hoyed a brick through the Labour Exchange window, they reckoned! The master would explode this time, and no mistake. Even the missus wouldn't be able to do much to help the lass. She'd come in for her share of his wrath and all, Margaret guessed, for Mrs Mayfield had openly sympathized with the women's movement before now. Encouraging her daughter in her foolishness, he'd say.

It was after ten-thirty before Margaret came back upstairs with the summons for Iris to attend her father in his study. Several times Iris had stormed to the door of her room, and opened it, setting foot on the landing before courage failed, or good sense prevailed, she wasn't sure which it was, and she withdrew back into the room again. In a way, it was an added challenge that the door was not locked. It merely served in the most galling manner to emphasize her father's authority over her that there was no physical barrier to prevent her freedom, only the invisible might of his word which kept her secured.

In spite of her resolve, she had not been able to hold back the tears when she made her confession on Saturday night. She had been banished immediately, despite the imminent arrival of their dinner guests, one of whom was Lionel Strang, a young man three years older than herself whom her parents saw as a very eligible contender for her hand – and every other bit of her, she acknowledged, with a secret frisson of both horror and shameful conjecture. Marriage was, it would seem, her chief purpose in life, from her parents' point of view. Lionel was a little on the short side, though with a square, muscular frame, and dark good looks.

Almost a hint of foreignness in his slightly beaked nose, the dark eyes, lustrous black hair.

He was pleasant enough as a companion. Easy going, jovial. As well educated as he needed to be. Had come down from Cambridge just last summer, had almost got his blue in rugger. Far more important, though, than these achievements, was the fact that he was one of the shipbuilder Strangs. His father, Sir William, had yards on all three north-eastern rivers. Which made Lionel a prize devoutly to be wished. But not by her, she was quite determined on that. Anyway, she reflected, with a guilty smirk, chance would be a fine thing now. What on earth would he, and his illustrious bald eagle of a father, think? Sent to bed without any supper, for flinging bricks through the Labour Exchange window. What price an alliance between the house of Mayfield and Strang now?

Her father's attitude was far from the fury she had anticipated. Unable to dismiss from her mind the image of a naughty schoolgirl, she stood in front of his desk, disturbed by the realization that she had absolutely no idea what lay behind the steady, enigmatic gaze he directed at her, under which she grew more and more discomfited.

'I feel it's partly our fault,' he said musingly at last. 'I'm not excusing your conduct, mind you. Not in the least. Damaging public property, making a nuisance, not to say a spectacle, of yourself like that I can't pretend both your mother and I aren't deeply shocked. And hurt, too. Deeply hurt. We thought we'd made a better job of bringing you up than that. That we'd taught you a proper respect for law and order.'

This tone of dignified sadness caught her off guard. She felt herself growing redder. She wondered if she dared sit down uninvited, decided she'd better not. She cleared her throat.

'Believe me, daddy, I didn't do it just for the fun of it. I thought a great deal—'

He held up his hand. 'I have no intention of entering into a philosophical argument. There is no justification for what you did. Nor for these acts of hooliganism that those who think like you are committing every day. You're your own worst enemies. But, as I said, I'm not arguing with you. If you'd come up in front of me on the bench I'd have been tempted to send you off to gaol. I think a number of girls like yourself are a bit too protected from some of the harsher realities of life. Incidentally, I wonder if you have any idea of how much you've embarrassed me by your foolery. As a member of the bench, I mean. Perhaps not. Or perhaps you don't even care.'

Again he held up his hand, stemming her hot protest. 'Never mind! I'd rather you didn't say things, or give assurances you don't mean. For what it's worth, you won't have to face the disgrace of going to court. Though I fancy that might disappoint you. Your friends seem to crave publicity, the chance to make a spectacle of themselves. What you *will* do, from now on, is inform your mother or myself of your whereabouts at all times. You will seek our permission for any visits you wish to make, however short they may be. And you'll give me your word you will not involve yourself in any further activities of the women's suffrage movement. Is that clear?'

He waited. Iris swallowed hard. 'Father. It's something I really believe in. It's not something I'm doing just for a lark, or for any other reason except that I truly *do* believe it's right.'

'Will you promise me you will not break the law again?'

Their eyes locked. She knew he had made what he thought was a great compromise. She wanted to meet him half-way.

'I'll try, daddy,' she murmured. But at his next words, her expression changed to one of dismay.

'You'll be going down to Linbridge. With Helena. To spend some time there. We'll be down in August to join you.' Linbridge was Uncle Hugh's place, in far off Hampshire. Deep in its rural heartland, surrounded by tenant farms. Banishment! Shipped off with her younger sister, buried in the countryside. 'Lionel Strang will be staying near there this summer,' he added, with little attempt at subtlety. 'He asked if he might call on you. We said yes of course. He's a very nice young chap. Rather keen on you, I fancy.'

31

She glanced up, smouldering with resentment. 'Has he been given the go-ahead then?'

Her father's look was cold. 'If you mean do we approve, the answer's yes. Though, quite frankly, the way you're behaving these days would be enough to put any decent man off, I should think. I'm afraid you'll need to grow up a lot more before any young feller would want to take you seriously.'

'That's good!' she fired back, stung by his words. 'Because I don't feel inclined to be auctioned off in the cattle ring just yet, thank you.'

Her father showed no sign of losing his temper. 'You'd better start packing. You'll be going down at the weekend. It'll be a lengthy stay, so take plenty of things. Right. That's all.'

She was breathing heavily, and she fought to control her voice, to keep the tremor out of it. 'Oh, just one thing. I'd like to go out tomorrow, if I might have your permission.' He raised his eyebrows, said nothing. 'On Saturday, there was a girl. She helped me rather a lot. Things could have got quite nasty. She rescued me. I'd like to take her out to lunch. Thank her properly. If that's all right.'

'Why can't you invite her here? I'm sure your mother would like to meet her.'

The red head lifted challengingly. 'Oh, I don't think so. I don't think she'd be comfortable about coming here. She's from Sidney Terrace. In Gateshead. Her father works in a shipyard. A carpenter.'

'I see. What exactly did she do – to rescue you?'

'There were some people. A bit of a crowd. They were threatening to set about me. She stepped in. Got me away from them.' She paused. 'Or don't you think I should have anything to do with her? Perhaps I should just send her some money?' Her voice rang with condemnation.

'Not at all,' he answered calmly. 'Go and see your plucky chippy's daughter. Flinging bricks and brawling in the gutter. What could be more appropriate? You're quite right. I'm sure she wouldn't be at all comfortable here.' He stood, and his voice hardened. 'You can have the motor if you want, as long as you're back here by four. Though perhaps you'd prefer to ride in the tramcar. Oh, and one more thing,' he added, by way of a final insult. 'Make sure you have a bath and a complete change of clothes before you come down to the drawing room, won't you?'

FOUR

THE FIRST REAL kiss, the kiss of passion, as May privately dubbed it, with suitable drama, came on the last Sunday in July. It shocked both of them, May no less than Jack, though she had been anticipating it, longing for it, for some considerable time. They took the electric train out to the coast, along with hundreds of other folks making the most of yet another glorious summer day. They tramped a good few miles, past St Mary's lighthouse to the long stretch of sand fringed by the pale sand dunes. Among these, in a wonderful little hollow surrounded by the gently rattling tall, dry fronds of slender grass, they found the solitude they both craved.

'Not before time,' May sighed, dropping to her knees thankfully. She turned modestly away from him and swiftly unlaced her boots, then tugged down her gartered stockings, to hide them discreetly in the supple leather tops of her footgear. She wriggled and buried her bare toes in the warm, fine sand, and laughed with luxury. 'Alone at last!' she vamped teasingly, batting her eyes at him in the manner of the sirens she had seen at the cinematograph shows.

He was kneeling, unpacking the haversack, and they both paused, their eyes meeting, as they realized all at once the import of what she had said. She blushed, glanced down briefly, then up at him again, her face serious. He moved slowly, seemed to take an age coming across to her, while she waited breathlessly. He caught hold of her hands, squeezed them. His dark eyes blazed at her intensely.

'I love you, May,' he said hoarsely. Again, she thought of pain, in the way he said it. The starkness of it passed through her, making her shiver, scaring her at first.

He can't! she heard her brain protesting. I can't! We can't say that, we don't know each other. Yet it was something different, on a different level altogether; she could feel it, churning up her insides. That was when they kissed. She watched his mouth coming closer and closer, that cute little youthful line of black moustache along his upper lip, those vivid red lips. Her own parted, she felt the sharp pain of their teeth pressing together, then their open mouths were mixed, and their bodies, blood hammering as they strained against one another, fell back, clawing at each other, their mouths still locked together. Her breasts were crushed against him, bursting, and the world had spun giddily away from her, all she could do was cling to him, her whole body melting to him now.

She fought for breath, wheezing with the effort, when they finally broke. He was gazing at her, deeply shaken, as she was.

'I didn't mean—' he said, his voice breaking, tailing away, and she shook her head, her eyes crinkled, the tears spilling over, trickling into the wisps of brown hair at her temples.

She smiled radiantly through her tears. 'I love you an' all, Jack! I really do!'

They chose May's eighteenth birthday to announce their engagement, in spite of the disapproval, initially from both families. The women in both households exerted a formidable influence. Sophia Wright was unrelenting in her opposition, Edward, her husband, slightly uncomfortable in following her lead. Robina was more subtle, but equally effective in persuading George to her way of thinking. She was soon convinced after meeting Jack of the couple's sincerity of feeling for each other, and May wisely made sure of recruiting her as an ally.

'Remember when we started courtin'?' Robina asked her husband in bed one night. 'That night we stopped late down the Gut? You and me da nearly came to blows. He was sure we'd been up to no good. And he was right, wasn't he, bonny lad?'

George turned towards her in the darkness, felt the familiar soft shape of her settle against him. 'Aye,' he chuckled. 'He was that!'

'Ah was only eighteen,' she reminded him gently. The battle was won.

Iris Mayfield came to the party they gave at Sidney Terrace. She had braved the cold contempt of her father to do so. 'It's totally unsuitable and you well know it!' Nicholas fumed. 'You'd think the stupid girl would have enough sense to realize it for herself. It's obviously gone to her head, having the likes of you treating her as some sort of equal.'

Iris quickly finished her meal, taking no further part in the conversation between her siblings and her mother. Inwardly, she was furious. Ever since that dreadful business of the Labour Exchange, she had been almost a prisoner. Or at least, like some animal tethered on a long rope, she amended. Poor mama had suffered, too, for some of her friends were active supporters of the women's suffrage movement, and they hardly dared come to the house any more. As for herself, she hadn't been allowed to attend a meeting. Daddy had been as good as his word. She had had to account for her movements every time she set foot outside.

At first, it had been as much a matter of defiance as anything, her seeing the young girl who had stepped in so courageously to save her that day. On the Tuesday morning following the incident, May had been waiting on the corner of Sidney Terrace, dressed in what Iris guessed was her best outfit, of demure blouse and dark skirt, with a coat over all which was smart but really a little too heavy for the hot summer weather.

The motor had rather overawed her, so that at first she sat staring about her at the familiar street scene as though she had never seen it before. She had scarcely said a word until they were over the bridge and pulling up outside the County Hotel.

'What's this?' May asked, in some alarm.

'I said I'd take you to lunch,' Iris laughed, not realizing how distressed the girl was.

'Oh, not here, please!' May looked terrified, and Iris was imme-diately contrite.

She pretended to be nonchalant. 'Oh, all right. Where would you like to go?' She dismissed Goulding with the motor, and they strolled arm in arm up Northumberland Street, May visibly relax-ing all the while, until soon she was chatting quite animatedly, responding to Iris's infectious enthusiasm. They looked in the shops, and Iris led her into Fenwick's department store. She almost spoilt things again by purchasing a pretty, flowered silk scarf and thrusting it impulsively into May's astonished hands. 'I'd like to say thank you for what you did on Saturday. Please wear it.'

May blushed, and looked so shocked that Iris blurted guiltily, 'Oh, very well! If you don't want it, I'll have it! I didn't mean anything by it. I only wanted to buy you something. A gift from me. To remember me. I didn't mean to upset you—'

'It's very nice,' May managed. She took the scarf back, draped it round her shoulders. 'Thank you.'

Iris's face darted forward, and she kissed May swiftly on the cheek. 'There! Now then. What about the tea rooms in the Hay Market? We can get something there.'

They had a wonderful time together, and both were genuinely sorry when Goulding turned up with the motor carriage, as they had arranged earlier.

'I'd like to meet up again,' Iris said, kissing her once more. 'If you don't mind. You're not ashamed of me, are you? I mean, I'm not an embarrassment?'

And May had giggled, shaking her dark head. 'As long as you promise not to hoy any more bricks!'

Privately, May was more than a little hurt to see that Iris's presence, for all her easygoing spirit of fun, did cast a certain aura of restraint over the proceedings. Her folks were on edge, May could tell, and the others, too, were not their normal relaxed selves, while Nelly Dunn, and some of the other young people present, adopted an almost abrasive attitude, as though to prove they were not in awe of such a distinguished visitor.

But Iris did her best to win them over, largely just by being herself, until, to May's intense pleasure, she overheard one of them whispering in the intimacy of the crowded kitchen, 'She's a grand lass, isn't she? No side to 'er at all!'

Nelly, perhaps using the numerous glasses of punch as an excuse for the flushed cheeks and bold manner, was clinging demonstratively to Arty Mackay's arm. Arty's was the only name on the guest list which had been put there at Jack's request. Cissy would have loved to come, but Mrs Wright had been adamant in her refusal to allow her daughter to attend. Brother Dan had conveniently had a previous engagement which he could not break.

'You been up before the beak yet then?' Nelly asked Iris abruptly.

Iris smiled unperturbed, and shook her head. Inside, she was feeling more than a little guilty, for she knew her father's influence had ensured that charges had not been pressed. She was even more ashamed of her secret relief, for the idea of such unlawful demonstrations had been to seize as much publicity as possible. 'Are you a supporter of our cause, Nelly?' she asked.

Nelly gave a loud, derisive snort. 'Some of us are too busy earnin' a livin' to find time for that kind o' carry-on!'

'Ye'll be wantin' to get into parliament itself next!' Arty laughed, catching hold of Nelly by the waist and whirling her round. The gramophone was trying to compete against the bedlam of noise. 'Imagine this one in parliament, eh?' he cried, giving Nelly another squeeze and eliciting a shriek of encouragement. 'She'd have us at war in five minutes!'

Iris had kept a careful eye on the time and was waiting to slip discreetly away when the motor car appeared, juddering down the cobbled street. Jack and May had both escorted her out to the pavement. The August night was overcast, the warm wind moist with the promise of rain. The compounded smells of soot and the various industrial works further down, by the river, filled the air. Iris turned and hugged May, and they kissed. 'Thanks for inviting me.

I've enjoyed it so much.' She turned, to include Jack. 'I meant what I said. You're a lucky man. Take care of her. Congratulations to both of you. You'll be very happy together. I'm sure of it.'

She gave their hands a last squeeze, thrust a small package into May's palm, and turned away quickly, climbing up into the high interior of the motor. They watched while the uniformed chauffeur closed the door, moved round to the front of the vehicle, and clambered aboard. It rattled off, under the pools of light from the hissing gas lamps.

May had torn open the paper. Inside was a simple cardboard box, and inside that, in a bed of cotton wool, lay an exquisite little jewelled brooch, in the shape of a spray of plumes. In the darkly enamelled little circle at its centre was the engraved initial, 'M'.

'She shouldn't have!' May whispered unsteadily. 'It looks ever so expensive.' She put the lid back on the box. She gazed solemnly at Jack. 'We will be, won't we?'

'Eh?'

'Be very happy together – like Iris said?'

He pulled her to him, bent slowly, his mouth curving in a smile as it approached hers. 'Of course we will. It was practically an order. For years and years and years. And then some more.'

FIVE

'MRS WRIGHT!' Jack murmured, rubbing his nose against May's cheek The turned back veil clung mistily about her face. He gazed at her, still shaken by the power of the love the sight of her summoned up in him. There was something even more spiritual in the slender form draped in the white lace of the wedding dress. He was in awe of her, of the love and beauty that had been entrusted to him.

He could scarcely believe that the year and more of waiting was over at last. No more seeing each other twice during the week; no more good-night kisses, in freezing cold or summer warmth, under the flicker of gas lamps on the doorstep of Sidney Terrace.

'Here! Move over, man! Let the best man kiss the blooming bride!' Dan, with his usual bravado, elbowed him out of the way and enveloped May in a bear hug, which drew a cheer from the crowds of guests tiered on the high steps of the chapel, and the spectators beyond the railings, on the pavement below.

The photographer called out instructions, disappeared once more under his black hood, and they waited frozen in their instant of immortality. Mrs Wright senior held her smile, glinting brilliantly on her painstakingly made up features, like the bright paste of a false jewel. Beside her, George, striving not to be hidden by the profuse plumage of her wide hat, lifted his chin with challenging pride and tried to ignore the unfamiliar chafing of his stiff winged collar.

He'd shown them, he had, and no mistake. Paid for the lot, including the spread waiting round at the Institute Hall, and this studio photographer feller. It had given him a special pleasure to refuse Ted Wright's offer to help out with the catering. 'Why no, man! She's our lass. Our first born. We'll do her proud.' Not a bad sort, really, Jack's father. At least he didn't try to lord it over them. Not like that sour-faced bitch of a wife of his. By God, it'd be a hard boot planted right up that tight arse of hers if he had the running of her. They'd only met the once before, about a couple of weeks ago, when all the arrangements had been made. She'd sat there in the parlour of Sidney Terrace, looking like somebody had just broken wind right under her nose.

He hoped they wouldn't hang about too long at the reception. After a few ales inside him, he might be strongly tempted to tell her her fortune, especially if the newly weds were safely out of the way, as they would be before long. Not that she would stay longer than she had to. She'd already let it be known that she was organizing a do back at their place for her lot. And good riddance to 'em an' all.

May turned round, looking up behind her, and drew Iris in closer to her, as the bridesmaids clustered round, self-consciously smiling and clutching at their bouquets. She smiled at the grinning figure. 'You look lovely, you really do.'

'Rubbish! I feel like some great gallumphing elephant alongside you. You're beautiful.' Iris's fingers tightened on May's arm, squeezed hard. 'In case I don't get the chance later – good luck! Be happy!' She bent and kissed May's cheek, then smiled and dabbed at her eyes. 'Aren't we idiots? Happiest day of your life and all that, and here we are blubbing all over the place!'

She was glad she had resisted her father's sniping remarks, his oblique efforts to dissuade her from attending. 'Is this your latest cause, your little chippy's daughter? To display your democracy, your fellow feeling for the great unwashed?'

'Be discreet, dear,' her mother had warned, more sympathetically, and Iris knew full well what she meant. Knew how unorthodox it would be thought for the daughter of Nicholas Mayfield to be a bridesmaid at the wedding of a shipyard worker's daughter. She was even more fiercely glad she had come now, even though she heeded her mother's advice and kept as low a profile as possible. It was after all May's big day, and the last thing she wanted was to steal any of its limelight from her.

She was even happier, too, that she had managed, against considerable odds, to present, as an extra wedding gift, the use of the small fisherman's cottage at Runswick Bay for the couple's honeymoon. It was one of a number of properties her father had acquired, with some vague plans as yet unrealized, to convert it into a suitable holiday accommodation for the family. Once she had, with her mother's invaluable help, got her father to acquiesce to the newly weds having use of it for a week, she then had to persuade Jack and May themselves.

Jack had intended to book them in for a three or four day 'Bed and Breakfast' holiday at an inn somewhere in the Yorkshire Dales. 'This will be much nicer than staying in some stuffy hotel,' Iris had urged, with her usual verve. 'No one watching you, sniggering over you.' May blushed. She knew exactly what her friend meant. 'You'll be all on your own. A chance for you to get used to each other. To play at Mr and Mrs. It'll take some getting used to, I expect.'

Again, May had understood perfectly. And had been won over. 'Please, Jack,' she said. 'Iris really wants to do this for us. And it'll be lovely – a whole week on our own. It's a lovely spot, she says. Please!'

He gazed back at her deep, pleading eyes, and knew he could not resist her. And did not want to. 'All right, bossy boots!' he grumbled, his heart thumping with love when she flung herself at him to show him how happy he had made her.

'Are you tired, love?' May could hear the tension in Jack's voice as he turned from lighting the oil lamp and adjusting the wick to stem the thick, smelly flow of black smoke from the top of its glass cover. The small square panes of the bedroom window were quite black. She could see her dim reflection in them before she tugged across the thin, sprigged curtains. They smelt faintly of damp, and outside she could hear the unfamiliar, steady roar of the sea. 'Do you want me to wait downstairs?' he asked.

She turned quickly. 'No!' she answered at once. She *was* tired. And sticky and hot under her finery. After all, they had spent the hours since they had left the reception in mid-afternoon travelling, changing trains twice before they arrived at the quiet station above this fishing village.

Once down among the narrow, twisting alleys, whose shallow, cobbled steps led them ever lower towards the rhythm of the sea, they had to search for some time to locate the home of Mrs Gough. The young couple were glad to find she was a woman of few words, none of them unnecessary.

She let them in, handed over the key to the front door, and gave them a brief tour. It did not take long. There was only the one bedroom, with a tiny box of a room next to it no bigger than a cupboard. The high double bed was made up, with crisp clean sheets and pillow-cases. 'They're all aired,' Mrs Gough assured them.

Downstairs, there was the small living room and a tiny kitchen, from which a back door opened onto a miniature yard. She nodded beyond the low brick wall to a row of outbuildings on the opposite side of the alleyway. All had identical green doors, with gaps at top and bottom. 'Middens,' she said. 'Yours is the end one there.' The short flight of steep stairs led directly from the living room. There was one more door, near the entrance to the kitchen, which Mrs Gough now pulled open. 'Pantry,' she announced. 'Well stocked. Bread's fresh this mornin', and milk. There's tea an' eggs an' things. Miss Mayfield left orders. She was down herself earlier in the week.' She glanced around, and belatedly the newcomers identified the smell of whitewash.

'Whole place has been done up, special. Anythin' ye want, ye're to ask me. I'll be in Monday mornin' to give a bit of a clean round, like. Ye'll be left alone till then.' She retreated rapidly, as though she did not wish to stay to hear their thanks.

It was almost dark, and they had another exploration after she had gone, before Jack carried their bags upstairs while May prepared her first meal of their married life – tomato and cheese sandwiches, and strong tea, when she had called on Jack to help her with the little spirit stove in the kitchen. There was hardly room for them to stand without touching one another. 'Like being on a ship,' May said, and put her hands on his shoulders. She found herself blushing deeply.

The tension was there, all the while, though they both worked hard at pretending to be relaxed, almost chattering about the eventful day, in a vain attempt to overcome the nervousness. But now, up in the low-ceilinged bedroom, sealed in its intimacy, they could no longer forestall, or pretend.

May turned from the window. She knew Jack was giving her the chance to delay further, offering to leave her alone until she was safely under the covers, even to feign sleep and remain inviolate until morning, if she wished. He came to her now, in the narrow space between the dresser and the bed, and gently reached for her hand.

'There's no rush, is there?' he said. 'We've got the rest of our lives together.'

She nodded, drew in a deep breath, her voice catching. 'Yes. And it's time we *were* together. I don't want to put anything off, Jack. I want to be your wife – properly. Will you undo me, please?' She turned, knew that his hands would be trembling as he awkwardly unhooked the fasteners at her neck and at her waist.

She eased her arms out of the sleeves, shrugged the bodice off her shoulders, and pulled up the rustling cotton. She pushed down the elasticated waist of her layered underskirt, and now she could not prevent her face from burning. Iris's other present – 'For you alone, darling friend!' she had said with that mischievous grin – was a bridal trousseau, which she had ordered from the Army and Navy Stores in distant London, and which consisted of nightgowns, camisoles, vests, stockings – and beautiful items of underwear, all in the finest nainsook and embroidered with lace. And in the latest fashion, too, which was why she was glowing hot with embarrassment at this moment, in spite of all her brave resolution. In place of her customary drawers, she was wearing one of the four pairs of knickers contained in the trousseau. Knickers which scarcely covered her thighs and thus allowed a shockingly generous portion of her bare flesh to show above the black stocking-top secured to the suspender straps which stretched from the short ten-inch corset imprisoning her already slim waist.

Her lip quivered, she could feel her eyelashes moist with tears. She simply could not meet his gaze. 'I don't normally – this is the new stuff. Part of what Iris bought me. Do you think it's too – is it—'

Then Jack did something so unexpected she never forgot it, as long as she lived. He bent, knelt in front of her, and put his hot face to her bare leg, to her skin, and very softly kissed her above the knee, laid his lips against her, while his hands came up and held her hips, swathed only in the thin cotton.

'You're beautiful,' he whispered. 'Truly beautiful.' He looked up at her, so shockingly close, between her thighs, she could feel him touching her, feel his warm breath, her own tingling reaction to it. 'Never be ashamed, May!' he said, almost fiercely. His face burned intently up at her, so close to her belly, her most secret flesh. 'Nothing can ever be shameful between us, my love.'

Afterwards, she savoured the intensity of their closeness, their sweating, joined bodies, his head on her breast, her joy, despite all the soreness, the discomfort of the sticky mess. The room grew light while they lay peacefully together. They heard the cracked, doleful tolling of a single bell.

'Let's go to chapel,' she said, and they rose at last. She was largely pretending to be ashamed of his seeing her naked. She was more thrilled than anything at his watching her while she stood on a towel and gave herself a comprehensive, all-over wash.

They found the chapel, after some searching among the narrow alleys. It was down in the midst of the village, perched on what seemed no more than a shelf on the cliffside, and no bigger than some of the cottages. There were more women than menfolk, all with the close-fitting, encompassing bonnets, the long tapes tied under the chin. The men gave self conscious little nods, the women were more open, some staring with frank curiosity. 'Mornin', ma'am. Mornin', sir.' May was embarrassed and puzzled by their distant politeness. It was the same when they wandered round the village later, and walked down to the foreshore, and the short sea wall, with its projecting pier at the end nearest the towering overhang of the cliff. The glances, the 'sirs' and 'ma'ams', until a blushing May was hard put not to giggle at this unaccustomed deference.

It wasn't until they had passed the drawn up cobles, where several fishermen were gathered, sitting working at their nets and lines, or at the wooden cages of the lobster pots, and they were walking along the long curve of the shore edging the bay that light dawned. 'Of course!' Jack's face sparkled at his grin. 'It's because of the Mayfields. We're staying at their cottage. They must think we're gentry!'

'And why not?' May held out her arms, her bag swinging as she twirled round on the sand. 'We look smart enough to be real toffs, don't we?'

On one of their walks, they passed a man with a silvery beard, sitting on a small folding stool, in front of an easel. 'Are you going to do some sketching?' she asked Jack, when they had passed the artist, with polite exchanges of greeting. She knew how skilled he was, with pencil, and with brush, for she had seen the water colours he had done earlier in his youth, some of which were proudly hung at his home, and to her untutored eye seemed as good as any professional.

'I'm going to sketch you,' he said, smiling, and she glowed with pleasure.

But later in that magic week she was genuinely shocked when he slipped her dressing gown from her shoulders, gently drew her nightgown over her tousled head, and sat her naked where the full morning light from the bedroom window fell mercilessly on her slim body. 'Sit still. Don't move.'

'No!' she gasped. She looked really frightened, crossed her arms over her breasts, and folded one thigh over the other. She could feel the hard unyielding wood of the upright chair on her bottom, the cold wooden floorboards on her bare feet. 'Not like this, please, Jack!'

But he came and knelt, put both his hands gently on her thighs, eased one from the other. He took her wrists, pulled them gently away, placed her hands at the sides of the chair. Her pale nipples budded to hardness. She shivered 'Jack!' she said again, pleadingly, but then was caught by that ardent gaze.

'You're not ashamed, are you? Tell me you're not.'

She sat still then, striving not to be, and gradually her discomfiture faded, a measure of pride penetrated her thoughts. He thought she was beautiful; her unclothed beauty captivated him. He worked quickly, then allowed her to escape, to cover herself again. He spent a lot more time working on the drawing, finishing it days later, framing it in plain dark wood. 'Promise you'll never let anybody else in the whole world see it,' she begged. 'I'd die!' But he hung it in their bedroom, and she was both thrilled and shocked every time she saw it, which she did every day, often stopping to stare at it, in wonder, and in guilty pride.

After the week's honeymoon, they moved into the rented rooms he had found temporarily for them, in one of the quiet streets of terraced houses leading down towards the park, only about ten minutes away from his parents' home, in fact, and respectable enough. There was a small bedroom, a living room, and a tiny kitchen, all on the second floor. They shared the bathroom, on the floor below, with the house-tenant and his family.

Two rooms in a modest house in Gateshead posed no problems for them. May enjoyed playing housekeeper. She had had a thorough training at home already, had watched her mother manage the household budget, helped her with the cooking and cleaning and looking after menfolk, so that her new position of housewife posed no threat. Indeed, she was overjoyed at assuming the role in her own right. They were blissfully happy, both of them, though they had little money to spare, sometimes none after the necessities had been dealt with. It didn't matter. Being together was all that mattered, sleeping, and waking up together, loving. It seemed nothing could touch them, no outside event infringe upon their impregnable private world.

She and Jack would often go round to Sidney Terrace on a Saturday evening, and stay for supper, sitting with the rest of the family round the kitchen table in cosy if crowded informality. Young George was holding forth with a budding mechanic's enthusiasm about the launch of the navy's ultra-modern weapon, the battleship, HMS *Queen Elizabeth*. 'Powered by oil,' he told them, with all the fervour of a disciple. 'First in the world!' He sighed rapturously. 'If there's a war, ah'm gannin' in the navy.'

'War? Don't talk so daft, our George!' Robina chided. 'There won't be no war.'

Her husband looked thoughtful. 'Ah hope ye're right, lass. Ah think we've woken up in time. They're goin' ahead with this battle-cruiser programme an' all. Another one due here, an' one on the Clyde. Yon Kaiser Willy won't try anything now, ah reckon.'

'Why, man, he's the king's cousin, isn't he, for God's sake? He winnat make war on his own relations!'

SIX

'I SEE YOUR CONFOUNDED *sisters*' – he gave the word the full force of his scathing sarcasm – 'have resorted to their bombs again.' Nicholas Mayfield crackled his newspaper angrily in Iris's direction. 'Not content with destroying priceless works of art, they've gone back to trying to maim and kill.'

Iris's head lifted challengingly. 'Considering what this government's doing to the Pankhursts—' she pulled herself up short and gave a little shake of her head. What right had she to lay down the law on such things, when she had virtually thrown in the towel as far as the struggle for women's suffrage went?

'Do they really think they're going to convince anyone they can act responsibly when they carry on with such lunacy?' her father pursued. 'As if we haven't got enough on our plate with this damned Irish Home Rule nonsense. Asquith's playing a dangerous game there, if you ask me. He should have no truck with them.'

'But the Catholic majority, daddy—' once more, she stopped in mid-sentence, assailed by the familiar weariness of such argument. He was in full flow now, and she sank back on the sofa, resolved to say nothing further.

'Bolsheviks at work here, it's all so obvious. This building strike.' He slapped the paper with his fingers. 'Blasted railwaymen, and the pitmen, causing trouble as well. They'll be out soon, mark my words. They'll cripple the country between them. We'll have our timber jammed up in the yards all over the place. It could ruin us.' He cleared his throat disgustedly.

'More tea, daddy?' She leaned forward, poured out another cup, envying her mother, who had escaped on the grounds of a headache and was resting peacefully up in her room.

Well, at least while daddy was waxing forth vehemently on national gloom and doom he wasn't belabouring her with her refusal to be dragged into an alliance with the Strangs. She was privately amazed that Lionel himself hadn't given up on her. After all, there were plenty of others, she was quite sure, just as desirable a catch as she was, who would be willing to fall into his arms, and his bed.

Not so far away, some of them, either. Helena, her younger sister, would be eighteen soon. She had seemed quite keen on him at one time. Although she seemed to have cooled considerably towards him in the past few months, more's the pity, Iris reflected. Probably because of parental pressure. Why on earth couldn't daddy be happy to marry off his youngest daughter first? Why was he insisting that she should be the first to sacrifice her maidenhood on the bed of convenience, just because she was the eldest? Was he afraid she would be left on his hands, an old maid?

She sighed. The prospect of a lifetime spent here, doing endless 'good works' and playing maiden aunt to nieces and nephews was hardly more appealing than the sanctified marital bed. But hardly less. She felt once more that unpleasant stab of irritation when she thought of the visit she had paid to May's two days ago. It startled her, and upset her deeply, too, this unexpected emotion. So much so that she had tried to push it away, not to analyse it, to dismiss it merely as one of her strange wayward moods. Yet she kept dragging back to it, like the helpless little exploratory probes you kept giving to a twingeing tooth.

She had not seen her friend for more than two months. In fact, she had seen little of her since the wedding, the gaps between her calls growing wider and wider. The first time she had gone to the house near the park, she had made all the right enthusiastic noises

50

about the two drab, respectable rooms they inhabited. That was after she had abruptly dismissed their profuse thanks for the gift of the week's stay at the cottage at Runswick. She was embarrassed by their gratitude. Jack had been present, for it was a Saturday. May had insisted she should come for tea when they would both be there. Almost as if she wished to parade her wedded bliss, was the uncharitable thought which Iris had swiftly chased away.

But, more and more during the infrequent visits she made, such ideas kept crowding into her mind. Iris made sure her social calls now were always during the week when she could be sure of having May to herself, but still there was a different look about her which roused strangely antipathetic feelings in Iris. Look at me! I'm in love! Isn't it wonderful?

That look seemed to shriek at her, more and more stridently. That glazed look of utter contentment – smug was the word which popped into Iris's shocked mind. That wasn't right, either. It was more a sense that they had found the answer to everything, that nothing else mattered. Men – and women – might be dying for a cause, the world might be rumbling fearfully towards unimaginably terrible conflict, yet none of it mattered to them, none of it touched these two young people, sealed off in the bubble of their fulfilment.

And what was wrong with that? Surely she must simply be jealous of such consuming happiness, wanting it for herself? But, painfully, she was forced to admit to herself that it was not the case; jealousy was not the reason for her feeling. Or rather, not jealousy of their shared happiness, but – and here the pain of such mental self probing stabbed so intensely she flinched from a continuation of it – a jealousy of the young man who had taken up such an all important part in May's affections, and, in effect, stolen her friend from her.

In the little time she had known her, from the very first fraught minute when they had met, she had felt an extraordinary fondness, a bond with the young girl, from such a humbly different background, which she had treasured, which she had hoped fervently

51

would grow, become a mutually shared affection. But, at the very moment when their valued friendship had begun, along had come this other one, the young man who had gradually come to take over every bit of the capacity for love which May possessed.

Sex, its mysteries, did not enthrall her the way it seemed to absorb so many young girls. It disturbed her, she knew it was a vital force which sometimes unwillingly intrigued her. But the notion of ever wishing to enter into such a union with a man was something she found shockingly repugnant to her.

Perhaps that was why she flung herself into so many causes, why she had become involved so passionately with the women's movement. She was happy, could devote herself fully, to such things. Maybe that was why her life seemed so empty now, and so irksome. And why the threatening pressure from her family for her to become affianced to Lionel weighed so heavily upon her. And why – she forced herself to go on, to acknowledge the painful truth – she mourned the loss of a friend. For that's what had happened between her and May, whether the dear girl realized it or not. She was lost to her, and the loss brought many bitter tears behind the safely bolted door of her room.

May dug out the framed nude portrait of herself from the top drawer where she had hidden it under her clothing. She always put it away when mam, or anybody else, was coming round, just in case they should for some reason need to go through to the bedroom. She had taken it down for Iris's visit the day before yesterday and forgotten to hang it back on the wall again. As always, she blushed a little as she replaced it. She felt the irresistible urge to smile tugging at the corners of her mouth, and she stared at herself in the mirror, strove to assume a solemn, matronly expression. She failed, and grinned at herself like a sniggering schoolgirl.

Her heart was beating quickly, and she was longing for Jack to be home. She had almost given way to her temptation to pull on her coat and walk up to meet him on the road. The louring April clouds and threat of rain was not what put her off. She wanted to be in here, in their own little haven, when she broke the news. She was more than ever glad that she had also resisted the urge to confide in Iris. It had been a strong one, too, but she told herself she had to wait for confirmation from Dr Welsh, though she scarcely needed it. And besides, no one should be told, not even her own mam, no matter how much she might have conjectured already, before Jack.

The tea was all ready, the hot water on for him to wash. She had already spread the towels in front of the fire, which was smoking under its burden of fresh coals. She found herself playing with her fingers, wandering about the room, crowded with the old pieces of furniture, glancing every minute at the clock, listening for his footfall along the passage, the sound of his voice calling out to her. Oh, why was he late, today of all days?

She thought again of Iris's visit. She had seemed in a funny mood the whole time she was here. On edge, almost relieved, in a strange way, when she jumped up and announced that she had to be going. She'd refused May's invitation to wait until Jack came in almost curtly. Just as well. Jack might have been embarrassed appearing in his work things with Iris there. May wouldn't. She'd have been proud for her friend to see him. He was skilled. An artist. The kind of work he did, with the stone carvings on the churches, the wooden screens, was really clever. And his water colours were on the walls. He had brought them from his home, for all to see.

Nobody's seen his picture of you, though, have they? She registered her discomfort with the thought. You're not ashamed of it? Jack always asked her, and always she denied it. 'It's just that me mam and our lot wouldn't understand, Jack. They wouldn't know.' Iris would, though. Why had she never shown it to Iris, or told her about it? *She'd* understand. Yet May knew she herself would be hotly scarlet with shame if Iris should look at it.

Her mind dwelt on the visit, troubled by it, without exactly knowing why. Her friend had seemed preoccupied, tense. Not at all her normal, jolly self. That was what May had always found so attractive about the tall, red-haired figure. Her exuberance, her independent spirit. Perhaps the troubles at home were worse than she made out. She had talked about this Lionel lad, pulled a comically lugubrious face as she described her family's efforts, and those of the young man himself, to get her into some understanding with him.

Maybe it was just the difficulty of maintaining a friendship with someone from May's background, so far beneath her own. The thought pained May a great deal, even as she acknowledged the possibility. Perhaps her folks were making things difficult over her wish to keep the friendship going. It was certainly out of the ordinary, to say the least. Something had upset Iris, that was for sure. Then all thought of Iris and her problems flew from her mind as she heard Jack's step, his cheery voice.

He came in through the back door, into the gloomy little kitchen, tossed his haversack and cap on the top, beside the sink. She wondered if he would remember, then was ashamed at herself when he said at once, 'Well? Did you go to the doctor's?'

She nodded. He knew before she said anything, she saw the dawning, awed expression take over his face. 'Yes. He's sure I've fallen. Early January, he reckons.'

'Oh, my God! Lass! May!' He caught hold of her, hugged her tightly, and she was crying, then laughing, the tears streaming down her face, and he was kissing her, his own eyes were wet, and then he let go of her suddenly, as though she were made of the thinnest china, and she laughed joyously again.

May regarded the visit to her in-laws, which they made the day after they had broken the news of her pregnancy to her own delighted family, as a duty. The tension was palpable. They had waited until they knew Jack's father would be home from his work, so it was quite late. The house was full of cooking smells and Dora, the live-in maid, was waiting to serve up the supper.

'We've got something to tell you. Something important.' Jack's voice shook slightly. His chin lifted. 'May's going to have a baby.'

There was an instant of absolute stillness, no one moving, then there was a general exhalation of air. 'By God! That's wonderful!' His father's voice seemed to thunder, shattering the stillness. He stepped forward, enveloped them both in his thin arms, pulled them in to his embrace. 'Well done. I'm so pleased for you!' He turned, pulled May even closer, and she felt his moustache graze as he kissed her full on the lips.

He took her by the shoulders, pushing her forward, almost thrusting her in front of his wife. 'Well?' His voice was still shockingly loud, raw in its challenge. 'Aren't you going to congratulate your daughter-in-law?'

Again there was that instant of awful tension, then May breathed in the scent of Mrs Wright's perfume, felt her cheek brush against hers, the ruffles of her blouse as she was drawn to that small but formidable bosom.

'Congratulations, my dears. I'm very happy – for both of you.' The voice was a hoarse whisper, the frame against her shook. She was actually crying! Then May was joining her, and for a second they were in genuine communion, for the first time, their heads together as they wept.

SEVEN

EVEN WITHIN TWO months of the outbreak of what would become known as The Great War, and would claim somewhere between ten and thirteen million lives among the armed services of the combatants, most people's minds were still preoccupied with matters which seemed far closer to home. By June, Nicholas Mayfield's gloomy prognostication had come true, and over two million men were on strike. Sylvia Pankhurst was arrested for the eighth time, and Lords and Commons wrangled bitterly over the Irish Home Rule bill, while in Ireland itself both camps were already armed and killing, and things looked set to degenerate into full-scale civil war.

May's greatest worry was her continued good health. She had waited apprehensively through the early days and weeks of her pregnancy for the dreaded morning sickness to strike. She lay in bed – Jack made such a fuss if she so much as stirred before he set off for his work at seven o'clock that she decided it was easier to let him have his way, and lounge in bed while he brought her a cup of tea. The mornings were usually bright with streaming sunshine and he would sit on the bed drinking his own tea while she lay propped up with pillows.

'How are you feeling?' he asked, and invariably she would smile at him with fond irritation.

'I'm fine. Honest. Never felt better.' And it was so true, her appetite so good, her health so blooming, she began to worry about

56

it herself. Yet there were undoubted signs of the changes going on within her. Her breasts were fuller, hung ripely against the thin cotton of the nightgown, the nipples pushing their shape through the cloth. She shivered when Jack touched them, gnawing at her lip, gasping. They were so sensitive. He would push down the sheet, gently trace the contours of her belly curve under the thin material.

'I'm not showing yet!' she would protest, pretending to push his hand away, suddenly intensely aflame with her longing for him to stay with her, go on caressing her.

'Oh, I don't know, lass. You're getting a bit of a pot, I reckon.' He would bend forward, kiss her gently, chastely, on her proffered lips. Stand up. 'Now don't go doing too much, all right? See you tonight. Bye.' She would hear him, getting his things together, then he would appear in the doorway again. 'Love you,' he said, abruptly, shyly, then ducked out of sight and she heard the door bang, his footsteps fading.

It was odd. She never wanted him to go, yet she enjoyed intensely these moments of solitude just after he had gone, the warmth of his love, the light touch of his lips lingering on hers. The dancing motes of the new sunlight filling the silent room, the indentation at her side, the warmth of where he had been, the feel of her own unfettered body as she stretched her legs in the width of the bed. And the lazy, animal freedom of her body: she was ashamed of the tremors of desire, of sexuality, that drifted through her, so that she lay, for long drugged minutes, replete, thinking hazily of the love making they still indulged in, gentle and slow and careful, his concern for her, his caresses which released such shockingly powerful sensations and fulfilment in her.

When he came home on Friday night, she could tell at once that he had something on his mind. She waited, increasingly anxious at his preoccupied air, until she could not stand it any longer. 'What's wrong?'

Mr Redmond, the general manager at Waller's, had asked him to go and take a preliminary survey of the parish church of St Mary's, at Whitby, on top of the high east cliff, beside the ruins of the abbey. Substantial restoration work was needed to the tower, and also to other parts of the roof. May could tell how pleased Jack was to have been entrusted with the initial investigation. As she listened to him, and heard the apologetic tone in his words, she caught the unspoken meaning behind them.

'It's a big job, all right. Months of work there. And well worth doing. It takes a battering, stuck up there.'

'He wants you to take it on. Mr Redmond,' she said quietly, understanding all at once. 'Oh, Jack! It's such a long way. You'd only get home on a weekend.'

'I know. I told him how difficult it would be. The way we're fixed now.'

But she also understood his pride, the honour of his being offered the work. 'You'd be doing it yourself? All on your own?'

'I'd take on a local lad. To help out. But yes – it'd be my job, all of it.' He stopped, coloured a little. 'But you're right. It's too far. And with you being the way you are, I couldn't think of leaving you—'

She swallowed hard, got the words out in a rush, before she should change her mind. 'I'll be all right, you know I've got mam just down the road. She'd keep an eye on me, you know she would.' She hesitated. 'And your folks are even nearer, aren't they? I'll be all right.' She put on a bright smile. 'And it'd be a good bit more money, I expect, eh?'

He nodded, said nothing for a while. 'There's another way,' he said tentatively, then shook his head as if already dismissing it. 'But with you ... I know you want to be near your mam.'

'What? What do you mean?' she asked quickly, eagerly, sitting up, alert.

'Well, we could both go. Move down there.' He was blushing, sounded ashamed of the suggestion. 'Mr Redmond was saying ... you can get furnished rooms. Cheaper than here. He knows a place up on West Cliff, he said. He could recommend us.'

'Jack! Why didn't you say so? I'd love it! It'll be wonderful, living there!' She kissed him on the cheek, then pulled his face round, to kiss him fiercely on the mouth.

'Whoah there!' He held her a little away from him, staring at her. 'Remember your condition. I didn't think you'd want to be so far from your folks just now. It'll—'

'There's months to go yet, you silly ha'p'orth! I can always come back nearer me time if I want to. Besides, they have babies down in Whitby, too, don't they? And midwives to deliver 'em, no doubt. Oh Jack! I'm so happy! And I thought you wanted to leave me behind! To get rid of me!'

'Now who's a daft ha'p'orth?' He kissed her, more tenderly this time. 'Time for bed, fatty.'

'We'll go round and tell me mam first thing in the morning,' she said blissfully.

It was not first thing. In fact, they lay lazily abed until almost mid-morning. By the time they were all assembled round the table for their Sunday meal, an event had taken place, a minute of violent madness over a thousand miles away, which would change their own world irrevocably. In Sarajevo, a young Serbian student stepped forward and fired three shots at point blank range into the passing motor car, killing the Archduke Ferdinand, heir to the Austro–Hungarian throne, and his wife, Sophie, and thus precipitating the final inexorable slide towards a tidal wave of destruction and death which even then was beyond most people's imagination.

'It's fine, love. Honest, it really is.' May struggled to make her tone as reassuring as possible. She glanced once more round the large room on the second floor of the high building. There was another storey above them, also private accommodation, and above that the narrow dormer-windows projecting from the steeply sloping roofs, where the staff who worked in the hotel which took up the first two floors slept. Amity House occupied most of the block known as Langbeck Terrace, part of the long, curving street lined by similar solid buildings which led off from the impressive arc of Royal Crescent facing out to sea, across the floral gardens.

May went and stood in the big bay window, peering over the wooden sill which bisected the long, right hand panel of glass. 'And you *can* see the sea. So we do have sea-views, after all.' She turned back, grinned at him. 'I love it.' She would, too, she vowed, when she got used to living in one room. Ahead of her, beyond the shabby sofa and the two armchairs, stood the raffia screen which separated the bed area from the rest of the room.

Outside, across the narrow little landing, was a recess with a sink and a small two-burner stove which was their kitchen. The shared bathroom was up another flight of stairs, on the floor above.

But what did it matter, how cooped and crowded they were, as long as they were together? And they needed to be together now. She had an uneasy feeling, a fear she resolutely held at bay, as July forced people to turn their eyes and thoughts outward, away from home affairs. Suddenly everyone was talking war, there was a belligerent feel to the very air itself. A great many seemed almost savagely excited and happy at the prospect of a conflict with Germany. For that's what everyone was assuming. All the talk of these other nations, of Serbia, and the Austro–Hungary Empire, meant nothing. It was Kaiser Bill squaring up to John Bull that mattered.

'They've got to be stopped now,' people declared emphatically. 'Getting too big for their boots. They need to be taught a lesson, before it's too late.'

'Ah'm gonna join up!' her brother George had announced, on Jack and May's last visit to Sidney Terrace before their move. 'The navy. Stoker mechanic.'

'Ye'll do as you're told and finish your apprenticeship,' their father had grunted.

'There'll be none of that if we go to war,' his son answered roundly. 'Ah'm eighteen now, any road. Ah can please meself.'

'There won't really be a war, will there?' May asked Jack, on their last night in Gateshead.

'I shouldn't think so,' he told her comfortingly, with far more assurance than he felt.

'Jack,' she said slowly, 'you wouldn't go off and leave me if there was, would you?'

He caught hold of her, folded her firmly against his body. 'No fear of that, lass. They'd have to drag me off screaming and kicking. I'm no hero.' He grinned, kissed her on the nose. 'And if they did I'd run off home first chance I got.'

The excitement of living in the seaport, of such a new and different life, buoyed May up. She enjoyed the walk down through the narrow streets leading to the harbour, or strolling down the steep slope of Flowergate to the quayside. Then over the swing bridge, to Old Town, browsing through the wares when the stalls were set up in the old market place, picking her way through the crowds, shopping along Church Street before she began the slow, toiling ascent up the steps to the abbey, where she would meet Jack, and share a picnic lunch sitting on the grass at the top of the cliff, the whole town spread before them.

'You'll have to stop this soon, you know,' he chided her gently.

She folded her hands over her stomach. 'I don't show at all yet, do I? And nearly five months gone. I feel a right fraud, not wearing a corset and all that. But Dr Butcher says everything's fine.'

'I must say it looks good to me.' He gave her that special look, narrowing his eyes as he took in her figure, and she pinked with pleasure.

But she could not remain immune to the growing atmosphere about her. She was moving fairly rapidly one morning past the laid out piles of freshly caught fish down by the fish quays. The strong smells, and even the sight of the silvery and mottled gleaming skins, the roundly staring, sightless eyes, made her feel a little queasy. She heard a startling eruption of cheering all about her. Men took off their caps, waved them in circular motion above their heads, the shawled women shrieked like banshees. They were all clustering along the harbour side, and she saw, through the masts of the fishing boats tied up alongside, a naval vessel, in dark grey, slowly nosing ahead as she lost way. Clouds of thick black, greasy looking smoke were still billowing from her slim funnels. She had just steamed in, between the piers, and was about to drop anchor in the outer harbour. She looked sinister. May watched the dark jerseyed figures bustling about the upperworks. She jumped as a hoarse voice bellowed right behind her, 'We'll give 'em hell, lads!' and there was another burst of cheering.

She felt a frightening sense of helplessness as the events of the end of that month rumbled on inexorably. She understood nothing of it, not even when Jack patiently tried to explain things. She wasn't stupid, she knew she wasn't, yet it felt somehow as though her brain was paralysed, refused to take in the enormity of it, though she could see the outcome. It began to lie on her, like some dead, icy weight on her mind, so at odds with the quickening life she could now feel flutteringly awakening in her body.

And that's what she clung to, what she had to cling to, so fiercely. 'Look, Jack. Come here. Feel. You can feel it. It's moving, I'm sure of it.' No longer embarrassed, she lifted her nightdress, took his palm, pressed it to her side, below her ribs, held his warmth comfortingly against hers. There was a ripple, a soft gurgle.

'That's your tea going down,' he teased gently, and she slapped at him.

On 23 July, Austria–Hungary gave Serbia an ultimatum, but gave her no chance of even agreeing to the humiliating terms. On the 28th, the newsboys were racing round the streets crying, 'War declared on Serbia!' Two days later, Russia was mobilizing. It was coming up to the bank holiday, and Whitby was filling up. The weather promised to be glorious, the traders and boarding-house keepers were getting ready for a bumper weekend.

May passed two of the girls scrubbing down the flight of steps which led up to the front entrance of Amity House. They were being supervised by Mr Brand, the chubby head porter. He nodded a greeting. His apple-red cheeks over his impressive set of greying whiskers glinted as he smiled. 'Make the most of it, eh, Mrs Wright? Eat, drink, and be merry, as they say! Might be our last!'

'Cheerful codger, in't 'e?' one of the girls said, pushing at a strand of hair peeping from under her mob cap with a red wrist.

May went on, through the high arch which led into the back lane, and the narrow wooden door to the yard. Another door gave access to the dark service stairs which led to their own rooms and those on the higher floors which were not part of the hotel accommodation. Her heart was thumping, and she was distinctly out of breath when she reached their landing. She pressed her hand to her side briefly before she let herself in with the key.

Bit early for you to be puffing and blowing, she chided herself. You've a long ways to go yet. She felt a bit nauseous, too, even a little giddy. She flopped into the nearest armchair, stared unseeingly at the huge bright window. She had just left Jack, not half an hour ago, but she wished it was tea time and he was coming in from work. Was it her condition, or her fear that made her feel so out of sorts? she wondered.

She heard the sudden clatter of a motor below, and dragged herself up out of the depths of the chair. She went to the window, moved the curtain, peered down to the street. She saw the square, box-like shape of one of those charabanc things they used to transport people from the station at West Cliff. Hardly more than a few hundred yards, but too long to stagger when you were loaded down with luggage.

And this lot certainly were. The women all had floral hats and parasols, the men, who were greatly outnumbered, in boaters and the striped blazers. There seemed to be swarms of children, too, pinafored and sailor-suited, who were threatening to take off immediately for the siren delights of the sea-front beckoning them only yards away.

The engine spluttered and coughed to a halt, and she could hear the excited cries, the laughing voices, full of the anticipation of the holiday. 'Eat, drink, and be merry,' Mr Brand had said. How did that go on? 'For tomorrow we die.' As the happy laughter drifted up to her, muted through the distance and the glass, May shuddered, and put her knuckle to her mouth, biting down until it hurt.

EIGHT

THE SENSE OF unreality dogged May throughout that last week-end of peace. The contrast between the breeziness of the summer weather, the jollity of the holiday crowds that packed the town and the great, numbing weight of fear that surrounded her was nightmarish. Even Jack was part of it. 'Are you working tomorrow?' she asked him, on the Friday night, and it seemed to her there was something evasive about the way he looked at her, then looked away.

His thin face closed a little as he murmured, 'Aye, lass. I'll have to put the morning in, at least, Bank Holiday or no Bank Holiday.' He knew very well she was not thinking of the holiday weekend, and she was shocked at the secret blaze of anger she felt which made her briefly want to bite shrewishly at him. He was just like all the crowds of red, laughing faces pressing on her when she wandered down past the pavilion gardens the next day. She wanted to scream at them, too, for their wilful blindness. Mr Brand's words kept running through her mind. Maybe they weren't blind, all these folk. Maybe they were just snatching what might prove to be the last moments of normal happiness they would know for some time.

Next day, however, there were crowds pouring in to the solid edifice of St Hilda's just across the way from Amity House. Jack needed no persuading to attend chapel, and they walked down the hill through bright sunshine to the Methodist church, which was packed, too. The preacher prayed for peace, for the world leaders who held all their fates in their hands. But even as they came back out into the sunshine, May comforted by the service, and the unity she had felt binding them, they heard the strident blasting of a bugle.

There were several blue jackets, in their best uniforms, from the naval ship which was in port for the weekend. 'Hey up! That's the recall!' one of them said, his face solemn, yet glowing, too, with importance. Jack and May made their way past Station Square, to the upper harbour where crowds were jostling. There were repeated bursts of cheering. The naval vessel was getting up steam, the crew hastening to get back on board, ready for an abrupt departure.

Newspapers were producing special editions by the hour, it seemed, and Jack bought the latest sheet from a bare-footed, patched-breeches lad who was screeching, 'Germany declares war on Russia! France mobilizes!' May clung tightly to Jack's arm as they made their way along the quays, held up by the volume of the strolling crowds. There was a great comfort in the solidity of his hand gripping hers. He squeezed hard, knowing exactly how she was feeling.

They passed the low, circular building of the old battery. Below them, on the level sand over the sea-wall, a great throng of children were sitting cross-legged, the adults ringed thickly behind them, watching the Punch and Judy show. Jack and May stopped to listen briefly to the raucous voices, the children screaming in delighted, horrified reply to the pantomime of violence.

'It's going to happen, isn't it?' May said quietly, as they continued along the foot of the cliff, the crowds thinning out a little as they left the vicinity of the pier.

He looked at her, paused very slightly, then answered, just as quietly, 'Looks like it, love. We've got to do something if Germany moves against Belgium. And it looks like they're going to, all right.'

The Bank Holiday Monday was a day of waiting, for what by then was the inevitable to happen. Jack took the whole day off. Again they walked, this time away from the town, along the beach to Sandsend. Suddenly, everyone seemed to be waving little paper

Union Jacks, and little boys dashed in and out of the holiday-makers, straining their throats with the sounds of war. May wanted to reach out and grab them, shake some sense into them.

When they came back in the late afternoon from their walk, there was a charabanc again parked outside the front entrance, this time loading up with departing guests. Red-faced men grinned and cheered at the couple, the women laughed tolerantly. There was a burst of 'Rule Britannia' as the vehicle pulled noisily away. While Jack and May lay in bed, they kept on hearing drunken snatches of the same song from the streets below, as well as bellowed lines of the national anthem.

All at once Jack felt May shaking against him, and he realized she was crying silently. His own throat closed and his eyes were wet with emotion as he hugged her to him.

'Folk've gone daft,' she wept. 'They all seem to want war.'

He kissed and stroked her hair, held her close. 'Don't fret, love. We'll be all right. Nobody's going to harm us. I'm not a coward, May. Leastways, I hope not. But I'm not going to leave you, and our baby. Not for anything. You're all that matters to me.'

'Bu—but what if they make you?' A great sigh shook her body and transmitted itself to him. 'Like they do – Mr Brand was saying the other day. The French are made to join the army. They have to do three years.'

'No, not here. They won't do that here.' He grunted. 'There'll be more than enough breaking their necks to get out there and fight, I reckon. Besides, you can't make a man fight. Not if he doesn't want to. You'll not get rid of me that easily!'

The nation was still not at war when Jack went back to work the following day. The official declaration did not come until 11pm that night, when German troops were already fighting on Belgian soil and Britain, honouring its pledge to guarantee Belgium's neutrality, plunged into the world conflict, 'just for a scrap of paper', as the German Chancellor contemptuously put it to the British Ambassador in Berlin.

At first, all eyes turned with anxious pride to the sea, and the might of the Royal Navy. It took time for the land forces to mass into positions. It was two weeks before our relatively small professional army was installed across the Channel, but even before they had gone, in towns and cities all over the British Isles there were long queues outside recruiting offices as boys and men flocked to join up by the thousands. A hysterical patriotism spread like an epidemic. Many were persuaded to volunteer, carried along on the spur of the moment. Suddenly, everyone had the chance to be noble. The romance of war made heroes of the dowdiest labourer, the scruffiest errand boy.

The old folk were caught up in it, too. Old soldiers wore their medals from the Boer War, forgot the miseries of sickness they had endured, and wished they were going too. Women and children supported the nationalistic fervour to the hilt, cheering on the volunteers, singing, waving flags, exchanging bold kisses with perfect strangers, on cheek and even on lips.

' 'Urry up, lads!' May heard a wag call out one day, in the long queue waiting to enlist. 'It'll all be over afore we get there at this rate!'

She felt a sense of helpless disbelief at the atmosphere all around her. She was secretly worried at the closed expression she now saw on Jack's intense face when he faced the outside world each morning. And when he came back from it each evening. As though he was doing his best to shut it out, not to see or hear it, a task she knew was impossible. There was proof enough that the madness was close to home.

There was a letter pushed in with the birthday card her mother had sent for May's twentieth birthday, which was celebrated on 10 August.

'Hope this finds you well,' Robina had written, 'and that you have a happy birthday. We all send our love and will be thinking of you. I hope you can get up soon to see us.

'Now for our bit of news. Your brother George has gone off and joined the navy like he said he would. He left yesterday (Friday) we couldn't talk him out of it, he had made up his mind. Your father says he's better off in the navy than the army. Anyway, there's loads of young ones from round here going off, I suppose they've got to do it. They've sent him hundreds of miles away, past London, Chatham, the place is called. I'm proud of him of course, we all are, but I pray that he'll be all right and come home again soon.

'Is your Jack talking of joining up yet? There's lots of married men signing up as well. Tell him that mate of his has already joined. Arty. I saw Nelly the other day. She still sees him. I thought she was keen on him a while back but you know what Nelly's like. Mind you, the way she was going on about him the other day you'd think they were engaged or something. Now that he's gone off to the war she's all sweet on him again and says she's going to write to him every week. I wonder how long that'll last.'

Jack read it as soon as he came in from work. May had prepared a special tea to celebrate her birthday, and put on her best dress to mark the occasion. She had already let it out, and it felt tight again, a sure sign of her changing shape. He glanced up at her when he finished reading. His face looked strained, tired, though that was just because of the heavy work he was doing up at the church, she tried to reassure herself.

'You have a strip wash and change before we eat,' she smiled, but he continued to sit there, gazing up at her.

'May . . . you *do* think it's right, don't you? Me staying here, with you? You don't think—'

'Don't be daft!' she cried, lowering herself to her knees and leaning against him. Her hands sought his, felt their work-roughened coarseness, lifted them to rub her lips softly against them. 'This is where you belong, you know it is.' And she let the soft bulk of her upper body rest against his knees.

'Iris. Would you mind awfully if I asked you something?'

Iris stared at Lionel Strang's dark eyes. She felt trapped by their steady gaze. For once, she felt she was seeing total honesty in them, and she was shocked by the depth of her response to his pleading look, the unspoken message there. You're just being a sentimental fool, she upbraided herself angrily. Just because he's going off to war, you're going all mushy on him. After months of keeping him at arm's length, holding him off until you were almost certain that he'd given up on you.

Now she was shaken by what suddenly seemed a very real emotional tie between them. Part of her was angry, as though he had somehow tricked her into this unsought intimacy, part of her was thrilled and moved. After all, it was rather pathetic, in the truest sense. A handsome young man, going off to face possible death, ready to give up his life for his country. How could she fail to be moved by the nobility of it?

And it *was* noble, the way young men all over the country were rallying to the flag. She had just read yesterday, in daddy's paper, of some of the terrible crimes the Huns were carrying out in Belgium. The murder of innocent women and children. At a place called Dinant, over six hundred civilians had been shot down in cold blood, in the town square. There were tales of brutal rape, of child murder. She felt a choking rage, and that old sense of feminist outrage in all its full force that she was unable herself to take any direct part in this crusade against evil. She would willingly take up arms, learn to shoot straight, wished that it was she who was going off to war, instead of this passionate, good-looking young man who was holding so clammily and apologetically to her hand to say his farewells.

'Of course not. Fire away!' she said cheerily now, ashamed of the perverse little thrill his soulful expression gave her, and her knowledge that she was responsible for it.

'I know you don't feel – well, there can ever be anything between us – other than friendship, I mean. We will always be friends, won't we, Iris?' Inside, she still felt that mocking, bitter rage at herself for her duplicity. He's right, of course he's right. You know you've despised his running after you all this year.

She returned the pressure of his hand. 'Certainly you're a friend, Lionel,' she murmured. 'Always.'

'Is there truly no one else who occupies a special place in your affections?' he asked earnestly. A flash of her habitual, self-mocking humour bubbled up internally. How typical! He could not imagine how she could fail to fall swooningly into his arms, unless she had already metaphorically fallen into someone else's. As though that were a girl's whole *raison d'être*, to be waiting for some swain to pluck her like a ripening fruit. Then conscience panged again at her new image of him as the knight waiting to ride out to battle.

'There's no one,' she said gently. She was tempted, dangerously, to succumb, to grant him the favour he had been seeking for the past year and more. Indeed, she put a tentative foot forward, gropingly, to possible danger, by adding promptingly, 'What was it you wanted to ask me?'

He was holding her hand in both of his now, she could feel his fingers pressing on her flesh. 'Well – if there *is* no one, would you mind keeping in touch? Would you allow me to write to you? And would you drop me a line now and then?'

He said it so humbly, with that pleading look, that she blinked rapidly, swallowed. There was a suspicious gleam of tears in her eyes. 'You silly boy! Of course I will. I'd love to. I'll write every week, give you all the news of home. And you must tell me everything. It'll be so exciting.'

'Yes. Perhaps, when it's all over—' he was even more hesitant now, an altogether new, uncertain Lionel whom, if he had but known it, she was far more stirred by than his old male animal, pursuing role, 'you might – feel differently towards me.'

'I'll always be very fond of you,' she murmured unsteadily, glancing down at her lap. She half expected him to lean forward, to take her in his embrace, as he had done several times before, to kiss her on the lips. Instead, he raised her hand, still held by his, and kissed it very softly.

'Bless you!' he whispered.

When it was time for him to go, and he had bidden farewell to her parents, and to an enthusing Helena, who clung to him impulsively and raised herself to kiss him on the cheek, in front of her parents, it was Iris who made the move, in the tiled porch, unmindful of the gaze of Beattie, the maid, behind them in the hall. She reached for him – she was as tall as he was – and cupped her palm along the back of his neck, pulling him into her, and kissed him passionately, her lips opening a little, lingeringly, full on the mouth. She felt the ardour of his response, the crushing of her body against him, his thighs and knees straining against hers briefly.

She stood, breathing heavily, her knees trembling, watching him drive away. She waved, felt a hysterical urge to giggle, then to cry, welling up inside, and blushed hotly as she realized she was dabbing furiously at her mouth, wiping his kiss from her and shuddering as she did so.

The atmosphere at Jack's home was electric with a tension he could feel as soon as he stepped inside the door. Its cause, he learned from his mother almost as soon as he arrived, was his older brother, Dan. 'He's gone and volunteered,' she informed him bitterly. 'Of all the stupid things to do! Left your father completely stuck, with his selfishness.'

Jack could sense, behind the bitterness, Sophia's anxiety for her eldest child, an anxiety which did not appear to be shared by her husband. Edward Wright was torn with conflicting emotions, not least of which was a fierce pride in Dan's impulsive action in signing on. 'Had his medical yesterday. Passed with flying colours. He has to report to Fenham on Monday. Joining the Fusiliers, of course.' He shook his head. 'Can't blame the lad, mind. I'd have done the same thing meself if I'd been younger.' Then he hurried on, aware of the thin line of Sophia's mouth, the flinty look on her face. 'But I don't know how we're going to manage at work without him, and that's the truth. And there's a lot more work coming our way now. Pamphlets. War work – posters and information sheets and that. I've had to get old Billy Knox back. Poor old blighter's seventy now, you know.'

'I hope you've got a bit more sense than your brother!' Sophia glared at Jack. Only then did she enquire about May. 'Not with you, is she? How's she going on?'

'No, she's a bit tired. With the travelling and all that. Trains are all mucked up. It took us hours to get through. We were stuck on Middlesborough station for ages. Troops everywhere. I'll bring her round tomorrow. She's having an early night.'

It was the first Friday of September. Jack had decided to take the day off work and travel up to Gateshead a day earlier than they had originally planned. He needed to go into the office over in Newcastle early the next morning, discuss things with Mr Redmond. The war was already affecting most areas of life, including the restoration of twelfth-century churches. It was two months since they had moved to Whitby and he had been promising May a trip back home for some time. They would spend the weekend on Tyneside, and travel back down on Monday.

'You could have stayed here,' his mother was saying, the hostility evident in her tone. 'I'm sure there's more room than round at the Rayners'.'

'It's only for a couple of nights, mam,' Jack said placatingly. 'We didn't want to put you out.' He glanced round at his younger brother, Joe. 'How's the birthday lad?' Joe would be sixteen on the following Wednesday. 'You're bigger than me already, by the look of you. What's happening with school then, Joe?'

Joe frowned unhappily. His father cut in before he could speak. 'He's done real well. Got him off to a flying start! There's plenty of positions he could take up now. Harrison's 'll take him on in the shipping office. But for a while he's coming in with me, to help out, like. Be worth his weight in gold, once he's learnt a few of the ropes.' Edward Wright's voice was rich with jollying enthusiasm. Joe glowered sulkily.

'I wanted to join up, same as Dan,' he muttered. 'They'll take you at sixteen if you get your papers signed by your dad—'

'Don't talk so daft!' Sophia interrupted vituperatively. 'Why on earth everyone's so blinking set on getting themselves killed—' she stopped short, and everyone began talking at once to smother the awful instant of silence.

'Well, I think our Dan's done a really brave thing,' Cissy put in, threatening to stir up the tensions all over again. Jack studied his sister's dark, mischievous looking face, which was set in a defiant pout. She was pretty enough, with a good figure, he acknowledged, gazing at her with a new objectivity. She'd have lads enough in tow, he surmised. She was almost the same age as May, would be twenty in less than two months. But she seemed so much younger, much closer to adolescence still. She was not a woman yet, for all her pert cockiness.

The chief object of their combined concern came in from town a few minutes later. He shook Jack's hand vigorously, gave him the ghost of a wink. 'You can tell your lass she can sleep easy in her bed now. This scrap won't last five minutes once I get out there!'

They made an excuse to get out of the house, and walked up the steep bank, past the rows of railinged houses, with the concealing privet and dour laurel bushes in the front gardens, up to the main road, and the Belle View Inn, where they went through the dark corridor to the Gentlemen's Parlour at the back. As they passed the spit and sawdust bar on their right, they could hear the loud chorus of the popular music hall song of the previous year, which was suddenly on everybody's lips in these stirring times. 'Goodbye, Piccadilly, farewell Leicester Square!'

'Listen to 'em!' Dan chuckled quietly, when they got their tankards of bitter and sat at one of the small round tables. 'They've never been further south than Durham in their lives!'

'You're sure you're doing the right thing?' Jack asked presently.

Dan nodded firmly. 'Absolutely! Can't wait! Just the ticket!' He gave the winning, wicked smile Jack recognized so well, had seen him use to impress and work his way through awkward situations since the days of their boyhood. 'Someone's got to do it, eh? Keep the world safe for you married blokes to sit at home and get fat in!' Jack smiled wryly, raised his pot in mock tribute before taking a sip.

Dan leaned closer, his beaming face transformed into a leer of parodied lechery, as his right eye closed in a broad wink. 'And you've heard all about those French ma'mselles, haven't you? Just dying to give their all to the brave Tommies from over the sea. A bachelor's dream, this lot, Jack!'

The soldiers of the BEF were in fact already mightily disillusioned. After their disciplined retreat from the area around Mons, they had marched steadily southward, away from the frontiers, with precious little singing as they swung along. On the day that Jack and Dan sat drinking in the pub, there was a pause, as Von Kluck's advance petered out, and the Allies prepared to launch a counter offensive. The British infantrymen in the front line were set to digging some rough, shallow trenches to give them shelter for the night.

'No need for anything too fancy, lads,' an NCO told them confidently. 'We won't be needing 'em for long. We'll be off and heading eastward tomorrow.' There were others, of far more elevated rank, who were to be just as spectacularly wrong in the insanities which lay ahead.

NINE

JACK HATED THE poster. It seemed suddenly to sprout pursuingly everywhere. On the wall by the railings of the Royal Hotel, on the hoardings at the corner of Skinner Street. Both sides of the swing bridge, which he crossed every day to get over to the east side and his work. Even on the pillars of the old Town Hall. That sternly implacable stare, over the great, symmetrical flow of the moustache, and, worst of all, that accusingly thrusting finger, pointed straight at you, picking you out. The red clarion call of the word above the picture shrieked at you. BRITONS. They didn't even need to put Lord Kitchener's name on. Just that stern face, that pointing finger, and underneath, the words 'wants YOU' And the 'YOU' blazed out in huge capitals made it very direct, very personal.

The tide of patriotic fervour swelled ever higher. Jack found himself alone in the draughty church one morning in early October, with driving rain and a cutting easterly wind flapping and rattling the canvas screens he had rigged up like huge sails to protect the interior of the building from the dust and rubble of the old stonework he was still hammering out up in the tower. He was outside, scouting about for his two assistants, when the verger came down the narrow path between the gravestones, from the cottage near the coastguard station. 'They've up and off,' he announced. Jack sensed a malicious glee in the elderly voice. 'Young Tommy and Frank Merriman. Both gone off to volunteer.'

75

He did what he could, working on his own, dressing the stone which was to replace the crumbling, faulty blocks, but he needed help to hoist them on the ropes up to the platform he had rigged up just under the roof, and to prise and ease and tap them into position.

Another full day passed before he could find a replacement. He was saddened to lose Tommy Wilkinson, for he felt he had established a good relationship with the youngster, who was no more than sixteen. The boy had shown a real interest and an aptitude for the work. Jack even sensed that he had caught something of his own fascination for the long ago past, the romance of dealing with the handiwork of long-forgotten craftsmen. 'Hundreds of years from now, somebody'll be looking at our work, Tommy,' he'd say, and had seen the lad's face stamped with reflective solemnity at the thought. Yes, he was sad to lose him so suddenly. But not surprised. The madness was everywhere.

His brother, Joe, had disappeared just days after his sixteenth birthday. His mother had been ill with frantic worry, until he had been traced, after almost a week, to the recruitment depot over the river, where Sophia herself had insisted on going along with her husband, and delivered a half-hysterical tirade to an elderly reservist lieutenant. 'We can't always tell if someone's lying, madam,' he said defensively. 'Your son stated on his form that he was eighteen years of age. The lad's keen to do his bit, I'll say that for him.' He did not add that recruiting NCO's were keen to turn a blind eye on such misdemeanours. A sheepish, exhausted-looking Joe appeared in the orderly room clutching a cloth bag with his few items in it, and had to endure the supreme shame of public chastisement as the slender, upright figure of Sophia, almost a head shorter than he was, stepped forward and clouted him resoundingly about his newly shorn skull before leading him away.

'Couldn't our Daniel have done something about it?' she asked her husband bitterly. She felt that Ted displayed nowhere near enough righteous wrath at their youngest son's errant behaviour and harboured a sneaking sympathy with the lieutenant's sentiment. She rounded on him vehemently. 'You'll not be content I suppose until all three of them are in uniform, including our Jack!'

Dan knew nothing of his brother's action, for he was several miles distant, living under canvas in a large camp at the coast north of Whitley Bay, and into a basic training so rigorous that crossing the Channel and joining the 'contemptible little army', as the Kaiser had dubbed the BEF, to face the Hun in action, was looked upon as a highly desirable goal. What Dan and his contemporaries did not know was that the army they were so anxious to join was in the process of being largely wiped out in the earliest bloody battles around Ypres.

Casualty figures were carefully doctored for home consumption, and newspaper reports were unfailingly optimistic, though the phrase 'home for Christmas' was heard less and less. The appeals for volunteers were more urgently strident than ever, and were met with continuing success.

One afternoon, Jack had to leave work to call in at the parcel depot of the railway. He had been waiting for some special supplies to treat infected timbers, which should have arrived from the works in Newcastle days ago He saw a crowd half blocking the roadway as he neared the bridge, the whooping kids and bold, brassy women that seemed to hang about the area permanently. Most of the men in the short line outside the recruiting office were red faced and loud with ale, and he felt that reckless, carnival atmosphere which seemed to have pervaded the town for weeks now, and which privately sickened him. It cheapened what should be a solemn undertaking. These men were offering their service, their very lives maybe, for king and country. Yet they acted as though they were off on some boozy holiday, and the girls and women who hung about them encouraged them in their light-hearted attitude. It degraded the whole concept of what they were doing, made a mockery of it.

As he passed onto the bridge itself, he found the way blocked by a gang of women. Some of them were the young lasses habitually found near the quays, with coarse aprons and woollen shawls pulled about their heads, but several were dressed more fashionably, in gowns and travelling coats and hats. A plump, matronly figure, close to his mother's age he guessed, certainly middle-aged, confronted him. Her chubby face set in a bright, friendly smile.

'Come on, laddy! You look like a fine young man. Are you going to answer the call? We need you, you know. Make your family proud of you!'

He flushed deeply, opened his mouth to speak, closed it again, moved around her. A younger woman, coarser in her dress and her manner, reached out suggestively, tugged at his sleeve.

'Ye don't want to miss the fun, me chuck!' Her eyes met his boldly, provocatively. 'Get yesel' over there. Sign on an' do yer bit.'

He shook his head and she was already turning as he hurried away, hot faced. His mind screamed obscenities, he felt himself quivering with a helpless rage, and he was breathing heavily, as though he had been running. His fist was clenched, he was ashamed of the savage longing he felt to smash it into that bold, leering face.

He said nothing to May about his encounter with the women. His conscience goaded him. Why? Is it because you're ashamed? Did they damage your manly pride? Do you really think they were right, that you should be 'doing your bit', joining in 'the fun'? He was sure the answer was no. Why then should he still feel so uncomfortable about it that he kept silent? Instead, he talked to her of his troubles at work, which were burdensome enough. The chap he had taken on as a replacement for the two he had lost was a dead loss himself. He turned up late, or not at all, and was sullen and uninterested when he was present.

'I'll have to advertise, I think,' Jack told May. 'I'll call in with a notice for the *Gazette* tomorrow.

'How does this sound?' he asked, after he had sat down with pencil and paper at the table in the window recess. ' "Young man wanted, 18–20. Strong and willing to work. To help in restoration of parish church." Think I should mention the wage?'

May looked over from her seat by the fire, and chuckled. 'Don't

want to put them off. Anyway, you'll be lucky. Most strong and willing young men are queuing up to join the army.'

He grunted, almost told her about the confrontation in town, but
did not do so.

'I wish Redmond could send us somebody from up home. I'm
fed up of these Yorkshire tykes. But they're short-handed up there
as well. There'll be nobody left at all to carry on at home if they
keep this up. They'll all have rushed off to sign up.'

'As long as you're not one of them.' She leaned forward, jabbed
at the small fire in the high grate. 'It's freezing for October. Are we
going to bank up the fire? You'll have to go down for some more
coal if we are.'

'Leave it. Let's have an early night.' He watched tenderly as she
rose, stretched and yawned luxuriously. Her waist had thickened
now. Even in the loose shirt which hung outside her skirt, he could
see the change in her figure. 'Look,' he continued carefully, 'we'll
have to talk properly about what we're going to do with you soon.'

She turned impatiently. 'I thought we'd settled that. I'll be fine
here. Mrs Wood is as good as anyone you'll find. And Dr Butcher'll
be there if he's needed.' It was true, Irene Wood was an experienced
midwife, and had already won May's confidence. She was more
determined than ever that she should stay here in Whitby for the
birth, and not subject herself to her mother's affectionate tyranny
for weeks on end. More importantly, she wanted Jack to be on hand
for the great event. Even if he *were* up in Gateshead when the baby
was born, he would be firmly relegated to a back seat by her mam
and the rest of the family.

She wanted him by her side, holding her hand, to the last possible minute, and back again the first possible minute he could be
there; she would have liked to have him there, be clinging onto
him, during the birth itself, though she was too ashamed to confess
such a notion to anyone, even to Jack himself.

'It's not just when the baby's born,' he argued. 'It's afterwards.
You'll need someone to look after you. The confinement—'

'Our Julia can come down. Mam'll let her, I know she will. She's fifteen now. She must 've got a bit more sense in her head, surely.'

'For that matter, I suppose we could ask Cissy,' he offered doubtfully. 'But what about Christmas? Your mam's going to want us to go up there. And you can't be travelling back and forth. Not by then. It's due early January. It'll—'

'What's wrong with us having Christmas here, on our own?' she said stubbornly. 'We had last Christmas with them. Why shouldn't we have this one on our own? We *are* married, after all. And I'll be in no state to go gallivanting about, partying and all that. It'll be lovely.' She paused, grabbed hold of both his hands, held them tightly. 'I'm a bit scared, Jack. A right cowardy custard for all me gab. I want you to be with me. I don't want you to be miles away, down here on your own, and me up there. It's our baby. We should be together.'

She leaned in close, lifting her face, puckering her lips for a kiss, which he gave her.

'Putty in your hands, aren't I?' he sighed, smiling.

'I love you,' she whispered, and returned his kiss, more passionately, her mouth open and working against his. Then she broke away, with a childish giggle. 'I'm off to the lav before I get undressed. It's bad enough having to use the po umpteen times in the night. I swear it'll be full to the brim one of these mornings. It's all this lemon barley water you keep forcing down me, you big bully!'

Jack woke in the black early hours of 30 October, wondering if the distant sounds of commotion he fancied he had heard were part of a dream he could no longer remember as he surfaced to full wakefulness. Then he heard the booming crash of the sea. At the same time, a fierce gust of wind rattled the bay window and the driven raindrops spattered like gravel flung against the glass. A full-blooded northerly gale hammered in direct from the sea. Aware of the raging elements only yards away, and of the warmth of the blanketed cocoon of the bed, he huddled down, fitted himself into the warm shape of May, curled with her back to him. His hand slid round, held the relaxed, full shape of her belly, then came up to cup the ripe fullness of her breast. She stirred in her deep sleep, pressed the soft yield of her buttocks into his loins, in unconscious acknowledgement of his enfolding touch.

The wildness of the weather both disturbed and excited him. He lay listening to the fury of the gale, savouring its contrast with his own snug warmth. He almost dozed off again, the temptation to lie on was wickedly strong. One thing was sure, he told himself, neither Jack Cameron, nor 'Ceddy' Burns, the lad he had taken on in answer to his advert in the *Gazette*, would be into work on time on a morning like this. In fact, Cameron, a feckless sort, about his own age and with a wife and babe in arms whom he cared little for, judging by the amount of time and money he spent in the various pubs around town, might well choose today to sign up for king and country, as he had been threatening to do for all the short time Jack had known him. Wild, stormy weather like this made people do some daft things.

In the end, conscience pricked away at Jack so much that he rose no later than his usual time, with the windows showing only the faintest grey through their rain-pocked surface. He looked out onto a flickering, lamplit desolation, the wind roaring up between the buildings of the street straight from the sea, and driving the rain in almost horizontal slants before it.

He dressed quickly, and went across the cold landing to put the kettle on the spirit stove. He made a pot of strong tea, came in as quietly as he could, and lit the lamp over on the solid dining table, shading it carefully so that as little as possible of its light fell on the darkened section of the room where the bed lay. His 'bait' box had been prepared the night before. He ate quickly, then poured out a second cup of tea, put in two large spoonfuls of sugar, stirred it thoroughly.

He edged round the screen, and reached across the bed, gently shook the humped shape beneath the bedclothes. The dark hair straggled lankly over the pillow as she surfaced, her face screwed up as though in pain. 'Eh? What?' She sighed and grunted to wakefulness, gave a huge heave, levering herself up on her elbows. 'Is it time? Already?'

He aimed a kiss somewhere near her ear. 'Here's your tea. You stay put, mind. Listen to it. It's blowing like mad. Don't you set foot out in this.'

'Yes, sir, no, sir!' She yawned, grinned sleepily at him. Only then did she become properly aware of the storm, and shivered. 'You're not going out in that, are you? I've never heard it so wild!' A childish excitement caught hold of her suddenly. She would get wrapped up later and take a walk, if only along the top of West Cliff. She no longer climbed the 199 Church Steps to meet Jack for lunch, though she still walked down into town most days, or strolled along past the pavilion gardens and out towards Upgang, to the north.

'I hope the tower hasn't blown down in all this,' Jack joked, when he was ready to leave.

'You take care,' she warned, stretching out her arms to embrace him. 'You won't be outside, will you?'

He decided to descend to the harbour by the Khyber Pass, in spite of the wind, which grabbed and buffeted him as soon as he stepped out of the back lane. He leaned into it, gripped by a boyish excitement, and pulled his cap off before it was plucked from his head. He knew there was something unusual afoot when he turned out of Royal Crescent and saw the knot of people huddled on the edge of the cliff, over the sharply curving road of the pass which led down to the harbour.

The louring grey clouds scudding by brought curtains of lashing rain which parted every now and then to make visibility varied and uncertain, but he could see the huge whiteness of the seas breaking right over the west pier immediately below. One of the standing men turned as he approached, not waiting to be asked. 'There's a ship aground. Ower yon, off Saltwick. It's a bad un!'

He hurried down the twisting road and ran into a crowd so thick it blocked the roadway by the lifeboat house. 'The' cannot get round to 'er!' a bystander told him. The lifeboat was an old-fashioned, open boat, propelled only by oars. 'The've been out two hours an' more. The' cannot get round beyond piers!'

He eased his way through and continued down past the fish quay. The boats were all still there, masts bobbing, thickly clustered by the harbour wall. The streets were already crowded. Many were making their way along Church Street towards East Cliff and the Church Steps, to climb up onto the abbey plain. Another considerable crowd had gathered on the high edge of the cliff, and more were coming every second. Jack joined them, peered out towards the sea. Curiously, the wind seemed to have dropped now, yet it made no difference to the vast waves driving in on the shore.

At first he could see nothing, then the grey cleared a little, and he saw a line of white breakers, and something dark like a rock sticking up. The light was growing stronger all the time, and soon he could make out the shape of the funnel and superstructure, and the tall slenderness of the foremast. The rest of the vessel was lost beneath the battering sea. The word passed among the crowd from the nearby coastguard station that a hospital ship, the *Rohilla*, had struck the Saltwick Reef at about four that morning. The lifeboatmen had been struggling to get round to her since dawn. The crowds on both sides of the estuary mouth watched the boat wallowing in the tossing but comparatively safe waters of the outer harbour, the distant figures of the crew slumped in the final stages of exhaustion over the oars.

'If they don't get them off soon it'll be too late,' someone muttered.

The wind rose again, and Jack realized he was drenched. He moved away, went inside the cold church whose clammy air seemed to wrap itself around him. There was no sign of his assistants, or anyone else. He glanced about him in the dimness. The sounds of the gale, and of the crowds, were muted, distant. He thought of the terrified passengers and crew, trapped out there in that hell, less than a quarter of a mile away. What did we need to kill each other for? he wondered savagely. He glanced up at this solid, ancient building. Nature could do it well enough, without our help.

There was a noise behind him, a hurrying of feet, then the dark jerseyed figure of one of the coastguards was there gasping for breath. 'Have you got a block and tackle? Some rope we can use? We're gonna try an' get the other boat over the spa ladder. Launch her from t'other side of East Pier.'

It was a desperate undertaking. The second boat, nigh on thirty feet in length and an open rowing boat like the other, was already drawn up at the foot of the east cliff, with a crowd of lifeboatmen and willing volunteers gathered round it. Everyone seemed to be bawling contradictory instructions at once, over the deafening roar of the surf, but order was quickly asserted. Ropes were tied to the wooden boat, some men, among whom was Jack, scrambled up the high sea-wall, the 'spa ladder' which joined the pier to the cliff itself, and with a great rhythmic chant, the many helpers began to raise the boat inch by painful inch, the rope fenders bouncing and scraping against the stone and iron work.

At last she hung precariously, teetering at the top of the wall. Soaked in sweat now, half blinded by it, the frantic men had to lower it down on the other side, where the full might of the sea was pounding in to break only yards away in the jumble of rocks below the cliff, with a solid thud that they felt travel up from their boots, through to their straining guts. There was a moment of panic when the stern dipped suddenly, and threatened to clatter the boat down in a heap, but, somehow, they held it, cushioned it as it made the final drop to the shelving grit and pebbles.

A corpulent individual, his beer belly tightly pronounced beneath his blue gansey, shook his head. 'The'll not git 'er out in this.' But his pessimism was disproved later, when the crowd, who had thought themselves exhausted, dragged and manhandled the narrow boat past the rocks, and out into the crashing surf. Jack was there, felt his hand slide from the gunwale, the fingers torn by the rough wood which soared suddenly way over his head, and he fell, staggered up in the icy foam, only to be crashed down by an onsurging wave. Heads and bodies and arms and legs tumbled together, hands clawed, holding one another, searching for the lifelines rigged up to the foot of the cliff. He was choking, doubled over, spewing wretchedly, and someone hauled him back by his sodden coat, and he fought and scrambled his way back to the strip of beach. Another wave caught him, battered him to his knees, but it was not so lethal; he resisted the pull of water, and was out of it, sinking to his knees on the shingle, before he heard a cracked cheer, and turned his stinging face towards the sea, where he saw the boat, already distant, tossed high on a wave, the oilskinned figures pulling together into the engulfing wildness.

They made two incredible trips, bringing back thirty-five people from the wreck, many of whom were nurses, white faced and stricken with terror. Jack waited with the others, to dash into the shallows and help lift and haul them to safety. They were stunned, many of them, paralysed almost with fright. They sat, shivering, wild eyed, huddled in blankets, unable to believe their fortune in being alive.

At the end of the second trip, the boat slewed round, dipping into the waves and almost spilling its contents, as Jack and the others dashed into the surf to grab frantically at the precious human cargo. The rudder had gone, and the planking at the stern had been stove in, while inside the water lapped almost to the gunwales. The beached boat was finished, its beached crew slumped in total exhaustion.

Eventually, one hundred and forty-five were saved, and eighty-four lives were lost, over a weekend of high drama and tragedy. Jack turned up back home in the early afternoon, still soaked and aching with weariness. May had watched part of the unfolding crisis from the vantage point of the west cliff, little realizing that her husband was directly involved.

A third lifeboat from Upgang was pulled by horses through Whitby, and over to Saltwick across the estuary, but the seas were too rough to launch it. By early evening, the Scarborough boat was on the scene, towed by a steam trawler all the way up the coast through mountainous seas which tragically prevented it from closing with the wreck.

Early on the Saturday, another effort was made to get near, once

again using another trawler to tow the Whitby boat as close to the
wreck as she could manage, and once again the mighty waves
prevented the oared craft from getting near the wreck. The Upgang
boat made a valiant effort, launched this time from the other side
of the piers, the crew struggling to row round and approach the
vessel from the north. After an hour of perilous struggle, the
exhausted crew were forced to abandon their attempt. The situa-
tion on board the *Rohilla* was now so desperate that many believed
they must make a last bid for life and began to leap overboard,
spurred on by the heart-breaking nearness of the shore and the
towering cliff. Ironically, the wind had died away, and the visibility
was good – agonisingly so, for May and Jack were among those who
watched in horror as the small black dots were clearly seen falling
over the side. Sixty people succeeded in passing safely across the
storm tossed stretch of water to the shore, where eager hands were
waiting to haul them out of the shallows. Many didn't.

Tragically, if they had remained on board they would in all like-
lihood have survived, for, at last, in the early hours of Sunday
morning, a motor lifeboat from Tynemouth reached the wreck,
having herself made the dangerous forty-odd mile voyage down the
coast in the still raging gale, to rescue the remaining fifty or so crew
members still on the *Rohilla*.

Bodies drifted ashore all along that stretch of the coast in the
days that followed. The wreck stood up starkly out of the water, a
grim memorial to the lives that were lost. Jack and May, along with
the other inhabitants of the port, had no idea that, in less than two
months, another drama would be played out, almost in the selfsame
spot, of entirely human origins this time, which would bring the
realities of war to their very doorstep.

TEN

J ACK HAD BEEN working steadily for almost an hour when the first shot was fired. He felt the deep, muffled thud simultaneously with the thunderous crack. It set all the windows rattling, and shook the planks of the narrow platform on which he and his young assistant were lying working away at the angled joists of the roof timbers. Bits of stone and plaster rained down, while a choking, billowing cloud of dust immediately filled the air all round.

The shell had ploughed into the face of the cliff itself, throwing up a huge gout of earth. The coastguards on duty in their station on the headland nearby were still staring open-mouthed, their stunned brains registering the swift flash from the sea seconds before the impact. One of them still had the telescope trained on the low shapes three miles out. They had watched the two warships steaming furiously northward, appearing off Saltwick, throwing up great white bow waves as testimony to their high speed. They had been sighted almost exactly on the hour, at nine o'clock.

'Those buggers are shiftin',' one of the men on duty said admiringly. Five minutes later, the first shell thudded into the side of East Cliff. 'They're bloody 'Uns!' he exclaimed incredulously. The telescope quivered as he trained it over the still conspicuous wreck of the *Rohilla*. 'Cruisers, ah'd say!'

He turned away, saw identical expressions of numbed disbelief on the faces of his fellow coastguard and the young lad, one of the Boy Scouts who were serving as runners. The lad and his companion were already making for the door, and were outside on the steps when the next shell struck the corner of the station itself and the world exploded with apocalyptic roar.

Jack was down the ladders in a second, followed by a wide-eyed Ceddy. 'Thunder?' the lad said, but Jack shook his head grimly. He knew from the reverberation that there had been a big explosion, underground somewhere. The gas-works behind the station? he wondered. The second shell detonated, with an even louder bang, and they both raced for the porch.

Running around the edge of the building, Jack saw the smoke and dust drifting up above the squat tower of the lookout station. One corner of it stood up jaggedly, its lines demolished in a pile of rubble. The white signal mast, its cross-spar still intact, was leaning over at an angle. Then he saw the distant, crumpled figures, and he raced across the uneven grass. There was a rushing, roaring noise and, ahead of him, he saw a mushroom of brown smoke rise from the row of coastguard houses, heard the crump of falling masonry, then the crack of sound which made him duck instinctively, and fall to his knees in the tufty grass.

A knot of women and children appeared at the end of the buildings, clinging pathetically together, and he screamed out at them, waving his arms frantically, urging them to get away from the houses, to move further inland. Another great whirring sound seemed to pass right over him, and he cowered down again, clinging to the damp earth. He lifted his head, and saw the great, ruined wall, the west end of the abbey itself, burst into tiny black fragments which arced high in the grey sky, then great stone blocks tumbled slowly from its upper portions.

Jack looked upward, scanned the haze above, thinking automatically that the attack must be coming from the air. It wasn't until the next shell went shrieking overhead that he stared seawards, realized that the firing was coming from the ocean. He was up and running again, drew near the ruined coastguard station. He reached the boy first.

The lad was moaning quietly. His eyes were closed, his face,

utterly bloodless, transfixed by pain. His right leg, in the grey
stockings and knee breeches, looked chewed and mangled, the
clothing dark and sodden with blood. A great wave of helpless
panic swept over Jack as he put his hand on the thin shoulder and
croaked, 'There! It's all right, lad. You'll be all right now.' To his
great relief, he heard hoarse shouts and saw several male figures
sprinting towards him. One of them was still in his long-sleeved
vest, over which was hitched the braces of his trousers They were
the off-duty coastguards.

Two of them swept the boy up into their arms and began to run
back, towards the ruins, and the parish church. Jack felt weak with
relief, then he moved on, accompanied by the rest of the newly
arrived group, towards the battered station. He stared at the body
stretched across the steps. Great fragments of masonry, and smaller
pieces, were flung all around the corpse. Jack's eyes took in the dark
trousers, the sturdy boots, jutting out at an angle. One arm was
flung out, above the head, dangling down over the side of the steps,
the fingers on the brown hand curled.

Head! The word rang sickeningly in Jack's dazed brain, for,
above the collar of the dark jersey, the dark hair was matted, the
shape of the skull flattened. The man's face was turned away from
him, Jack could see the pink right ear, then only a ghastly bright
curtain of blood and torn flesh. He could not look away, or move,
until one of the others jostled him roughly as they passed, made
their way up the crumbled steps, moved the body aside.

Another shell shrieked by. The men had entered briefly, now
they hurried out again. They had found a cloth of some sort, and
they tumbled their comrade into it, held the corners, using it as a
makeshift stretcher, and ran with their burden back across the
field. Another shell had landed on the row of dwellings, whose
roofs had collapsed. Black smoke was pouring through the gaping
holes in the slates.

'Better get off out of 'ere, mate!' someone panted, and Jack
turned, swallowing the bile which had risen, bitter and burning, in
his throat.

He found Ceddy still in the churchyard, on the landward side, crouching behind a gravestone, snivelling softly. 'A woman said the Germans are landing,' he wept. 'It's Christmas next week,' he added pathetically.

Jack grabbed his shoulder. 'Get off home!' he said, trying to encourage him. 'Your family'll be worried.' Oh God! May! The thought of her burst upon him with a rush, in an agony of fear, and remorse. She'd be terrified. And the baby due in three weeks or so! Why hadn't he thought? Why had he waited? He had to get to her, now. He raced for the steps. Women and children, carrying all kinds of bundles, were stumbling and tottering down. He saw one little girl carrying an ornate black clock under her arm. They must be the families of the coastguards, and others who lived on the headland. As he moved downward, there was a fearful explosion, and everyone screamed, crouching in frozen terror. The stink of cordite filled the air. He looked up behind him, to his left, saw the smoke clearing from a great hole torn in the long, tiled roof of the Tithe Barn, part of the Abbey Lodge outbuildings.

Thank God all the firing seemed to be directed towards the abbey headland and the harbour, not at West Cliff. The narrow width of Church Street at the foot of the steps was jammed with people, many sobbing, also clutching hastily grabbed belongings and scrambling along the cobbles back towards the town, away from the sea. Frantic parents were jostling and shoving their way along to get to the primary school at the far end. In the middle of the chaos, he came across a small ring of people standing stock still, outside a cottage, on the step of which an elderly man was holding up a twisted lump of black, melted metal. They were all staring wordlessly at the fragment of enemy shell as though it held some supernatural powers.

By the time Jack had fought his way over the swing bridge, he began to realize that he had heard no fresh explosions for the past few minutes. Yet he could still hear the panic stricken cries from some of the women. 'They're comin'! The Huns are landin'!' He was gasping, sobbing for breath as he made his way round the side of the Red Lion on New Quay Road, and started the steep climb through the maze of alleyways that would take him back up to the top of the west side.

On Silver Street, he paused momentarily, winded, leaning forward, his hand on the wall, his mouth hanging open, drawing in air. A man, in collarless shirt and braces, came out and stood on the steps of the Conservative Club. He eyed Jack phlegmatically.

'Doan't fret thisen, lad. The've gone.' Jack looked up at him, his shoulders heaving, and shook his head, still unable to speak.

In spite of the December morning, his body ran with sweat, it glistened on his brow. The man's calm expression changed, to a frown of indignation. His head jerked upward.

'T'buggers've put one through the roof. The've ruined t'bloody billiard table!' Now he, too, shook his head and went back inside. Jack had a sudden hysterical urge to burst out laughing. He forced himself to go on.

By chance, or mischance, May was outside when the bombardment started. She did not go far these days. With less than a month to go before her time was due, she was, truthfully, more than a little embarrassed at appearing in public, for even the voluminous maternity clothes could not hide her condition. She had, somehow all at once, put on weight and, more dramatically, changed her shape over the past few weeks. Her tummy had swollen to a vast, pale, blue-veined dome, tight as a drum, on which her heavy, achingly tender breasts rested. Irene Wood, who had been predicting all along that she would have a girl, because she was showing so little sign of her condition, had now imperturbably changed, and was stating with equal confidence that the baby would be a boy.

There had been a right battle, conducted through the post, with her mam, who was obviously hurt and disappointed that she was not returning to Gateshead for the confinement. Then had come the announcement, an inevitable enough decision following on her determination to stay here for the birth, that they would be spending Christmas in Whitby. 'I can't just up and leave your father and the rest of them!' Robina had written, prompting May to exclaim indignantly when she showed Jack the letter that evening, 'I never asked her to!'

It had eventually been agreed that Julia would come down a few days into the new year and stay as long as May thought necessary, while her mother herself would come as soon as she received news of the delivery, and stay for several days. 'Perhaps you could find me a cheap room somewhere. Or I could doss down on the floor,' she had written. 'She's still in a huff,' May told Jack regretfully. But she was still as glad as ever that she was having the baby here, with Jack.

May bought her milk from a young lad who came round the streets leading a donkey, with the churns strapped to its sides. On the Wednesday morning of the week before Christmas, she went down with her jug as usual, blushing slightly at the way the lad's eyes swept with furtive curiosity over her thickened figure. The morning was damp, and hazy, but not particularly cold. Glancing down towards the end of the street, she could see the grey sea, calm enough, the horizon cut out by the white haze, and she decided on impulse that she would have a stroll along the front. There would not be many people about, particularly if she stuck to the top of the cliff. She felt healthy enough these days, apart from the aching back and feet sometimes. All the queasiness had gone long ago. Not that there had been much to start with. 'Disgustingly healthy!' was how Dr Butcher had described her at his last examination.

She was strolling along the esplanade above the pavilion when she heard the first booming report from out at sea, so loud that it seemed to make the land itself tremble perceptibly beneath her feet. Somehow, she knew it wasn't thunder, thought instinctively of gunfire, though she had never heard the sound before. A naval battle, out there somewhere! Folk had said all along that that was what would decide it. If Jacky Fisher's Grand Fleet could catch the Germans on the high seas, it would all be over. She had a sudden fear for her brother, George. He had finished his training, had joined a ship just a few weeks ago. A destroyer, she thought it was. HMS *Doughty*, her mother had said.

May clenched her hands inside her woollen gloves and said a silent prayer for his safety. Then she jumped, the shock passing right through her body, at the second report. That was too loud to be out at sea, surely? The few people who were out had turned questioningly, looking back down towards the town and harbour, and the headland across the mouth of the estuary. She saw people coming out of the rows of elegant houses on Royal Crescent, all moving down towards the headland above the Khyber Pass, and she began to hurry in that direction.

'It's Hun battleships!' a man called out to her, eyes popping with excitement. 'They're shelling us!' Some of the gathering crowd began to turn, to run back the way they had come. Among them were weeping women. 'Get the kids! Get back!'

'It's the coastguard station they're after!' she heard someone cry, and she went cold with new panic. That was across the other side. Right next to the church! Next to Jack! She started to cry, standing there in the milling crowd, tears beginning to roll down her cheeks.

A man grabbed her arm, tugged her forcefully. He glanced down at her bundled figure, recognized her condition.

'Get yeself 'ome, luv! Get down in t'cellar! Quick!' There was a loud whine, then a fearsome report. Everyone flinched, the women screamed. 'That one was at us! Get off out of it!'

A plume of smoke was rising from the corner of East Terrace, where a house had been hit. May felt the solid bulk of the child she was carrying, felt her clumsiness as she tried to hurry, her heart pounding. She should go to Jack! She wanted to be with him. She was sobbing now, but no one took any notice of her, they were all racing off, away from the sea, and the harbour below. She moved after them, hating herself for her indecision, the clutching fear that possessed her.

Go to Jack! You're leaving him! You're running away! But the baby! The baby! You've got to keep it safe! Why? Why? I don't want it if Jack's not here with me. She was round into the dignified sweep of Royal Crescent, still making for home, when there was a whooshing shriek in the air above her, then a horrifying bang which made the pavement jump. She dropped to her knees as a blast of hot air seemed to waft past her, and she was staring at a shallow crater in the middle of the roadway, only yards from her.

People surged about her. She felt herself plucked up by her shoulders, she was trembling and sobbing while a man held her. He took her by the arm, led her along like a child.

'Where do you live, love?' he asked gently.

She nodded. 'Just round the corner. Langbeck Terrace.' He took her all the way to the back lane entrance, holding onto her all the while. She was glad of his touch, his solid, comforting presence. 'It's my husband,' she said, her cheeks still stained with her tears. 'He's over on the east side. Up on the abbey plain.'

'He'll get to you,' the man said. He patted her gloved hand. 'Are you all right? Is there anyone I can get for you?'

'No. Thank you. There's the girls downstairs, If I need . . .' her voice trailed away, her chest heaved in a great sigh. 'You've been ever so kind,' she said, offering her hand formally. 'Thank you. I'm all right now.' He moved off, touching a crooked finger to his brow and she went inside.

The yard was full of figures. She recognized a couple of the maids from the hotel. 'I'n't it awful? Are you headin' off? The's loads o' folks up on t'fields at Upgang. Get outa town, the' reckon.'

Jack would come to her, May was sure. She eased her way through, onto the stairs. 'Come down to cellars!' someone else urged her, but she shook her head, smiling politely. She made her way back upstairs, fumbled the latch key and got inside the room.

She sank down in the armchair, suddenly unable to move, apart from the trembling which shook her like an ague from top to toe. She couldn't rise now if a bomb landed right here beside her. She suddenly thought of the day she had met Iris Mayfield, the accident which fear had brought upon the tall, red-haired girl, and how it had brought them closer together. 'At least I haven't wet meself!'

she said aloud now, to the empty room. and her lips formed a quivering little smile, while she continued to weep.

Iris had already sent through the parcel post a great chest containing a complete layette for the birth. Nightgowns, day gowns, an embroidered, lacy robe, wool and silk bootees, towels, flannel swathes, napkins and pilches, slips and fancy bibs – everything she would need or could think of for the new arrival. 'There must be shillings' worth here,' May had exclaimed wonderingly, when she showed Jack the contents, which she had laid out on the bed for his inspection.

'You can never have too much of this sort of thing, so I'm told!' Iris had written, in her offhand, cheerful way May knew she was trying to ease any embarrassment they would feel at her generosity. 'So I don't suppose it will matter if you've already got them all. You can always keep them for the next arrival! You can count it as an early Christmas present as well as a gift for the baby.'

May thought of her own mother's thrifty caution, evidence once again of the great social barriers which divided them from Iris. 'Best not to get too much beforehand, just in case.' The practicality did not lessen the secret dread May had felt at the unspoken warning that things might not go well, that tragedy could always strike.

Perhaps it had struck now. May tensed, sat there, every muscle clenched, waiting to feel some mortal pain, or some other dreadful sign that something had gone wrong. The baby was stirring, kicking strongly, but that was quite normal these days. Panic for Jack's safety swept in again, and set her off on a fresh bout of helpless blubbering, which left her feeling even more wretched and weak. She had just forced herself to lumber up from the chair and take off her outdoor coat, and her shawl and scarf, when she heard clattering feet on the stairs. She turned to the door as Jack, dripping with sweat, burst into the room and they were together, clutching each other, and she was in his arms.

'Oh, thank God, thank God!' she moaned. 'I was so frightened for you, Jack! I couldn't bear it if anything happened to you! I couldn't!'

He kissed her, tasting her tears, ready to weep himself. 'Nowt's going to happen to me, lass. I've told you. I wouldn't let it. I'm here, aren't I? Are you all right? Are you sure? Come and sit down. I'll put the kettle on.'

The raid had lasted precisely seven minutes. No one was sure how many shells had been fired on the town from the two German cruisers. Some claimed as many as two hundred. Several had fallen three miles inland, on the village of Sleights. Miraculously, only two fatalities had occurred, unlike the two ports of Scarborough and Hartlepool, which had been bombarded about an hour earlier, with considerably greater loss of life. The young boy scout whom Jack had found outside the coastguard station had had to have his leg amputated, but he had survived.

That Friday's *Gazette* carried a detailed list of all the properties damaged, together with a variety of accounts of how the terrifying bombardment had affected the town. In the boys' school of Meadowfield Hall, the headmaster had just uttered a prayer for 'deliverance from our enemies', when the first of a whole series of shells had burst close by, and he and his staff had led the pupils, who all marched out steadily, away from the nightmare explosions. It was in that area, and in Fishburn Park, that the majority of the shells had fallen.

Although St Mary's had been in the direct line of fire, the church had remained untouched, though the force of the explosions had broken most of its windows.

'More ruddy repairs!' the verger grumbled, as Jack and his men gave him a hand with the clearing up. 'And more work for you,' he muttered, with a suspicious glance in his direction that seemed to suggest that Jack had secretly organized the bombardment himself, in order to add to the list of renovations Waller's was carrying out. 'You'll be here for ever at this rate!' Jack was beginning to feel that way himself. What with difficulties with labour, and obtaining supplies, not to mention shipwrecks and enemy raids, it looked as though the verger's gloomy forecast might prove to be correct.

The attack had certainly caused a sensation. The town was normally very quiet and undisturbed during the winter, but the ensuing week saw hordes of visitors, mostly day-trippers, who came to troop round the streets to look at this firsthand evidence of war, which they had never thought to see. No mention of 'Home by Christmas' now, not even from the most naïvely optimistic.

Still, Jack was determined it was not going to dampen the holiday spirit. He decorated their room until it was a jungle of paper chains, and rigged up some evergreen branches with baubles and silver paper, and cotton wool, giving it pride of place by the large window. He wouldn't let May stir, so she sat by the fire making the decorations, and issuing laughing instructions while he clambered about, balancing precariously to fasten them on the high ceiling.

He finished at dinner-time on Christmas Eve, which was on a Thursday. 'That's the best thing about being your own boss,' he told a delighted May. 'Besides, it's never going to get done, anyway.' He had bought a duck from the poulterer's in Church Street, where hundreds of newly plucked birds hung outside the shop in long rows. 'It's one of the gulls. I found it up on the abbey!' he teased. May had already arranged with the cooks downstairs that they would roast the bird in their ovens early the following morning.

Jack managed to sneak one of her black stockings, and stuffed it with sweets, an apple and an orange, and some slides for her hair. He had bought some port, and allowed her a glass, as they sat before the glowing fire, in unbuttoned ease. 'I'm doing everything tomorrow,' he declared fiercely. 'Cooking and all!'

'Don't be daft.' She groaned. 'Mind you, I've got some chronic pains in my back today. They're not half giving me gyp.'

'You're all right, though?' he asked, his face at once serious, and she smiled tenderly.

'Never better, love. Let's get to bed. Though I bet I won't sleep a wink. I never do at Christmas.'

He felt he had not been asleep more than a few minutes, though he found out later it had been about two hours. It was half-past midnight, just into Christmas Day. The fire was still casting a red glow about the room. 'What is it?'

She was kneeling up in the bed, her hands cupping the bulge of her belly, which showed prominently through the tightened white cloth of her nightgown. Her dark hair was tumbled down on her shoulders, her face pale.

'I feel awful, Jack. I've got pains.'

'You can't!' He scrambled out of bed, stumbled over to the table, fumbled for the lamp and eventually got it alight. Her eyes were enormous, and deeply shadowed in the gentle glow. She sat on the edge of the bed, the gown caught up, showing her pale, slim legs and bare feet.

She turned to him, and he could see the fear stamped on her face, felt his heart clutch with it. 'I feel bad, Jack. Griping pain.'

She can't be starting now! he told himself again. There's three weeks to go yet. January, they said. He saw her clench herself, bite at her lip, unable to suppress a low moan. She was hunched forward, still holding herself. He stood indecisively, until she bent and groaned again, rocking softly. 'I'd better go,' he said. She looked up at him, nodded.

He flung on his clothes, racing up the narrow flight of stairs to the attics, where he knew Joan, one of the chamber maids who had become a good friend to May, slept. He hammered on the door, heard some protesting moans, and called out her name.

'Can you come quick?' he said desperately.

She appeared, her face stamped with sleep, her hair all over the place, still in her nightgown.

'Hell!' She vanished, came out again wrapped in a heavy over-coat, and followed him down the stairs.

'It's Joan, love!' he called. 'She's here now. I'm off to Mrs Wood's.' May was sitting on the chamber pot, by the side of the bed, but she showed no embarrassment. The time for such niceties had gone.

'Be quick!' she gasped. He did not need to be told.

ELEVEN

'WHAT? SHE CAN'T BE! She's nowhere near due. Christmas Mornin'? You must be jokin'!' But Mrs Wood knew he wasn't, and was ready to accompany him after only a few minutes, grumbling all the way through the wet, deserted streets. 'If she's got me out of bed on Christmas Mornin' for nothin', I'll kill the young madam!'

Jack was reduced to a hovering, wretched presence, banished beyond the screen, useful only for nipping back and forth across the chilly landing to boil a pan and a kettle of water. Dawn came, the morning advanced, louring and drizzling rain, spotting the windows. At one stage, May, feverishly bright eyed, appeared quite animated, almost high spirited, sitting up on the pillows in a clean nightgown, hair brushed and neatly pinned back, her lower half decently hidden beneath the blankets. Reluctantly, Irene Wood agreed he could cross the boundary of the screen and perch nervously at the bottom of the bed, while they all drank tea. Risking her wrath, Jack boldly leaned forward and kissed his wife's shining forehead before he retreated again.

'Have ye got your bunny rabbit there, May? Ye can start chewin' his ears off now, if ye want.' Mrs Wood had taken one of Jack's white handkerchiefs and knotted it so that it had two large protuberances, flopping like rabbits' ears. The idea was that she should bite on the cloth during the final, most excruciating stage of the labour. The midwife came bustling round the screen once more. 'Go and get that lass. The one that said she'd help. Be quick!'

'What's wrong? I can help if you need—'

She looked scandalized. 'It's no place for a man to be! Fetch the girl, quick!'

He froze at the wailing cry which turned to a full-blooded scream, and only just prevented himself from sweeping aside the fragile barrier which kept him from May's agony. He went over to the table, and slumped down, his head on his hands, and listened to the last cries of pain before the baby came.

Then everyone seemed to be laughing and crying, and the first thin wails of the new life thrilled him. Joan came out, carrying a dish of pinkly discoloured water, and Jack was calling out. 'Is it all right? May! May! Are you all right, love?'

Mrs Wood came out, holding a swaddled bundle. Jack saw the tufted dark hair, the wrinkled, astonishingly tanned, tiny face, and the midwife said, with a smile which transformed her red, ordinary features,

'Here! Make yourself useful and hold your son!'

'I'm really sorry to bother you, miss – er, Iris. It's just, with it being Christmas Day and everything. It's hard to get hold of anyone. My dad – my father – he's got the telephone in at work, but not at the house. And the telegraph office—'

'No, Jack, it's fine, honestly. I'm glad to help. And you're sure May's all right? Everything's all right?'

'Yes. She's a bit tired. You know. Worn out, in fact. But he's a fine healthy chap. Bawling his head off!'

'That's great news. Give my love to May. And congratulations to both of you.'

'If you wouldn't mind sending someone round to Sidney Terrace—'

'Of course. Take care now.'

Iris hung the receiver back on the stand. In her thin evening gown, with its low cut bosom, and her arms bare from the shoulders, she was shivering in the draughtiness of the tiled hall. The piano had stopped playing across in the drawing room, and the voices of the family had quietened somewhat. They all looked up curiously when she re-entered. Her mother had an expression of apprehension on her face, which vanished at Iris's excited smile.

'It was from May's husband,' Iris announced brightly. 'Jack Wright. May's had her baby early. A boy!'

No one seemed to know what to say, except for her mother, who asked quietly after the health of mother and child. The aunts and Uncle Colin were looking blank.

'One of Iris's new chums,' her father said, with his sneering smile. 'A shipyard worker's daughter, no less.' There was an instant of embarrassed silence, then he went on, 'I would have thought that even such an earth shattering occasion as the birth of another member of the proletariat could have waited for a more appropriate time to be announced.'

Iris coloured. 'It's something of an emergency. They've moved, you remember. Her husband's work. They're down at Whitby. They want me to let the family know.'

'It couldn't have waited until tomorrow, I suppose? Or a telegram wouldn't—'

'I said I'd let May's parents know right away. I won't be long.'

There was a murmur of surprise, and protest. Mrs Mayfield said, 'You can send one of the servants round, dear—'

'No one's turning out tonight!' Nicholas Mayfield interjected cuttingly. 'The girls are finishing early. And Goulding's already gone off. Not that I'd dream of asking him to turn out tonight! And you certainly aren't going out, young lady. Not to such insalubrious quarters as — where is it your chums live?'

'Sidney Terrace, father. It's a perfectly respectable neighbourhood.'

'And how are you proposing to get there? Wander through the streets alone? In the pitch dark?'

'I thought Bertie might—'

Her fifteen-year-old brother's eyes lit up at the prospect of escape. 'Yes, rather!' he volunteered. He was already rising from the stool on which he had been sitting when his father waved him down imperiously.

'Certainly not! It's altogether—'

Mary Mayfield stood up, and said quietly, 'That's quite enough, Iris. We're not having you upset things tonight of all nights. Come with me. You can help me see about dinner. The staff will want to be away early.'

She led her daughter from the room, and turned to her in the dimly lit hall. 'See if you can call a cab. I'll tell Margaret to go with you. You're to come straight back, mind. Promise me.'

'Oh, mummy! Thank you!'

The sight of Iris's elegantly cloaked figure standing on the step of Sidney Terrace caused a sensation almost as great as the news she brought with her.

'Oh my God! She's far too early! Is she all right? What did they say, miss? Are you sure she's all right? Oh, Ah'm ever so sorry, miss! What'll you think of us? Step inside.'

Iris moved into the narrow passageway inside the front door. The rest of the family were crowding behind Robina, staring in some wonder at the exotic sight Iris presented. She beamed at them.

'I can't stay, I'm afraid. The cab's waiting. And my – Margaret is with me. I have to get back. You understand? But I told Jack – they wanted you to know right away, of course. Jack assured me though, everything is fine. Mother and baby doing well.'

George stepped forward, took her gloved hand in both his. His face was working with emotion, enhanced by the amount of alcohol he had already consumed. His breath wafted beerily to her.

'God bless ye, miss! It's so very good of ye to go to this bother!' For a second, she thought he was going to hug her to him. She was as tall as he was. He was not wearing collar or tie, but his shirt was clean, and buttoned to the neck, and he was sporting his best dark waistcoat, matching the trousers of his Sunday suit. The silver chain of his watch drooped across his chest.

'Congratulations!' Iris smiled, gently withdrew her hand. 'Your first grandchild, I believe? And born on Christmas Day, too.'

George nodded, rendered momentarily speechless by the solemn thought. They all stood on the step, and waved as the cab drove away.

'I'll have to see about trains,' Robina said decisively as they turned back and closed the front door. 'I'll be away down there tomorrow.'

Iris was not sure whether her father was aware of her brief absence or not, but they were almost ready to sit down to dinner when she got back, and he said nothing. She felt a little uncomfortable when her Uncle Colin, her father's brother, called across the table, 'This girl you know who's had the baby. Her husband away in the army, is he?'

'No, he was the one who telephoned me. He's a very clever chap. Quite a good artist. He works on restoring churches. They moved down to Whitby in July. Just before—'

'Good Heavens! Whitby? They were bombarded by those Hun battleships last week! Damned disgrace. Hartlepool, and Scarborough, too. Yarmouth last month. What's the navy up to, eh? Well, now that she's safely delivered, I expect he'll be itching to enlist. Do his bit, eh?'

'I'm sure he will, uncle. His brother's already in the Fusiliers. The Pals' battalion. He enlisted back in August. They should be over in France now.'

Jack settled down with his back against the weathered, blackened headstone. He read through May's letter a second time, savouring it, almost welcoming the bittersweet emotion it aroused, which made him feel churningly hollow inside. This was no life, he told himself disconsolately. Spending the lonely week in his room – *their* room, the room where John had been born – then the rush on a Saturday, to get away as soon after midday as he could, and even then it was usually after tea before he reached Sidney Terrace. And starting off on the return journey just twenty-four hours later.

And he'd been doing that for three months and more now,

through all the bleakness of winter. Last week he'd been held up for what seemed like hours, outside Middlesborough, his head stuck out of the carriage window as the afternoon dragged by, until, eventually, a seemingly endless train had clanked slowly past them, wagon after flat wagon, each with a motor vehicle fastened down on it, heading for the Front, no doubt, that mythical place which was developing an insatiable appetite for men and supplies.

At least the weather was improving, after a late start. Today was full of bright sunshine, of high, billowy white clouds, racing shadows over the sea. Fine if you were moving, or sheltered from the breeze as he was. But he wished he could be going home to May. He used to love staring across the harbour mouth, thinking of her there among the chimney pots over on West Cliff, waiting for him to come home.

He felt disloyal, but he could not help nursing a secret resentment against his in-laws, and in particular, Robina. 'It's not safe for a new born baby there!' Robina had argued forcibly. She had made a great fuss over the fact of the bombardment, they all had. 'The poor lamb could've been killed before he was born! Ye cannot think of takin' him back there!'

His mind seethed once more with anger as he recalled his first arrival back here alone, in the gloom of a biting January evening, after he had left a tearfully clinging May in Gateshead, her mother's fondly mocking words unheeded by either of them. 'Howay, lass! No need to blub. He's not joinin' up, for goodness' sake! He'll be back in a week's time!' Didn't they realize? Hadn't she felt like this about George once? He couldn't ever imagine feeling any different about May. It would always be painful, however long, or short, the parting.

Then, on the steps of the station, as he prepared to walk up through the lamplit streets to the cold cheerlessness of the empty room at Amity House, he saw a group of women standing there. He thought at once of Iris, of votes for women, which had all magically seemed to die away with the outbreak of war. A young girl stepped forward. She smiled brightly at him, with just a hint of shyness in her dimpled cheek which added to her prettiness. Her eyes were light, clear with youth and innocence. She was a young lady, he could tell, not only from her smart winter clothes, the stylish little hat which set off her looks.

'Please. Take one. Thank you.' Again, that lovely smile, as she pushed a single printed sheet of cheap paper in his hand, turned to the next traveller hurrying by.

He moved a few yards onto the street, glanced at the bold letters under a flickering lamp.

'Men of Yorkshire. Join the New Army. Avenge the murder of innocent women and children in Scarborough, Hartlepool, and Whitby. Shew the enemy that Yorkshire will exact a full penalty for this cowardly slaughter.' In a storm of choking emotion which he scarcely understood himself, he crumpled the bill savagely and cast it from him.

Now, almost three months later, he sat on the headland, reflecting sombrely on his loneliness. He would have to speak with May, tell her plainly that he wanted her and the baby to come back with him. There had even been the argument that his work itself might not last. And it was true, it looked for a while as though the whole project might have to be shelved, left incomplete until things settled down again. But the rector himself had come up with a good local man, a middle aged craftsman from Ruswarp, whose own business had sunk into decline, and who was an excellent workmate for Jack. And Ceddy, though leaving much to be desired as the third member of the team, was becoming more reliable, and was not inclined to go running off to war. Mr Redmond had eventually agreed that he should keep on with the work, even though it had fallen well behind schedule. Jack reckoned it would be well into the summer now before the work was completed. Perhaps as late as the end of August. The prospect of being a weekend husband and father all that time had no appeal whatsoever.

He put May's bulky missive back in his pocket. There was a lot in the letters that was not spoken, as there was in his to her. It was much easier, they both found, to express your love in words on paper. There were other, far more powerful ways of showing it when you were together.

He turned now to the second letter. One from his brother, Dan. Only the second he had received in the eight months since Dan had joined up. He still had the first at home, in the sideboard drawer. It had come a few days after Christmas, before Dan had known about the baby. He had just arrived in France then.

'They took us up the line for Christmas. To give us our first taste of the Hun. It's amazing, like a miniature city all of its own. Trench after trench. They've even got names. We were chuffed to find "Northumberland Street", though it's not exactly like the original. Three foot wide, full of mud, and not a shop in sight – only miles of dug-outs where blokes are crowded in like mice, living in candle-light and trying to keep warm.

'We were in the reserve trenches, but then this sergeant led us up a few at a time to the front line. And guess what? The ruddy war had stopped. We looked over the parapet and asked what all the lights were. The Huns had put up decorations. There was even some sort of tree. They started singing. The company commander assigned to look after us seemed really embarrassed. He got some of his lads to loose off a few rounds, but our own chaps looked pretty fed up with him. There was a lot of muttering, and they got us out of there double-quick.

'We had our Christmas Dinner back behind the lines. We even got a present from Her Majesty. How about that? I think they were intended to go up the line for the lads in the trenches, but a whole box finished up in our billet. So I've now got a new baccy tin and a smart wallet thing with some notepaper and a pencil in it. From Queen Mary herself! See what you're missing back there?'

The second letter had just arrived. To Dan's vehemently expressed disappointment, that trip up the line on Christmas Eve had been the nearest they'd got to the enemy for weeks and weeks. Apparently, they had spent an endless time training all over again. Lord Kitchener seemed in no hurry to put his New Army into the field, despite the heavy losses that had already occurred to the regulars, the 'contemptibles' who had faced the Kaiser's troops from the first.

'Just as well, maybe,' Dan wrote, in the letter Jack had just received. 'We're part of a Terriers Division. Some of them haven't even got full uniforms yet, and there aren't enough rifles to go round, so some of the chaps have to make do with broomsticks! If the Hun breaks through now, we'll have to whack him to death!'

Jack was surprised at this disclosure. In his other, earlier letter around the turn of the year, Dan had mentioned the censorship of letters. Perhaps their officers were getting careless, or tired of prying into their men's personal lives.

'At least we've been blooded, at last. We've had a spell up the line. Not long, but enough to make you appreciate the comforts we've got back here at the R and R area. And to think we thought we were roughing it. All very boring but we'll be going up again soon – can't tell you where – and there's rumour of a big push, so we might see some action soon.

'I've saved the important bit till the end. Congrats on making me an uncle. Glad that May and sprog are both doing well. What a sensible fellow you are to stay at home and get on with the business of real life! I'll try to bring back a souvenir for your son and heir.'

Jack glanced up. He was breathing rapidly, his fingers curled with a sudden desire to crunch up the paper he was holding and fling it furiously away, as he had the poster which the pretty girl at the station had thrust at him.

TWELVE

I RIS REACHED UP and took hold of May's hand. May leaned over and gathered up her heavy skirt to jump down from the high step of the dog cart, while Iris steadied her with a hand at her waist. The mare was already cropping at the grass which grew in high tufts by the gatepost and along the fence.

'There's a place through here. Under the trees. Jack and me used to come up here a lot when we were courting.'

Iris grunted as she lifted the hamper from the back of the cart, and gave a knowing laugh.

'Oh yes? This is where he had his wicked way, is it?'

'Certainly not! All we did was hold hands and talk. I was a good girl, I was!' She giggled. 'We were married six month before I fell with John. My mam was beginning to get worried.' She was leading the way along the narrow path She ran ahead to the copse, stopped and did a pirouette. 'Here. This is it.'

Iris was several yards behind, the heavy picnic basket bumping against her leg as she lugged it along.

'Sure you can manage?' she asked, putting it down on the grass. She knelt to open it up and spread out the rug which lay on the top.

'All right, sarcy! Don't forget I'm a poor old married woman. Not a great strapping lass like you.'

'Yes. Well, don't *you* forget, this strapping lass is a full two years older than you.'

May sat down, holding her skirt round her drawn up knees,

watching Iris place the provisions out on the rug's tartan surface.

'Poor old soul. You'd better watch it, you'll end up an old maid if you don't get a move on!' Her voice changed, she continued archly, 'Have you heard from Lionel lately?'

Iris glanced up sharply. This time May did notice the colour which rose to her friend's face. Her serious expression drove the smile swiftly from May's face, and it was her turn to look embarrassed.

'Not lately,' Iris answered. 'Not for a couple of weeks or so. He's got rather a lot on his plate, I expect.'

May sensed the rebuke in Iris's tone, and nodded contritely. She gazed affectionately at the red-haired girl as she busied herself over the food. They had become closer than ever over the past three months, since May had returned to Sidney Terrace with the baby. During May's stay in Whitby, they had seen nothing of each other, had corresponded infrequently, and, once again, May had thought their friendship was slowly waning, a fact she regretfully felt was inevitable, given the differences in their circumstances. But since John's birth, Iris had made sure they met at least once a week, had shown her so many instances of her regard and kindness that at times May had been embarrassed, her sense of pride, and propriety, forcing her to put a curb on Iris's generosity. 'It's nothing!' Iris would protest, when she brought yet another gift, for mother or baby.

She was even accepted more easily at Sidney Terrace, and had been an enthusiastic godmother at the Wesleyan chapel Christening, along with Cissie Wright, and an awkward Joe Wright, who was the godfather. May had enjoyed a private, malicious sense of satisfaction at the effect Iris's presence, and obvious friendship, had had on Jack's mother. Since then, the two girls had met regularly, spending whole days together during the week, going off to Newcastle, or, as the weather improved, for trips out into the countryside, like today. May's mother was only too happy to look after John. 'It does her so much good, mi . . . Iris!' Robina said. Try as she would, the older woman found it hard to make such familiar use of the Christian name.

Now, the two girls leaned against the rough bole of a tree, shoulders touching, while they ate. Iris put her hand over May's, their fingers entwined, then Iris raised their clasped hands and gently rubbed May's knuckles along her cheek.'I'm going to miss you,' she murmured.

May turned, her dark eyes wide with appeal.

'You can come down to see us!' she cried. 'We can put you up. Jack can sleep on the sofa. If you don't mind sharing a bed, that is.'

'Are you sure you're doing the right thing?' Iris asked. May looked at her with a wounded expression, and she went on hastily, 'It's just, your mother was saying Jack wasn't sure how long the work would last—'

'That's all sorted out now. He'll be there until September at least.'

'And he won't . . .' she hesitated, carried on carefully, 'he won't change his mind? I mean – decide to go off?'

'You mean enlist, don't you?' May said accusingly. 'That's what you're getting at, isn't it? You think he ought to go off and join the army.'

The subject lay like a suddenly exposed, raw wound between them. May knew what Iris's views about the war were, knew that she had espoused the cause as ardently as the women's suffrage campaign. She had even gone to public meetings, supported the recruitment drives that her father was involved in. 'He can't believe there's actually something we can both agree on!' she had laughingly told May. But it was a topic both girls carefully skirted. They avoided talking about the war if they could possibly do so, for they knew their views were diametrically opposed.

Now, Iris coloured yet again at the hot accusation in May's voice. She did not shy from it this time.

'I think it's a duty men shouldn't shrink from,' she replied slowly. 'For king and country. It's not just an empty phrase, you know. And if everyone left it to the other chap to do the right thing—' she paused again, the tension between them mounting, then plunged on, 'well, there'd be nobody to stop the Hun, would there? And such unspeakable evil has to be stopped.'

Iris was squeezing her hand tightly, clinging onto it, and May had to pull away to disengage her grip.

'What about me? And John?'

'All the more reason for him to do the decent thing. If not for king and country, then for his own wife and child.'

'He could be killed!' May's voice was still quiet, though it contained the full horror with which she made this appalling statement.

'We can't shirk from our duty just because it's unpleasant.' Iris was pleading now. 'It's a simple question of right and wrong. Of good and evil. We can't just sit back and let wickedness triumph. Think of all the murder of innocent victims. Of women and children. Babies – like John. The raping, and terror—'

'But is it all true?' May cried out desperately. 'Don't you think that's what they're telling them as well? That—'

Iris gazed at her, deeply shocked. 'You don't think our boys are killing and torturing civilians! Raping women and innocent girls! Do you?' May shook her head helplessly. Iris knelt up. 'You know I'm right!' she pursued relentlessly. 'However painful it is, I'm right. It *is* his duty, every fit man's duty—'

The dam of May's suffering burst, and she cried out rawly, 'You're damned great on shouting about duty! Telling men to go off and get themselves killed! What about you? You – you women? You were keen enough to go about blowing up things with your bombs, screaming about your votes for women! Seems to me you should be the ones going out there to do the fighting!'

'I wish I was! I wish I was a man! I want to do my bit! I'd do anything—'

Roughly, May knocked Iris's hand off her. She scrambled to her feet.

'I love Jack! And he loves me! That's all that matters to us. I wouldn't send him away for anything! Anything! And he'd never leave me! Never! You hear?'

She began to cry, and her grief smote at Iris, who made to rise, stretched out her arms.

'May! Love! I'm sorry! It's just—'

'Leave me alone! Why can't the whole damned lot of you leave us alone?' With an anguished cry of rage and pain, she flung away, stumbled, picked up her dark skirt and hurried, half running, along the narrow path of bare earth by the side of the field. She didn't stop until she was a small, distant figure, dark against the new budding greenery of the hedge. She looked frail, and forlorn as she bent over, her shoulders quaking.

Iris stared after her. The scene dissolved in the blur of her own tears, and she felt the weight of her despair. Oh, my darling! she cried silently, inside herself. I don't want to hurt you. Of all the people in this world, I wouldn't want to cause you a second's pain. I love you so much. She ached, her spirit and her body ached, to say these words to her.

She rose, waited a while, then walked slowly towards the distant figure. May was clutching a small handkerchief, holding it to her wet face. She shook her head at Iris's approach, turned away from her, but the red-haired figure continued to advance, put her arm out to encompass the narrow, sloping shoulder.

'Darling May!' She felt the shrug of resistance, the stiffening rejection, but she stepped closer, hugged May forcefully, drawing her close, and all at once, the slender form yielded, relaxed, turned and came into her embrace, and they clung together, weeping, holding one another. Iris kissed repeatedly at May's cheek, tasted the salt of the tears on her lips, and a great, quiveringly sweet tenderness flowed right through her.

On the first Saturday of Jack and May's reunion in Langbeck Terrace, the liner *Lusitania* was torpedoed, with the loss of 1,200 lives. The following week, the British press whipped up anti-German feeling to a new pitch of hysteria. Particularly painful for May was the latest in the incessant stream of posters which appeared in every public place where the least space was available.

112

This one showed two women, one dark and one fair, clinging together as they gazed with sad pride through an open window at a line of marching soldiers, while a curly headed infant clung to their skirts. 'Women of Britain say – Go', was its simple banner of declaration.

It was little wonder that May and Jack felt the weight of the outside world pressing ever more heavily upon them, and looked on their furnished room as a private sanctuary, the only place where they could feel safe from the madness surrounding them like a besieging army. When Jack had travelled up to Gateshead to bring back his family, he had found the atmosphere strained, and brittle with tension. The disapproval of May's folks at the move was all too clear. He could understand that it was Robina's love for the baby which was making her so astringent towards him, but it hurt, deeply, more so because of his genuine affection and gratitude to her for all that she had done for his wife and child. She had sniffed, and said cruelly, 'I shouldn't've thought they'd be that bothered about your work now. Doin' up old churches doesn't seem that important. Not now, when the's more serious work needs doin', any road.'

For once, Jack, flushing darkly, was stung to reply. 'What are you saying? That I should be off to volunteer? Is that what you mean?'

She sniffed again. She looked away, unable to meet his piercing stare, but her chin lifted aggressively.

'It's not for me to tell ye how to go on, is it? All I know is I've got a son that's out there, at sea, and your own brother is away over in France—'

'Mam!' May's face was pale. Her voice trembled, but she spoke with quiet resolve. 'I believe in the Bible. I don't believe it's right to kill. And if Jack went away – left me and the bairn to go off and fight – I don't think I could bring myself to forgive him! Ever!' Though there were hugs and tears when they finally left, the altercation had left a bad taste, which lingered long after the event itself.

The month which shared its name with May ended on a note of continued disaster which made others besides May privately ponder on whether they could make the glibly automatic assumption that God was on their side. All within a week, there was a horrific train accident near the Scottish border, in which over 200 lives were lost, the vast majority of them being soldiers on their way to the war, a naval auxiliary vessel blew up at Sheerness, killing 270, and the first air raids on the capital took place.

'You won't leave me, will you?' May asked him, yet again, one night in early June. She had just settled John down in his crib the other side of the raffia screen, and was still fastening the bosom of her cotton nightgown as she clambered into the high bed beside Jack. The lamp, on top of the locker at his side, cast its cosy pool of light over the bed, an oasis against the dimness of the rest of the room. Her face, shadowed like an actress by the lamp, added to the drama of her words. With her dark hair hanging richly loose onto her shoulders, she also looked very young, and vulnerable, and, as always, he felt the love in him tighten his throat. He shook his head, reached out for her, and drew her into his side.

They had not had sexual intercourse since several months before John's birth. They had made love. He had shocked her, profoundly, at the gentle, patiently tender skill he revealed, and the knowledge, with which he was able to bring her such shattering release, and relief. And she had brought him relief, too – he had guided her, shown her what to do. 'It's love. It's all part of our love,' he had told her, and she tried not to feel ashamed. The shame, in any case, only came later, when she contemplated the shocking things he had done, they had done, to each other. There was no one she could talk about it to. She did not know anyone so intimately, it was a subject she could never imagine discussing with another soul. Most shocking of all, she felt, was the fact that she loved these months, loved what they did to one another's bodies, felt that the releases he brought her were every bit as consuming as any they had known previously.

But this night, when he lifted the hem of her nightgown, and she felt his warm fingers tracing their course up her leg, her thigh, she wanted him inside her, his hard manhood driving inside her, and

114

she reached down for him, impellingly, moving onto her back, squirming underneath him, parting her legs widely, raising her knees. 'You're sure?' he asked, tensely, and she gazed lovingly at his dark eyes, and nodded.

'I want you,' she whispered. 'I want you to do it to me.'

'We have to be careful,' he murmured thickly, holding himself off her, stopping himself from entering her. He had talked before about 'precautions', she knew about the ugly, thick rubber sheaths, the various methods they could employ to avoid her getting pregnant, all of them filling her with secret revulsion.

She smiled. 'You know nowt, you! Don't you know I can't fall again while I'm nursing John?' She wondered if it were true, what so many women had told her back home? Her breasts were still ripely heavy with milk. Right now they were sore, and wincingly tender. She thought about another baby growing inside her. In the days after the birth, she had privately and tearfully dreaded the idea of having to go through such a trauma again, felt the clutch of real fear at the contemplation of having seven, like her mam. Most had four or five at least. Now, it held no such terror for her. She reached down, boldly, wantonly, between their bellies, felt his hardness. 'Don't you want me?' she breathed, pulling him to her, lifting herself, opening for him.

They did not, after all, take any precautions. They had intercourse regularly, and, despite her private moral discomfiture, continued to practise those other methods of arousal, and relief, she found so erotically powerful. She clung to such physical intimacies with increasing desperation as a way of binding them tighter together against the looming threat of the outside world, of which she was becoming more and more frightened as the war advanced through a splendid summer towards its first anniversary. It seemed to be changing the tenor of life in so many ways.

The flood of men to military service left a gap in the workforce at home which itself threatened to create its own crisis, until women stepped into the breach, to fill the vacancies in works and factories, and, in turn, to experience a measure of independence and liberation they had never dreamed possible.

Robina wrote, 'Nelly Dunn's working at the munitions works at Armstrong's. The place is filled with lasses, making more money than is good for them, working all hours of the day and night. They've even got some lasses working on the trams. Your da was horrified, they've got themselves dressed up just like the men, trousers and all. Though apparently a bunch of women down the town gave one of them a good sorting out, debagged her and sent the little hussy running off home in her drawers. Quite right too.'

Though May's mouth twitched in an involuntary smile when she read it, she could not help a pang of sympathy for the unfortunate victim. It seemed that many of the women on Tyneside were not in favour of such revolutionary changes. She thought all at once of Iris, and the hostile reception those Gateshead females had given the poor girl that day outside the Labour Exchange. Not surprisingly, Iris had availed herself with all her characteristic enthusiasm of these unprecedented opportunities.

Although they had bidden each other a tearfully fond farewell, and since then exchanged several affectionately intimate letters, Iris had not visited them in Whitby, and the memory of the fierce confrontation between them just before May had left Gateshead for the second time remained, at least in May's mind, with all its painful clarity. She hoped that the fierce recriminations she had flung at her friend were in no way responsible for the red-haired girl's present action, for she had written with touching eagerness that she had embarked upon a motor driving and engineer's course, with the avowed intention of joining a newly formed Ambulance Corps which was to employ women drivers. 'Who knows? I may even end up over the water. Next stop Gay Paree!'

Meanwhile, May watched the set expression which crept over her husband's features each time he prepared to leave for work, the haunted quality of his eyes which he could not quite hide, and it frightened her more and more. She imagined the inner torment he was enduring, for she was sickeningly afraid that, secretly, he felt more and more strongly the urge to volunteer, like the million and more of his fellows who had already done so. That was why she tried so hard to shut out the terrible world, to build their own private world for just the two of them. 'Don't leave me!' She kept repeating it, over and over, hoping that he would see her as the weak one, the one who would crumble, fall apart if he should ever go from her. She would, too, she told herself. But she didn't even know if that were true.

She began to pray desperately that she would fall pregnant again, for she saw that as yet another strong tie to bind him to her. Blushing hotly at her own shamelessness, she would play the siren, almost every night, urging him to make love to her, praying fervently as each month's period approached that the absence of her regular discomfort would manifest her changed condition.

Even the pleasures of a walk out in the crowded town at the weekends was sullied, for once, as they wheeled the pram along the esplanade at West Cliff, a stout woman, dressed in widow's black, her red, fleshy face wild with emotion, suddenly came up to them and caught Jack by the sleeve.

'You look like a healthy enough feller to me! What's wrong with you? Why aren't you in khaki?'

Passers-by stopped to stare in surprise at the raucous tone. Jack angrily pulled his arm away. His face was white.

'Mind your own business!'

'It *is* my business! I've got a dead son over there that says it's my business. He never got the chance to have a bairn – or a wife!'

'Come on, Jack!' May muttered wretchedly.

But his torment made him untypically cruel. He turned on the plump black figure, his eyes burning.

'Aye! And did you tell *him* he should get himself into khaki? Did you?'

The woman flinched, her mouth fell open, her fleshy lips shining, and Jack swung away, striding out so quickly that May had almost to run to keep up with him.

THIRTEEN

Following hard on Jack's encounter with the corpulent woman on the sea-front, came a letter from his brother, the third he had received in the nine months that Dan had been away. It was addressed to 'Mr J. Wright'. There was no 'and Mrs' on the envelope, which May left, pointedly unopened, propped against the clock on the mantel shelf.

'A letter from your Dan,' she said unnecessarily, trying to hide the hurtful sense of exclusion she felt. But they were too finely attuned to each other for him not to notice.

'He probably doesn't think you'd want to hear too much about what goes on out there,' he said apologetically, holding the envelope in his hand, studying it as though reluctant to open it. 'He tells me – I've noticed. I've seen the letters he writes to mam and dad. They're always short, more like notes. He's always cheerful. Doesn't want to worry them. Doesn't tell them anything about what it's like – out there.'

'He does *you*, though, eh?' Her voice was brittle, almost harsh with accusation.

He knew what lay behind her words, could feel the pain she was undergoing. After all, it was more or less the same as his, he was sure. The same guilt made him hesitate. He was ashamed of his unwillingness to open it, to be brought helplessly closer to the horrors that pressed in upon them remorselessly, against which they tried so desperately to raise the barrier of their love. He

118

cleared his throat, dug his finger into the corner he had torn open, ripped along the thin paper. There was a thick wad of folded sheets, closely written upon.

He looked up at her sadly, held it up. 'Do you want to read it?'

'No! I don't!' She flushed, moved away from him, across the cluttered room, fussing with the pots on the table, which was set for their evening meal. It sounded as though they were quarrelling. He was about to speak, then compressed his lips, unable to think of anything that would ease the sudden tension. He sighed, turned to the opening page.

Dan had been fully 'blooded' at last. Though they had had two spells 'up the line' as relief units, they had not had a prolonged spell of trench duty, nor had they taken part in any big 'push'. They had spent practically the entire bitter winter in the vast network of training camps and supply depots and reserve areas which were still being established behind the lines. 'Some of the training camps are bally awful,' he wrote. 'Worse than England. Makes you almost look forward to getting sent up the line, even if we *are* so short of ammo we've no more than a few rounds apiece.'

Once again, Jack pondered on the careless censorship which was prepared to allow such harsh truths to slip by. Of course, there were thousands and thousands of such letters being dealt with every day now. He wasn't sure of how the actual details of censorship worked, but obviously it would take a good number of men the entire war, day and night, to sift conscientiously through every line that was written by the troops. This letter had the smudged ink of the censor's stamp on the back of the envelope's flap, but there was not one instance of the official pen being put to use on any of its contents.

'A couple of weeks ago, we got our chance at some real action for the first time – I can't tell you where, but I don't suppose it would mean very much to you in any case. Unfortunately, we were on the receiving end. We were called in double-quick to plug a gap where our froggie allies had allowed the Hun to break through.

'I don't know if there's been anything in the papers back home –

119

it's weeks before we see any of them – but the Huns were using this poison gas everyone has been so worried about. Pretty awful stuff, too, if you get a whiff of it. We were lucky, we missed it. The poor old Canadians got clobbered rather badly. Mind you, it's a bit of a chancy game, and the Huns were caught by their own devilishness. This great green cloud just hung about, there was no wind to disperse it, so although the frogs had legged it, the Hun couldn't really push forward very far because of his own gas!

'We haven't got any of those respirator things yet, so the Service Corps wallahs will have to get cracking and get some out to us pretty quick. Meanwhile, you'll never guess what they've told us to do in the event of a gas attack – we have to piddle in our hankies and hold them over our noses and Bob's your uncle! What a lark, eh? Anyway, we put up quite a good show for new boys, and the Canadians did absolutely splendidly. The upshot of it all, and the result of a week of really stiff fighting along the whole of our sector, is that we've had to fall back two miles or so, but we've stopped what could have been a serious break through, so we're feeling quite chuffed with ourselves.

'It didn't really bother us all that much, dropping back. We hadn't been in the line that long, but some of the blokes in the other units are pig sick. I suppose when you've been living in the same trenches for weeks on end, you get quite attached to them. Some of the dugouts are real home from homes, curtains up, the lot!

'We took a bit of a beating ourselves – our first real losses, apart from the odd one or two who were unlucky when we were in the line before. You might know about it already if you keep an eye on the papers, I should guess there've been some long casualty lists in the *Chronicle*. Mind you, now you're living down there among the Yorkshire tykes, I don't suppose you're up to date with local news, you traitor!

'How's the job going, by the way? You mentioned in your last letter that it might not last all that much longer. Oh Gosh! I've suddenly thought. It'll be a b—— if you've already left Whitby. Still, hopefully this will get sent on to you, wherever you are. How's

your pretty wife and bonny bairn? Still blooming, I trust. Give
them my love. I expect you're developing quite a paunch now, with
all that good food she's ladling down you. The grub here varies, as
you can guess. When you're up the line of course, it can be pretty
basic. Or maybe disgusting would be a better word for it. Most of it
is quite unidentifiable, probably just as well. That's when you get
any at all. If there's a flap on, or a bombardment, you crouch there
in your funk holes and chew on bully-beef. I usually smoke instead.
It's amazing, though. Some of the lads seem to find the grub not
bad at all. Makes you wonder just what on earth they've been used
to back home. I must admit, some of them are scrawny specimens,
especially when you see them in the buff.

'By the way (he said modestly!) you'll have to address your
letters to "Corporal" D. Wright from now on! I was made a Lance-
jack when we finished our basic training, but I've got my other
stripe now. We've lost a good many NCOs in the last two weeks, I'm
afraid. Promotion could be fairly rapid out here.'

By the time he had read through the rest of the letter, Jack was
sure that the push Dan had been involved in was the assault on the
Ypres salient. With a shameful sense of reluctance, Jack felt that
somehow he ought not to shirk following the progress of the war in
the newspaper, and so he read the *Daily Mail* assiduously, trying to
assess the truth behind its belligerently optimistic reports. It was
becoming increasingly clear with this emphasis on trench warfare
that both sides were bogged down, like two prize-fighters, standing
toe to toe and slogging it out. And the one with the biggest punch
was the one who was going to win.

The punch in this case meant armaments. That was the worry-
ing thing. Dan's cheerful letter laid bare the reality. Not enough
bullets to go round. Not enough guns to put them in. And, even
more important, a shortage of the big guns, the artillery that would
make the crucial difference, surely, in the horror of this revolutionary, technological warfare. The munitions factories were only
just beginning to get geared up for the massive production needed
to keep pace with demands. Would they ever succeed?

The fervour of the patriotic thousands who had flocked to answer Kitchener's call had stripped British industry of half its work-force. What good was it sending men out in droves to the battlefields if they had nothing to fight with? And how could we expect women, who were beginning to come forward to take on the absent men's work, to perform the tasks for which only those men were fitted?

It was all such a terrible mess, a tragedy. And yet the drum thumping and flag waving went on as furiously as ever. 'Enlist now!' The words screamed at him from every hoarding. He could not help the guilt which dogged him every time he stepped outside, went off through the town to work, or walked with May and the baby at the weekend. A helpless rage boiled almost permanently inside him, for he despised himself for what he saw as his own weakness. Weakness not in refusing to dash off and obey the urgent posters, but in feeling this guilt about not doing so. About appearing in civilian clothes when so many were hastening to put on a uniform.

It *was* weak, for in his heart he felt no moral compunction to join up. He 'loved' his king and country, he supposed, whatever that meant, as much as the next man, even if he wasn't joining him in running off to the recruiting office. Was it the kind of love that made you want to be a part of the wholesale slaughter going on across the Channel, and now in other, more distant battlefields? Like the Dardanelles campaign, which had got under way in April, and was now taking on a fearful similarity to the war in the west, with its own ever-growing casualty lists filling the papers each day. May's brother, George, was part of the naval force which was supporting the landings.

Though, undoubtedly, some appalling atrocities had been committed, he found it hard to accept the popular version of the Hun as the devil incarnate which the press nurtured. Thousands of Germans were ready to die, too. They could not all be devils. They believed in 'Kaiser and country', just as powerfully. Could anything really justify so many, many young men setting out to slaughter one another? Was any kind of 'love' worth that?

The only love he was certain of, knew in full measure its strength, which ran through and through him like a core of iron, was his love for May, and for the baby. Yes, he would die to protect them, fight with every last ounce of his strength to save them from any harm. But he could not honestly believe that that was what he would be doing if he volunteered to go off to the fields of Europe with a gun in his hand. He was not sure who, or what, he would be protecting by so doing. King and country, maybe. Or the way of life of a privileged few who were happy to send the youth out to carry out their slaughter for them?

He had seen the *Chronicle* a few weeks ago – his father sometimes sent him a batch of the local papers – and there had been a prominent picture of Iris's father, speaking at a recruitment rally. The article had said that Mr Mayfield, head of the large, well-known timber firm on Tyneside, was sending timbers to the Front now, to be used in constructing vital defences, as well as continuing to supply the coal-mines of the region, whose production was also vital to our war effort.

It made him sound like a selfless patriot. But it was beyond doubt that he would be getting well paid for his goods, as were the armaments manufacturers like Armstrong's, and all the uniform and boot suppliers. Was that who the young men like Daniel were really dying for? If the Hun came sweeping ashore here, if they really threatened the life of May and John, he would fight to his last breath, as fiercely as he could. But until then – he steeled his jaw, felt the clenching tension inside him once more – he would not let himself be blackmailed by this climate of nationalistic hate.

'Tea's ready.' May's voice was soft. He could sense the penitence there, saw it at once in her luminous, troubled glance at him. 'How is he? Is he all right?'

'Yes, he's fine. He's being made a corporal now, he says.'

As May put his plate in front of him, she leaned against him, put her hand lightly on his shoulder. 'Listen, pet. I'm sorry. I didn't mean to sound . . . you know. It's just – I don't want his letters to upset you. Make you feel bad about . . . about him being over there.'

'And me not, you mean?' He looked up at her, smiled wryly at her blush. He half turned, put his arm around her hip, pulled her belly against him tightly, feeling the uncorseted softness of her flank under his hand. 'I don't,' he said, with quiet firmness. He did not release her, holding her into him, feeling the concavity of her thighs and loins against him, and she put both her hands on his shoulders now to keep her upright. 'I feel bad about him being there, in danger. But I've no wish to join him. You can be sure of that.'

'Oh Jack,' She gave a kind of muted cry and bent, pulling his neat, dark head into her breasts.

A few days after the blaring triumph with which the British papers reported the return to work of the striking Welsh miners at the end of August, May told Jack with quiet satisfaction,

'My monthly hasn't come, Jack.'

'It *is* what you want, isn't it?' he asked. They were lying quietly side by side in bed, and she snuggled into his right arm, savouring the solid reassurance of his warm, calm body alongside hers. He had known she did not like the precautions against further pregnancy any more than he did, and, as the weeks slipped by after they had recommenced sexual intercourse, he had accepted and adopted her own placidly fatalistic approach.

'We'll have to wait and see, of course. Another two months before we can be really sure.' She gave a quiet laugh, hugged him companionably. 'But I know now, really I'm sure I am. That means sometime in the spring.'

'So much for your theory about nursing mothers. That means there'll only be fifteen months or so between them.'

'I hope I can give you a little girl this time.'

He turned towards her, folded her tenderly into his body. 'It doesn't matter. Whatever, it's ours. We made it, that's what counts.'

The impact of the new phrase, 'total war', was making itself felt more and more, in civilian as well as military life, as the war moved through its grim second year. Those with more privileged lifestyles suffered greater hardships. Or so it seemed to them. Food became limited, there began to be an increasing number of things which money could not buy. One of the most painful bugbears was the acute shortage of domestic staff, as more and more girls left service to go into the organizations and industries which had opened up a new way of life for them.

Mary Mayfield coped stoically with the disruptions to her household, while her husband scarcely seemed to notice. He was away so much of the time nowadays, involved not only with the rapidly expanding business and the problems of meeting its demands against the ceaseless threat of U-boats, and a clogged transport system on land, but with his work on a large and varied number of war committees, for which he was 'sure to get a knighthood at least', Mary's friends assured her.

Iris was away, still training somewhere within striking distance of London, where her parents were convinced she was having the time of her life, in spite of all the scares of the air raids.

'Please, dear, don't let your father see you in that,' her mother pleaded, during one of her daughter's rare, brief visits home, when she gaily paraded in front of Mary her new frock, of the very latest fashion, which showed her ankles and almost a foot of silk-clad calf. Mary strove to disguise her shock as she watched Iris laughingly step out of the dress. 'Don't you wear corsets any more?' she asked, and Iris laughed again

She posed, pirouetted in her flimsy silk and ruffles of ribboned lace. She picked up the petticoat hem and showed off the frills of her knickers.

'Oh, mummy! Girls aren't bothered by that sort of thing any more. We need to be able to move.' For what? Mary wondered privately, but she managed to maintain her silence.

It was late at night before Iris saw her father. She was sharing a cup of coffee in the drawing room with her mother, still trying to digest the fact that Beattie was the only live-in servant left, and that the clumsy, surly girl who had helped to serve dinner, as well as the cook clattering noisily in the kitchen, was a local girl who came in every day. Iris was secretly dismayed at the strain she could see on her father's fleshy, newly lined face. She rose and gave him a brief hug, kissing him on the cheek as he entered the room, then he flopped down onto the sofa with a luxurious sigh.

'Oh God! These committees! How some people love the sound of their own voices.' He eased off his shoes, using the toes of one foot to prise off the shoe from the other. He glanced about in some bewilderment, but his wife was already coming forward, dropping his leather slippers on the carpet beside him. 'Ah! Thank you, dear.'

Although Iris was struggling to stifle the yawns which were threatening to erupt, the result of a good number of late night wining and dining at the capital's crowded, frenetic night-spots, she stayed to converse with her father, who said presently, 'How's Lionel? Have you heard from him?'

She was sure he already knew the answer, for he was still on intimate terms with Sir William, Lionel's father, who was no doubt well aware of his son's continued correspondence with her. A correspondence which troubled her more and more, with each passing week and each scribbled, bulky letter.

Although she felt that she had made it abundantly clear, when they had parted over a year ago, that there was and could be nothing but warm friendship between them, Lionel's letters, particularly since he had gone over to France at the end of his training, had assumed an increasingly intimate, tender tone, until they now read more and more like the love-letters they undoubtedly were. Though she felt a deep compassion for him – how could she not when he was in danger of losing his life at any moment? – she felt also a deep seated anger at what she saw as a kind of emotional blackmail. She should have put a stop to these impassioned outpourings, but, again, how could she, given the circumstances of his precariously uncertain existence?

'I think about you constantly, darling Iris,' he had written, just two weeks ago. 'The vision of you, of your clean and wholesome beauty, keeps me going in all this unbelievable chaos and violence

126

that surrounds us here.' He was commissioned as a second lieutenant in the Fusiliers, but was attached to some sort of Signals
unit, which meant that he was moving around a lot, sometimes in
the front line, sometimes behind the lines, at Divisional HQ. 'I'm
lucky, in a way,' he told her. 'A lot of the chaps I trained with who
stayed with their PBI companies (poor b——y infantry, by the
way!) have bought it already, whereas although we sometimes get
shot at spectacularly when we have to deal with front-line communications, we also get our share of dossing down with the Staff and
living in comparative comfort.'

She had resolved a number of times to write firmly to him and
put their relationship on the more ordinary, platonic level she
wished it to be. But the insidious thought kept creeping into her
mind that each letter he wrote might be the last she would ever
receive from him, and so she put off her day of reckoning, penning
instead her usual jolly, indeterminate replies, wishing him well,
and leaving him to make what he would of the 'All my love' with
which she invariably ended.

In October, she completed her training course, and began work
in earnest. She saw at first hand the evidence of what modern
warfare could do. She spent long hours of the day and night ferrying wounded from the disembarkation points on the Thames to the
various London hospitals, then, further afield, from southern coast
ports. She was moved by the pathetic bravery of the wounded men
she came into contact with, their unfailing courtesy.

She quickly realized, and was ashamed of the fact, that she and
the other girls of the new units of Ambulance Corps, were only
dealing with officers. 'Not suitable at all for you to handle ORs!' the
elderly, 'dug-out' Medical Corps officer told her, with what she
presumed was gruff kindness.

One day, she was part of a large convoy which was sent to
Waterloo Station, where a whole train load of walking and stretcher
cases had arrived. She pulled her ambulance into line in the station
forecourt, and climbed out to open the rear doors. 'Officers only!
Officers only!' She heard the cry echo down the concourse under

the great arch of the roof. Orderlies were starting to come forward, in the direction of the vehicles, carrying the stretchers. Other bandaged figures were making their own slow way.

A military policeman stepped forward, looked uncertainly at her drab dark skirt and battledress blouse.

'Right . . . er, miss. Graveney Street, is it?'

Iris nodded. 'What about the other ranks?' she asked.

Hs smiled cheerily, shook his head. 'Don't you worry your pretty head about them, miss. I think there's some lorries bein' organized for them later on. Lucky bastards won't mind waitin'. Whoops! Pardon my French, miss! Only too 'appy to 'ave copped a "blighty", most of 'em.' She was beginning to pick up the lingo of the Western Front, both from Lionel's letters and the daily contact with the wounded troops she brought in. She understood therefore that a "blighty" – a soldiers' term for England – was also slang for a wound which was serious enough to warrant treatment and convalescence back home, but not serious enough, hopefully, to finish you off.

London was still buzzing with the shocking news of Nurse Cavell's execution by enemy firing squad when Iris found a letter waiting for her one sharp October evening on her return to her billet. She recognized the neat, square hand of May, and opened eagerly, unmindful of the grumbles and chatter of her four room-mates. Already, she was used to the lack of privacy such crowded conditions entailed, and she stretched out on her narrow bed, pulling her dressing gown like a shawl about her shoulders. She smiled at the involuntary formality which May always seemed to adopt in her writing, with her 'I hope you are quite well', and the polite queries about the rest of her family.

There was more interesting news towards the end of the short missive. 'I'm pleased to be able to tell you that I am in a delicate condition once more, and that the new arrival will be here, God willing, some time in early April, we think. As you can see from the above address, we are still in Whitby, though we expected to be leaving much earlier, at the beginning of September, as I told you earlier. Jack has had lots of difficulty getting the work completed but it is nearly done now, and we think we will be gone by the end of the month. It would be safer to send your reply to my mother's address, which I will write below, as it is sure to reach me from there.'

Pregnant again, already. Iris was startled at the stab of resentment she felt against Jack. But really! Why did men seem so eager to turn their wives into breeding machines, from the moment they got them wedded – and bedded? Especially men of . . . she felt the warm colour mount to her face as she tried to stifle the completion of her uncharitable thought. Men of the lower orders, was the phrase that had sprung into her mind, she acknowledged guiltily. Oh God! I'm sounding just like daddy! she scolded herself ashamedly. Besides, it was palpably unfair to place Jack in that category. She knew very well that he was a sensitive, deep-thinking soul. Like her darling May, she added loyally. But her roots, certainly, were those of the labouring class. The shipyards, Sidney Terrace. Liberated as she was, and self-congratulatory about her democratic outlook, Iris could not deny the gulf between their families.

Not between her and May, though, she avowed. She would not allow any social distinctions to sully the closeness of their relationship. She was still overcome with tenderness when she thought of that day of their first meeting. Of how that slim, petite figure had appeared from nowhere, the resolute bravery with which she had literally put herself in front of those harpies. And all to protect her, a meddling stranger. Taking her so readily to her home like that, too, however humble she might have thought it.

Once more, a storm of emotion bubbled up as she thought of her friend, the slim beauty of that body threatened by the mystical distortion of yet another pregnancy and childbirth. If he was so caring and so sensitive, how could he possibly put her through such a dangerous and painful experience so soon? The ambivalence of her feeling towards the unsuspecting Jack disturbed her a great deal. She strove hard to feel sympathetic towards him. After all, to May he was the most important person in the whole world – a fact which caused Iris to wince involuntarily, like the stabbing pain from an over-sensitive tooth. He was certainly fully prepared to honour his commitment to the ancient, God-given marital rites. He was going forth and multiplying all right, even if he wasn't prepared to do his bit on the broader world spectrum.

It was largely due to these cloudy sentiments regarding May that when, a couple of days later, she received a hasty, scribbled note from Lionel telling her excitedly that he was coming home for leave in two weeks' time, and asking humbly if it would be possible for her to get some time off and spend it with him, she sat down immediately and wrote a warmly enthusiastic reply affirming that she would do her best to comply with his request.

'I can't tell you how much I'm looking forward to seeing you again!' She put three crosses after her name, then stared down at what she had written as though shocked by the clear, bold words. Abruptly, she thrust them inside the envelope, licked at the flap and pressed it down against the blotting pad before she could change her mind.

FOURTEEN

MAY RETURNED TO Gateshead two weeks ahead of Jack, who had to stay on in Whitby to see the final threads of his task pulled together.

'Sixteen months,' Mr Redmond mused, when Jack finally turned up at the works in Jesmond, on the first Monday in November. 'A darned sight longer than we thought, eh? Still, you've done well, lad, everything considered. You've done a good job. How's the family? Are you fixed up all right for accommodation?'

'We'll find something,' Jack answered. 'Just a question of keeping looking. At the moment, we're living back with the folks.'

They moved in with Jack's parents, establishing themselves in the large back bedroom which Jack and Dan had shared since they were young boys. The atmosphere was uncomfortably tense, particularly on that first day, when Sophia stood, a rigidly corseted figure, with her folded hands clasped in front of her, and welcomed May formally. 'You must tell me if anything doesn't suit,' she said stiffly. 'We want you to feel at home. You and John. You're welcome to stay as long as you please, I hope you know that.'

In the days, then weeks, which followed, a sometimes uneasy truce existed between Sophia and May. Little John proved, surprisingly, to act more as an unconscious peacemaker than otherwise. May had expected that the baby would prove a great bone of contention between them, but, though they certainly did have differences of opinion, not always voiced, on various matters

131

concerning his well-being, May could see clearly how much his grandmother loved the boy. And she was prepared to forgive a great deal in view of that sentiment.

The rest of the family, too, worked hard to make May's stay easier, from Mr Wright's over-exuberant jollying along, to Cissy's casual, unaffected friendliness. Jack's sister, now just turned twenty-one – her birthday only two months after May's – was working as a 'lady typist' for a large retail firm down by the river. She was more than happy to have a female confidante of her own age in the house, and would regale an intrigued May with all the gossip involving her work-mates, and, in particular, the unattached males, who showed a lively interest in such a personable young lady.

'You'll be settling down soon enough,' May laughed. 'One of them'll get a ring on your finger.'

Cissy, who pretended to shuddering horror whenever John's nappy needed changing, would make a vehement denial and insist she was perfectly content with her present unencumbered state.

May was equally glad of the feminine company Cissy provided. She had realized how much she missed the friendship she had shared with Iris. She was delighted therefore when, during the Christmas period, she went round to her mother's one morning (there were very few days when she didn't drop in at Sidney Terrace at some point in the day, while Jack was at work) to find a letter waiting for her. 'It's a note from Iris,' she told Robina happily. 'She's home for a few days over Christmas. She wants to meet up.'

'You look absolutely gorgeous! And so smart, too! The uniform really suits you!'

Iris flushed with pleasure at May's ardent praise. She crossed her legs, studied the length of black-stockinged leg revealed under the dark skirt. She knew herself she looked good. She was a little ashamed of the amount of money she had spent having the uniform tailored, so that the dark green jacket and skirt were fitted alluringly to her tall, slender figure. The soft felt hat, its brim pulled low at the front over her carefully styled hair, trimmed short in the latest fashion, completed the fetching outfit, in a military yet thoroughly feminine manner which pleased her greatly.

She gazed fondly across the small table at the neat form opposite, who was now pulling a face of comic dismay. 'You just make me feel even more like a house end. You can see now why I didn't want to go anywhere where anyone would see us!'

They were in a quiet café on the corner of Hood Street and Grey Street, on the ground floor of a hotel, and ensconced in a cosy window seat. Between the net curtaining, May could see the lofty monument to Earl Grey, standing darkly against the strip of grey sky. Iris laughed, stretched out her hand and placed it over May's.

'Stop fishing for compliments. You're the one who looks gorgeous, as always. Your condition agrees with you, I have to admit. You look blooming!'

'Right! That's enough of the mutual admiration society, yes?' May leaned forward confidentially. 'Now then! Tell us all about this life of yours down in London. Or as much as you can without shocking me to death. Hey! Have you seen Lionel? Didn't you say—'

May was silenced by the unquestionable expression of pain she saw fall on Iris's face at the mention of the name. She coloured, the eyelids lowered for an instant as though she would hide that pain from her friend's compassionate gaze. The grip of the hand was returned. 'Oh, love!' May went on feelingly. 'What's wrong? He's all right, isn't he? He hasn't been . . . hurt?'

Iris shook her head. 'No. He's just gone back, as a matter of fact.' She glanced up at May, tried to smile, and May was touched by the look of vulnerability, the uncharacteristic shyness and hesitancy she saw there.

May took her hand in both hers, held onto it. She sensed that, underneath this strange reluctance, Iris had a strong urge, a need, to confide in her. She waited. When she went on, Iris's voice was quiet, clipped with an uncomfortable embarrassment.

'Things have got – rather complicated.' There was another

pause, and still May waited patiently, holding onto her hand. The violet eyes suddenly sought hers, with a deeply earnest, searching need.

'May! This . . . this love business. Is it really – how do you feel about it? Really. Is it—' she stared helplessly, floundering, then went on, 'Is it good? Do you like it? The sexual side of it?'

Now, the colour swept up, flooding May's shocked face. She couldn't help it, it was the openness of Iris's question, bringing such a subject out in front of them like that. But she could feel the desperate urgency in her friend's voice, her whole manner, and she knew at once there was nothing prurient about her friend's startling words. She nodded bravely. Her voice was even quieter as she answered.

'Yes. It's wonderful Between Jack and me – I didn't think I would, I was so frightened. But when it happened, he was—' she stopped suddenly, realizing the import of Iris's question now, staring at her solemnly. 'You're in love with him?' It was half-question, half-statement.

Iris shrugged, made a hopeless gesture with her free hand, turning the palm upward, as though she were not sure of the answer herself.

'He thinks I am! I couldn't – I don't want to hurt him. He's different. Since he's been out there. He's not so . . . he's so quiet. He seemed – oh, I don't know.' Once again, that hopeless, questioning gesture. 'Desperate. It's like – he was clinging on to those feelings – about me. About us. I feel so terrible, May. I couldn't disillusion him. I didn't want to. But I don't feel deeply enough about him – about . . . any of that sort of thing.' For the third time, she shook her head.

All at once, May knew what she was trying to tell her, that she had given herself bodily to him, made love with him. Part of her was shocked, she couldn't help it, it was an instinctive reaction, because of her own conventional, strictly moral upbringing. But only part of her. Much greater was her immediate wave of sympathy, and love, for her friend's distress.

'Oh, Iris!' She squeezed her hand tightly, to convey the depth of her feeling. 'You must care for him – very much. You'll learn to love him—'

She was startled at the violent head shake of negation.

'No!' Iris said at once. 'No! I couldn't! I can't.'

With a kind of helplessness, Iris's mind went back yet again to the afternoon five days ago. The musty, damp smell of the great, rambling attic at Ferncliffe, the Strangs' mansion north of Newcastle, out along the road to Morpeth. It was cold, so cold that their breath was steaming. Iris had stared, distracted by it as Lionel's shining lips approached hers, then descended on her mouth, smotheringly, wetly, cutting off all thought except that heart-banging panic.

They had kissed before, several times, passionately, in the gloom of porch, or stairwell, or wildly in a briefly abandoned drawing room for a snatched moment before returning footsteps sent them leaping apart. She should have stopped it, right from the start, put an end to it, that fevered clutching, that sealing mouth. Now she lashed herself with the bitterness of hindsight. She had hesitated. Had even thought that maybe she would somehow get more used to it, that it was an aberration on her part which she would recover from. Besides, there were not many of such moments, she could endure them, when she saw the desperation, that strange, raw need of his. The quiet, haunted quality, the uncertainty and loneliness which had transformed him so utterly from the confident, preening, egotistical male she had known formerly.

Just as with his letters, in his presence, she found herself quite incapable of delivering the cruel truth to him. Instead, she even tried to fool herself, unsuccessfully. After all, she would argue with herself, I *am* fond of him, in a way. Very fond. He means a great deal to me. But it was that new loneliness, that stillness inside him, that made her keep back from telling him the truth. She could not be that cruel, did not want to be.

He made it hard for her, though, pressing her, almost begging her to wear his ring, to declare that she would be his love. 'We ought to wait, Lionel,' she said, unconvincingly. Perhaps, deep inside, there was a part of him which knew the answer already, could see beyond her diffidence, and balked from facing it. At any rate, his leave progressed, until the day before it was due to end, he had led her through the great house, in the lead dull afternoon of a new year's day, to the deserted upper regions, just below the crenellated roof.

He was searching for his old nursery toys, the forts and soldiers, horses and carriages. He seemed anxious for her to see them.

'Gosh! I wish I'd known you then,' he smiled wistfully. He was holding her hand tightly. She didn't mind. With secret shame, she acknowledged her pride in this worshipful admiration of her, the moonstruck quality of it. 'Mind you,' he was continuing, as he led her along the dark corridor past the rows of oak doors, to the narrow, twisting staircase that led to the series of low rooms under the roof itself, 'I'd probably have tormented you wickedly. Yanked you by your pigtails. I was a horrible bully.'

She laughed. Tugged against his hold on her.

'I'd have given as good as I got, I should think. I was a bit of a tomboy, myself.'

He found the attic with the old toys in. He dragged out a wicker box, took out the battered painted soldiers, the dented fort, started setting them up, in an old-fashioned military formation. She flinched as, all at once, he swept the line of gaily coloured figures aside, scattering them with one savage blow of his outflung arm. She saw the line of his jaw, standing up beneath the clean shaven skin like a miniature reef. He was shaking. Her heart ached as she saw the chilling, haunted look descend across his features again.

'Lionel!' she whispered. She put her hand out, gently, hesitantly, touched his arm. 'It's all right.' She watched his mouth come close, saw the little cloud of his breath before his lips pressed hard against her own, and she felt the pressure of his teeth against hers.

She was close to tears, aching with her sorrow for him. She had a strong urge to hold him, to mother him to her breast, to whisper soothingly to him, like a mother with her baby.

'There's a blanket!' he said tightly. His fingers clasped her by the arm, he pulled her through the cluttered floor space. Then they were down, kneeling, on some old cushions, and he had a thick rug in one hand. 'God! Iris!' Her name came out in a kind of sob, then he was sprawling, pulling her down beside him. In any other circumstances, it would have been laughable, the absurd indignity of it, her sprawling there too, the skirts of her dress turned back, the lace of her petticoat, her high boot, and her thick ribbed, black-stockinged leg showing far too liberally.

But there was nothing funny, now, about his tortured gaze, the nightmare quality of his eyes, burning right through to her. Then his weight was on her, for the first time she felt a man's urgent body thrust against her. A voice cried out inside her head. A voice that shook her profoundly. Let him have you! Let him take what he needs, he is in torment over you! She began to sob then, the strength ebbing from her, so that she lay when he turned her, her arms around him, her hands gently resting on the rough cloth of his shoulders. She felt his knee between hers, driving her limbs apart, and his mouth was savaging at her neck, she could not breathe.

She did not know, thought she would never know, whether she had intended there and then to let him have her. But his mouth was slobbering all over her, as he moaned out her name, his hand was clawing, clutching at the shape of her breast through all the thick-ness of her clothing, then his other hand was clawing up her leg, on the coarse worsted stocking, burrowing under the stiff material of her dress, the lace of her petticoat, digging into the softness of her flesh above her knee, through the thick pink flannel of her draw-ers. Another agonizing, shrivellingly embarrassing afterthought, a savagely mocking, ridiculous one, as she relived it, the thought of that ugly, sensible, winter undergarment, elasticated almost to the knees, over which that blind hand roved, to the fullness of her thigh, then to the hot, damp, beating shame between, as she squirmed and clenched, then, madly, with a cry of revulsion, caught his wrist, flung it from her, fought out from under him, flung him bodily from her, striking out at him, sobbing, quivering, until she found herself outside the low room, alone, weeping and shivering still as she clattered down the iron stairs.

She found a bathroom, sat there behind the locked door, wept until she could cry no more, bathed her face, and wearily steeled herself to face the world again. He was downstairs, white, silent, while his mother came to her, full of concern, briefly touched her hand in a coded acknowledgement, a purely female message of complicity.

'I understand you're not well, my dear. Lionel will see you home. He'll drive you. Effy is packing your bags. I'm so sorry. We'll see you again soon.'

She was too weary to protest at his accompanying her. She did not mind, in any case. She was sure he would do her no harm, would not even touch her. She could sense the despair oozing from him, the craven defeat. She even felt vaguely sorry for him, but with none of the intensity of her former compassion for him. She was not really surprised when he wept, at the end of their journey.

'I won't come in. I'll say goodbye here, if you don't mind.' His voice broke. 'I'm sorry – I can't ask you … it was unforgivable, I know that. I didn't think—' he shook his head, very quickly ducked and kissed her hand and she felt the wetness of a teardrop. Then he looked up at her. He did not try to disguise the tears, they glistened on his cheek, above the dark curve of his moustache. 'If only you knew—' he began intensely, then once more shook his head.

Pity took over then. She put out her gloved hand, softly caressed his cheek.

'It's all right. Really. It's just – I'm not brave enough,' she lied, blushing deeply but meeting his gaze. 'You'll continue to write to me, won't you?'

The sadness she saw, the humility of his gratitude, moved her.

'I *do* love you,' he whispered brokenly. 'Honourably. Deeply.' He did not attempt to kiss her, but swung away abruptly, moving from her to climb into the high cab of the automobile. She gave one wave, and turned to run swiftly through the gloom, her feet crunching on the gravel of the curving drive.

Tears were running down the steam-fogged windows of the café. Iris smiled sadly at the concern she saw reflected in May's eyes. She returned the caring grip of the hands on hers.

'I'm still unsullied,' she murmured, and smiled again, this time with pure love at the pink she watched rise enchantingly to tinge May's cheeks. 'I thought I wanted him to – to make love to me. I wanted to ease his pain. To make him feel better. But I couldn't. Couldn't bear him to – anywhere near me.'

Once again, May was shocked, felt the blush increasing.

'Of course not!' she said. 'But it's ... it'll be different. When you're married—'

Iris laughed tremulously, picked up May's hand, rubbed it against her face in that impulsive gesture of hers.

'I love you.'

Outside, before they stepped into the motor which was waiting for them, Iris bought an evening paper. The date was 6 January.

'Only horrid war news, I bet!' May said, when they were seated in the covered rear of the car. Iris had been studying the front page.

'Commons vote in favour of conscription,' it read. 'Home Secretary to resign.'

'You're right,' she said, and flung it beside her on the seat before May could see it. There was no equivocation this time about the pain of the love she felt in her heart for the girl sitting at her side.

PART II – Today

FIFTEEN

THE BIRTH OF the second baby was a quicker, and easier, affair altogether. May was delivered in the back bedroom at the Wrights'. 'I'd like it very much if you'd have the baby here,' Sophia Wright said, in what, for her, amounted to a plea. 'In the room Dan and Jack shared as boys. It would mean a lot to us, Ted and me.' The inclusion of her husband made it all the more difficult to refuse, not that May had any serious intention of doing so, even though she knew it would probably upset her own mother. Robina had grudgingly come to accept her daughter's lodging with her in-laws, largely because May made a point of spending several hours each day round at Sidney Terrace, with John.

It was undoubtedly very handy, especially as her pregnancy advanced, for May to have so many willing helpers on hand to help her look after her son. Both grandmas vied with each other to indulge the infant, while, whenever they were free, Cissy and Julia enjoyed the role of aunt, and were happy to take him out for walks in the high perambulator, or even to give him his bath in a bowl in front of the kitchen fire.

The rivalry between the two households could still sometimes be a strain. Christmas had been a time of special tension, because of the double celebration of Jesus' and John's birth. May felt torn, had almost fallen out with her mother. 'He's Jack's bairn as well, mam!' she cried. 'We'll have to have Christmas dinner with his folks. We'll pop round after dinner, let you see his presents.' Instead of the row which was threatening cracklingly to erupt, mother and daughter had ended up hugging one another, and Robina had painfully settled for Boxing Day as their time with the young marrieds.

This time, Dr Smith, the Wrights' family physician, was in attendance for the birth, together with his nurse, though the delivery was uncomplicated, after a labour of only eight hours. Jack was downstairs, puffing away at his pipe in a highly nervous state, leaving cups of cold tea in various places around the dining room, drifting in and out of the kitchen where his mother and the latest in the part-time and wholly unsatisfactory domestic help were boiling pans and generally trying to keep themselves busy.

They had been pretending not to listen to May's muffled but increasing cries in the last stage of her labour, and they all nearly collided with one another as they rushed into the passage on hearing the rustle of the nurse's starched apron as she came hurrying down the stairs.

'Congratulations, Mr Wright! A fine boy. He's just perfect.'

Another three quarters of an hour, and Jack was allowed into the bedroom at last, where May was sitting up, her hair shining and dampened as it was brushed back in two parted folds from her brow, her dark eyes animated, her face only a little pink, and shiny, too, like a child who has been freshly scrubbed. She had her embroidered bed-jacket on, and smelt of fragrant cologne. Jack was amazed at how lively and glowing with health she looked. Remembering vividly the last time, he had expected to see her dark ringed and wan with exhaustion.

She stretched out her arms, pulled him down to her waiting lips.

'Isn't he beautiful? He's bigger than John was. Handsomer, too. Look at him.'

Jack stared at the peaceful form, heavily wrapped in blanket and shawl, the tiny features angelic in repose, the downy fair hair raised in delicate wisps of gold threads. He was lying on the pillows beside his mother, deeply asleep.

Jack swallowed hard, his emotion choking him as he nodded and murmured, 'Perfect, isn't he?'

Later that night, his father was almost equally overcome. He tiptoed in to greet his daughter-in-law and catch his first glimpse of his new grandson. May smiled as she lifted her face to be kissed, and said, 'We're going to call him Edward, if you've no objection, after his grandpa Wright.'

May was restless, anxious to be up and out of bed, trying not to be irritated by all the fuss that was lavished on her. 'You must have rest, the doctor says,' Sophia would insist, picking up the vigorously protesting toddler who was playing about the bed.

John was not impressed with his new brother. 'Ba-ba!' he cried hopefully, while the adults kept a ready and wary eye out lest he demonstrate his enthusiasm by a sudden grab. But the baby did nothing, just lay there and slept, or yawned, or bawled, and he rapidly lost interest. He wondered angrily why his mama was lying in bed all day and why various people kept taking him away from her. It was a frustrating time for him altogether.

At the end of two weeks, May was on her feet again, and felt perfectly well, apart from the soreness of her tender, full breasts. But the period leading up to the confinement, the birth itself, had been in many ways a temporary escape from the fears that lay in wait for them outside. In March, a month before Edward was born, the Military Service Act had come into being. Conscription had begun. 'They're only taking the single men, though!' May had said, desperately trying to reassure herself. Everyone knew, it had been made clear from the start, that, although single men would be called up first, married men would follow. 'But you've got two little bairns!' May reasoned fearfully. 'They can't take you. They won't.'

Jack was carrying out a lot of fairly minor repair jobs, none of which lasted more than a week or two, in churches all round the Tyneside region, never too far away to prevent him from getting home each night. It was as if everything were in limbo, waiting to see what was to happen.

'Can't you find work somewhere away?' May asked him. 'A longer job, so's we could all move. Like Whitby.' He could hear the regret, the wistfulness in her voice. 'We can't stay here. Not with two bairns as well. It's not fair on your folks,' she added defensively.

Jack shook his head. 'There's hardly enough work to keep me on, as it is. They're only waiting—' He paused, drew in a deep breath. 'They'll be calling up married men soon. My age group. Twenty-four. I'll have to go.'

'No! Don't say that! You won't. Not with little ones. You can tell them – say I'm bad. Can't cope. It's true.'

He gazed at her sadly. 'I can't do that.' he murmured.

She flung herself at him. She wound her arms fiercely about his neck, pressing her head against his chest. When he put his arms round her, he could feel her shaking.

'No, Jack. You mustn't leave me. Please promise. You won't.'

He was close to tears himself, the emotion tearing so painfully at him he wondered how he could bear it. For now with a fatalistic certainty, he knew that he would go. Wanted to be gone, to have this tearing pain done with, to meet it as quickly as possible. With this new feeling came the equally sure belief that it was right. He couldn't explain it, not even to himself. He was still convinced that he had been right before not to rush off to volunteer, not to be one of 'the first hundred thousand' so many had cheered off to war.

But now the monstrous war was something he could no longer avoid. No one could, it was like some inexorable machine, sucking in men, a great nemesis that lay ahead, was unstoppably approaching. He was afraid, a vague, unformed fear of violence, of killing, and dying. His imagination worked fearfully from all the information he had received, from the endless war news, and the letters from Dan, the talk from others with relatives at the front. He had noticed that the few returning soldiers he had met, on leave, or invalided out after being wounded, talked very little, imparting only little pieces of trivia, almost unconnected to the dark truth he sensed lay out there. It was like a wall dividing them from all the rest, those back here at home. More and more, he had this sense of something inescapable drawing him towards it.

May felt it, too, in a different way. Her victim's helplessness grew, it was like the childhood nightmare she could not wake from.

146

She was going to lose him, was in some terrifying way losing him already, she could see him slipping away from her, from their life together, in the abstracted quality of his expression, more noticeable each day. In those first weeks of Edward's life, it was cruelly ironic that she should be suffering so much, when physically she was in the best of health, felt so different from the debilitating weakness she had suffered after John's birth. The new baby, too, was much stronger, much more placid, providing none of the anxieties and disturbed nights that they had known with his older brother.

A few days before the government brought into force its new Daylight Saving scheme, whereby, on 21 May everyone was supposed to advance the clocks one hour, Jack came home from work just after lunch. May was round at Sidney Terrace and she gasped in surprise when he walked in on her and her mother sitting at the long table in the kitchen.

'My God! What is it?' Robina cried, jumping up in concern. She could see at once the strained, tragic look on his face. He was still in his work things. 'Sit yesel' down, hinny. Ah'll get ye a cup of tea.'

May's face was pale, too. Their eyes met, stared at each other wordlessly for long seconds.

'They've not called you?' She whispered the words almost soundlessly.

He shook his head. Forced his words out. 'They're forming another Pals' Company – the Fusiliers. I'm signing on. Tomorrow.'

She nodded slowly. 'How long have you been planning this?' she asked, her words still hardly more than a whisper.

'I haven't planned it. I only just heard. Told Mr Redmond today.' He stepped forward, close to the table. Made to reach out his hand, then let it fall to his side. 'I'm going to have to go, anyway. You know I am. I'll be in the next batch. I want to be with the Fusiliers.'

'Oh, aye. The Pals! You might meet up with your Dan. All right having a brother who's a sergeant, eh?' Her words rang with bitterness. Her eyes glittered as they held his.

'Stop it, May!' Robina banged down the mug of tea, then abruptly flung her arms around the still figure and gave him a clumsy hug. 'Well done, lad!' she said emotionally. 'We're right proud of you.'

Jack's body swayed involuntarily at Robina's embrace, otherwise he never moved. He was still staring at May.

'I had to, May,' he said intensely. 'There's nothing else I could do.'

'No!' He flinched, and Robina started, at the piercing pitch of May's cry. 'No! You said, you told me – you wouldn't leave me!' She had stood, the chair scraped back over the stone floor. She was gasping, her breasts heaving, great, laboured breaths as though she could not find sufficient air. 'Never, you said! Never!' The sobs were deep shudders, coming from the depths of her despair, and he moved swiftly, unable to keep from reaching for her. 'No!' She screamed, wildly, and he tried to gather her in, hold her to him, and her fists flailed, struck at his face and his arms. She broke free, with a noisy wail, and crashed through the door, fled along the passage, up the stairs, her cries fading, while John set up a shocked and frightened screaming from his corner.

Jack sat on in the kitchen, stunned, sipping at his tea, staring ahead, Robina's hasty words of comfort flowing unheeded over him, a gentle background to his wandering thoughts. An hour later, at his mother-in-law's bidding, he went slowly upstairs, found her in the bedroom she had shared with her sister since she was a child. She was lying carelessly across the bed, on her stomach, her face hidden in her folded arms. Her hair was awry, her ankles crossed, he could see the high boots, the white hem of her petticoat showing beneath the dark, displaced skirt.

She was quiet, he thought she might be asleep. He swallowed, cleared his throat, advanced nervously.

'May.' He sat down on the edge of the bed, across from her, ached to reach out and stroke the rich waves of hair lying over the eiderdown, but he didn't. 'Please, May. I'm sorry, love. I didn't want to hurt you. I've never wanted that.'

She looked up then. Her eyes were swollen and red with weeping. Her nose was, too, her face blotched with grief.

'But you have,' she answered, with quiet, undeniable simplicity. 'You're leaving me. You can't hurt me any more than that.'

'I don't want to, May. It's the last thing I want. I've got to. I have to do it,' he said hopelessly, inadequately.

She gave a little nod, so that, for a moment, in the middle of his despair, he had a pinprick of hope that she understood him. She sighed, a shuddering remnant of a sob shook her shoulders, then she swung herself up, stood, and shook out her skirt. Her voice sounded croaky, as though she had a cold.

'You know what?' she said softly, again with that lop-sided smile. 'I'm glad you can't touch me.' She nodded towards the wide bed stretching between them. 'That way, I mean. That you can't make love to me. I think it'll make it a lot easier, don't you?'

He stood there as she moved past him and went out. He remained there, motionless, his head tilted back slightly, his eyes closed.

After a medical and the swearing-in, together with several fiercely patriotic talks designed to fire them up with righteous rage against the enemy, the new recruits were allowed home for one more night. They had to report at the Central Station to take a special train for the short ride up the coast to the tented camp north of Blyth where they would start their basic training. They had yet to be kitted out with uniform, so Jack was wearing his second best suit, and carried his few personal items in a cloth haversack.

They had said their own private goodbyes, through the long, sleepless night when they lay side by side. The bitterness was still there, overwhelmingly, in May. But the helpless rage had gone, leaving her weak, and almost apathetic with a depth of despair that seemed like a high wall shutting out any future. She did not tell Jack everything of how she felt. She couldn't. She lay and sobbed heart-brokenly in his arms, until she exhausted this outpouring of her grief.

'I don't know how I'll manage,' she confessed. Her whispering voice was stunned, like a child's. 'I don't know how I'll be able to go on – without you. I can't even picture it.'

'You'll be all right. You'll do it, for the bairns' sake. Be strong for them. For me.' Towards dawn, he lifted his head from her breast, and, leaning over her, his face close to hers, said fervently, 'Listen, May. I swear to you – and this time I won't let you down, I mean it, I'll keep my word to you. I'll come back to you, and the boys. I promise you.'

May pulled him down to her, moved her warm body underneath him, until their bodies touched along all their length, while their open mouths fixed passionately together.

'You'd better!' she gasped, when the kiss finally ended. With great bravery, smiling through her tears, she whispered, 'I'll kill you if you don't!'

At the station, they kissed again, open-mouthed and passionate, too, despite the jostling publicity of the embrace. It didn't matter. All around them, couples were doing the same, some laughing, many dissolved in tears. The tears were flowing down May's face, which made her wide, determined smile even more incongruous. The cries of parting were deafening. A burst of cheering rose as the train began to pull out. The little paper flags fluttered madly. More and more of the recruits crowding at the windows took up the refrain of the latest song which was proving to be a great hit at music halls everywhere.

> Nothing else would matter in the world today,
> We would go on loving in the same old way . . .

Please, please, God, let him keep his word to me! May prayed, still smiling, the scene of the departing train shimmering and dancing through her tears.

The wooden sign, leaning at an angle over the sandbagged redoubt, read 'Whiskey Street'. 'Look at the way the bastards've spelt it,' someone called out. 'Bloody Irish!' The long communications

trench was crowded, the men, bulky and clumsy in their equipment, squatted down. The earth walls of the trench were not very
high here, nor well timbered. There was far more protection up in
the front line, which this trench, part of a maze of such construc-
tions, led into about 200 yards further up. Overhead the morning
sky was paling, the cloud high and wispy.

'Gonna be a warm day,' someone said quietly.

'Aye, ye could say that,' a Geordie voice answered drily, and there
was a soft murmur of laughter.

'Thank God that bombardment's stopped. It's been drivin' us
daft.'

'Ye can thank your lucky stars for it. The' cannot be owt left of
the Huns after that lot.'

For a week, the British guns had pounded away practically non-
stop, the shells screeching over the men's heads in seemingly
endless succession.

'That's right, eh, sarge?' The young, pointed face, looking even
smaller under the tin hat tipped on the back of his head, stared
eagerly at Dan, watching his own face, desperate for confirmation.

Dan smiled confidently, saw the youngster's expression of gratitude spread over his features.

'That's right, bonny lad. It's a bit of a stroll for us this morning.
I reckon we'll just walk over there and occupy those trenches.'

' 'Bout time an' all.'

'Make way there. Signals party!'

The men cursed, jostling one another as they stood, unwilling to
raise their heads over the walls of the trench, making way for the
small group of men moving at a crouch, paying out wire from a
heavy coil, securing it at intervals in the churned up floor of the
trench, at the angle of the wall.

'That's it, Mr Strang, sir,' a corporal called out. Dan caught the
name, looked up with quick interest, saw a stocky second lieutenant, his uniform liberally covered with dust. He was wearing a
cap instead of the steel helmet. The dark bronze of the Fusiliers'
insignia showed at its brow.

151

Dan had heard the name before, knew that he was the son of Sir William Strang, the big timber man. He had joined up as early as Dan had, caught up no doubt in the local patriotic fervour. Practically veterans now, Dan thought, with a wry smile. Most of the lads were still local, though their numbers were becoming more and more diluted by newcomers from other regions. Mr Strang was lucky, Dan guessed. Second lieutenants had a poor life expectancy. Going over the top with a swagger stick and a pistol, and in front of your men to boot, was a job with only a limited future, or none at all.

The officer squeezed past him, and Dan touched his fingers to the rim of his helmet in what passed for a salute. Lionel Strang gave an equally casual return, smiled and nodded.

'Good man. All set, sergeant? You should be moving up soon. First wave's due over at seven-thirty.' He glanced at his watch. 'Seven minutes to go. Good luck!'

'Thanks, sir.' Dan watched him heading for the front line. The corporal was taking a breather, crouched beside him, fumbling for a fag tucked in his helmet. 'All right, is he?' Dan asked, nodding at Lionel's retreating back.

The corporal nodded tolerantly. 'Aye. Not bad for a toff, like. Daft bastard, mind, like they all are.' He grinned. 'Reckons he's dead lucky. Never wears his tin hat, see? Reckons he doesn't need it.' He nodded to the two fusiliers with the drum of wire, and they prepared to follow their officer.

'You going over?' Dan asked casually.

The corporal grinned. 'Not till you lot've cleared it for us, sarge. We'll see you ower in the Hun trenches when you've got 'em all ship shape for us. Good luck!'

Minutes later, whistles blasted piercingly all along the ten mile sector of the Somme, and the heavily laden troops of fourteen divisions climbed the ladders and went over the top, closely packed, advancing slowly in line. The ground ahead looked like a desert, pockmarked, desolate, blasted with shell holes. Yet, to their dawning horror, many of the attackers found even the enemy barbed wire intact in stretches. Many did not get that far, but were cut down by the raking machine guns, then the heavier guns which, suddenly resurrected, began to pound at the thick clusters of troops.

The 1st Tynesides knew early on something was wrong. They could hear the mounting fire. They were still awaiting the order to be called up into the front line when suddenly, with those terrifying rushing screams, shells began to fall all about them, then, inevitably, on them. 'Move!' Dan cried desperately, in the chaos of pungent smoke and showering earth, and torn, raw, bleeding flesh. 'Get up front!' He had lost half the company before he could get them to break from the trench and risk a rush over the littered ground, intersected by the support trenches, until they could reach the stouter protection of the front line itself.

The battalion commander saw him, waved him on urgently. 'Good man, Wright! Well done. Spread 'em out. We'll be going over soon.' He turned, to encourage the hurrying figures. There was a great whoosh, a hot blast of air, then there was no air to be had. Dan felt the ground lift, he was down, clinging to it, it was covering him in a roaring deluge. He struggled up, blinded, spitting the loamy soil from his black face, wiping his eyes clear. There was a crater, and a bloody mess of meat, with one highly polished, leather riding boot protruding, where the commander had stood.

Their battalion alone had lost nearly a thousand troops before they went over the top, at eight-thirty. As Dan climbed the ladder ahead of his men, and faced the horrors of the battle still to come, he did not notice the crushed, mangled khaki hat, a second lieutenant's cap, which lay discarded, trampled beneath the feet of the men who were going to face the hungry guns.

SIXTEEN

THE LIGHTS WENT up in the Empire Theatre to a stunned silence, then came the soft sound of women crying, until the tiny band of musicians, led by the jangling piano, struck out the obscenely vigorous chords of the *National Anthem*, the muted cheers which rose thinly from only a very few throats adding to its martial obscenity. May's face looked jaundiced in the garish light. She stared at her mother-in-law, whose own visage was etched with the deep lines of pain and shock. Instinctively, they reached out to hold one another. Edward Wright was unable to look at them, there was a hint of shame in the way he wordlessly took their elbows, steering them out into the crowded central aisle.

As a piece of propaganda, *The Battle of the Somme* was a colossal blunder on the part of the authorities. Brilliantly shot, its footage covered every aspect of the battle which was even now still continuing, in a nightmare landscape of mud and desolation. The documentary film brought the horror of the war starkly home to all who saw it, and the audiences were flocking in their thousands up and down the land, to music hall theatres like the Empire, to village halls. The reaction everywhere was almost identical: a horrified disbelief at the scale of the carnage and suffering presented so graphically, and fear for their friends and loved ones locked in the gigantic struggle going on across the Channel.

The silence continued between May and the Wrights during the tram ride home. They dismounted and began the walk down the

154

steep bank from Durham Road.

'They've got to stop it!' May cried suddenly, turning to Edward, who was stationed between the two women, giving an arm to each. She stared at him in anguish. 'They can't go on like this! They can't!'

'Now that Lloyd George has become War Secretary,' he started to reply, then his voice tailed away. He was still too caught up in the immediacy of the violence they had witnessed, the pathetic bravery of the smiles, the perky waves for the camera, the wide-eyed fear, the hollow eyed look of fear, and despair, the lines of maimed, bandaged figures waiting outside the casualty stations, the rows of covered bundles, incongruously neat on the stretchers where they lay lifeless. He thought of the phrases he had read in the papers this week. 'Battle of attrition . . . one last push . . . peace this year'. He knew that May was clinging desperately to the hope that Jack would not have to go out there, after all.

He felt sick with fear and tender compassion for his oldest son, and, as if for the first time, appreciated something of the anguish his wife must have endured all these long months. And a deep and disturbing shame at the pride he had felt at Dan's action in joining up so readily, the patriotic boastfulness he had displayed at work, and to his friends and colleagues – 'our Dan's in the thick of it. Been made up to sergeant now.'

Cissy had been looking after the children. She was nursing the baby in the kitchen, rocking the shawled bundle back and forth at her shoulder.

'I think he's ready for his feed,' she said, grateful for their return. 'How was it, then?' she asked brightly. 'You didn't see our Dan, did you?' She saw their faces, the glance that passed between them. She handed Edward over to May.

'I'll not bother with a drink or anything to eat,' May said. 'I'll go up, have an early night. I've got a bit of a headache.'

'I could bring you up a drink later, if you like,' Sophia offered.

May smiled. 'No thanks, I'm fine. I'll get off up. Good-night then.'

Upstairs, she left only the one dim lamp on as she swiftly unbuttoned her blouse, then her bodice. Edward was grizzling, and his little face rooted eagerly for her nipple when she put him to her breast. She was already having to supplement his feeding, for her milk was nowhere near as plentiful as it had been with John. She glanced down fondly at the dark head in the cot over in the corner before she settled herself on the bed. So wide and lonely, now that Jack was away. She felt herself blushing at her body's desire for him, at her sensual reaction to the infant nuzzling at her.

'I don't know what I'll do, how I'll manage without you.' She smiled again as she heard herself uttering those words, and Jack's forlorn reply, 'You'll be all right. You're a brave girl, May, the bravest I know.' But now she shivered, tried to shut out those stark images, of men lumbering over that arid wasteland, the falling clods of dark earth, the mushrooms of death. They had looked so insignificant, like scuttling insects, crawling out of their holes, dark little dots, running countlessly to destruction.

It seemed to be stretching out its fingers to so many that she knew, and loved. Not only Jack, and his brother. And her brother, George, too. Now even Iris had been drawn in. Only a couple of weeks ago, she had written hastily, and eagerly, a brief note to tell her that she was being sent over to France. It had come suddenly, there was no time even to come up north to say her goodbyes. It sounded like some sort of emergency, a response to the latest 'big push' which had started at the beginning of July. The push which had been the Battle of the Somme, the grim epic which had unfolded before her very eyes on the white screen in the smoky comfort of the Empire tonight.

Again, that sense of chilling fear swelled up, until the baby grizzled and whimpered at her breast as though he, too, could sense it. She found herself wishing that something might happen, that Jack might fall ill, even have some kind of accident, which would disable him in some way. Anything to prevent him having to go on into that terrible conflict she had seen tonight. The same helplessness seized her at the inevitability of it, the way in which everybody was caught up in this madness to some extent or other, and all incapable of calling a halt. He had promised her! Sworn he would return. He would keep his word to her, he must!

'Come on, you 'orrible conchie lot! Get fell in, and quick about it! You gotta learn to look smart when you march off to death or glory and we ain't got much time left!'

Jack studied the bristles on the bull neck of the drill sergeant with a detached pleasure at this confirmation of the stereotype. It appeared he was right about one thing, though. Their training had been accelerated, or, rather, abbreviated, and they would be rushed off to France well before Christmas, it looked like, instead of after the new year, which had been the original intention.

Rumours abounded. There was an undercurrent, whispered among the ORs, of seditious talk of mutinies across the water, and large-scale desertions. That was the real reason they were being shipped out early, big Geordie Blacker asserted, nodding his pitted face with the wisdom of one 'in the know'. 'The're all packin' it in, man. The's streams of 'em comin' away from the line every day, ah tell ye!'

Again with detachment, Jack reflected how much he loathed the sight of Geordie's long, scraggy frame, with its comical little pot belly thrusting out the thick vest and drawers, the dark, discoloured scabs at the crinkled elbows and knees which betokened his long service down the pits north of the Tyne. The drill sergeant's use of the term 'conchie' when addressing them was typical of the abusive scorn the recruits had endured throughout the four months and more of their training. To their instructors, the notion of a conscript was identified with that of a conscientious objector.

Jack had given up protesting that he was a volunteer. In fact, a third of the intake were volunteers, but their indignant protestations at the abuse heaped upon them met with little sympathy. 'Well, ye took yer fuckin' time joinin' up, that's all ah can say,' one three-striped veteran told them contemptuously, and they lapsed into injured silence.

It no longer mattered much to Jack. All he knew was that he was sick to death already of the brutalizing institution he had become a part of. There was no glory in the drilling and marching and learning to kill, though he performed all these actions satisfactorily enough to keep him out of bother. In the same way he fitted quietly into the coarseness of barrack-room life, smothering his shock and disgust at the lack of privacy, the physical discomfort, the endless monotony of the swearing and the feuding, the bullying of the weak, and the animal-like obscenity.

Even now, the sergeant's lips were parting in a leer of pure delight at his power to goad them, and their helplessness to reply. 'Ye've crawled out at last from under yer mothers' skirts or yer wives' skirts, or yer poxy little tarts' skirts, and we're out to make men of ye, ye snivellin' little snot rags. And when ye go off to get shot at or blown to bits by them nasty coal scuttles an' whizz-bangs, don't you worry about yer loved ones! We'll take care of 'em for ye.' His grin widened, and he held up his rigid forearm, fist clenched. 'In fact the'll realize what the've been missin' all their poor lives, cos we know more about fightin' and fuckin' than you'll ever learn, you miserable wankers!'

Jack was ready to admit that he was sadly lacking in any real killer instinct when it came to shooting or bayonetting the Hun. But he would gleefully murder the tall, carrot-haired Ginger Gardiner, who, unfailingly, rose every morning from the bed opposite clad only in his vest and exhibited his cock in a powerful erection, thrusting it lance-like ahead of him before he hung his towel proudly over it and headed off for the wash room with a cry of, 'How's about this then? Bet your lass would fancy a bit of this, eh?'

There had been bitter disappointment when they had been moved from the camp outside Blyth, on the north-east coast, for the journey down the length of England to this camp in rural Dorset. The majority of the men were local to the area, intended to swell the vastly depleted ranks of the 1st Tynesides. Desperately, they had prayed that they would be given leave, if only for twenty-four hours. Indeed, several had 'gone over the wall' before they entrained at Newcastle Central station. They were not seen again, though their sergeants assured the recruits that their miscreant colleagues had been swiftly picked up, and were already bitterly regretting their desertion. 'Time of war, that's a capital offence,' Sergeant Havelock told Jack's company. At the blank looks of some of them, he added with a grin, 'That means they could be shot, and serve 'em bloody right!'

But it was a cruel torment, for many besides Jack, to watch through the crowded windows as the train chugged over the King Edward Bridge south, past the rows of narrow streets of his home town, then out, where the houses thinned and he recognized the slopes of Silver Hill, the woodland surrounding Ravensworth Castle, the wheels of the pits of Ravensworth and Kibblesworth standing out to be identified. Cruellest of all, a blurred, fleeting glimpse down the embankment of a rutted track, a barred gate, a flash of the field with its copse of trees where he and May had agreed to marry.

Four years ago. And a different world, it seemed. A world which, since, they had tried so hard to shut out, to keep at bay. And failed. It was agonizing to think of that comfortable, modest house, the home he had known as far back as he could remember, sheltering his own two infant sons. May would be up now, organizing John's breakfast. She would have fed the baby earlier. She would probably be in her dressing gown, not yet dressed on this grey autumn morning. Less than two miles away, over there to the left of this crammed and rattling tube of a train, whose clicking wheels stretched out every second the yards separating him from all that he loved until he wanted to weep, and beat his hands desperately against the thick glass that sealed him so completely from what lay outside.

Iris stopped, stared giddily at the thin figure rising from the depths of the armchair, along with his fellow officers, at her entrance. The dim room, stripped of its pictures and most of its furnishings, still retained some vestige of its former stateliness, though a corner of

159

the chateau's roof had been blown off, and most of its windows shattered. It had been commandeered for the officers in this R and R section, well back from the line, so that the guns were merely a distant, unnoticed rumble.

She blinked, almost shook her head to dismiss the sense of unreality which had seized her. She was very conscious of her neat appearance, her trim dark uniform of jacket and skirt, her polished boots almost free of the mud which seemed to have covered their world for months now. She had spent a long time the previous night having an all over wash behind the makeshift, blanket draped screens, then washing her freshly clipped red hair, which her friend, Ollie Willis, had helped to style and to brush into shining, neat order.

One of the girls had washed and pressed her best uniform, another cleaned her boots, so that she was looking her best when she set out early in the morning for the village of Flixecourt, on the road between Abbeville and Amiens, where she had learned that the Tyneside-Irish had been quartered for their rest and recuperation after their latest spell up the line. Ollie had begun to make some joke about her 'getting off' with some smart young subaltern, then flushed and shut up quickly as she remembered the reason for Iris's visit.

'I don't really know what to say,' Iris admitted uncertainly before she left. 'But I feel I owe it to Lionel's parents. At least I can tell them I've met some of his chums. It might make them feel better.' It still hurt her to recall his last message to her. The letter had been forwarded to her by Lady Strang, with a short, exquisitely penned note.

'This was found in Lionel's things. He had clearly been intending to post it to you, so I thought I should send it on. I do hope you won't find it too upsetting or macabre, but I can't help thinking he would have wanted you to have it, as it must be just about the last thing he wrote. He was extremely fond of you, as I'm sure you know. I also know you did not feel as deeply for him as he did for you, but you were close friends. Sir William and I would have been more than happy to welcome you into the family.

'Please try to remember Lionel not as he was on that last leave, at Christmas – I fear the war had affected him deeply, he was not himself at all, as you clearly saw – but as he used to be before this whole dreadful business started.'

Iris's mouth curved in an involuntary smile of irony, for it was the old, cocksure Lionel that she had found so unappealing. She was far fonder of the newly uncertain, rather abstracted young man who had come home from the war. Except ... as always, she blushed hotly at her recall of those moments in the cold upper room, when he had assaulted her so wildly, the fearfully invasive touch of him, her fear and revulsion. And yet he asserted so strongly his love for her.

She looked again at the pages of his letter to her. She had cried of course when she first heard of his death. Then, only days after, in the midst of all their hectic work in the capital, had come the sudden opportunity to move across the Channel, which she had seized so eagerly. It seemed to come at such an appropriate time, almost as though it were being offered her as some sort of expiation, though she was not clear herself what she had to feel guilty about at his death.

Now, weeks later, his last words to her had reached her, from beyond the grave. Except that there was no grave, nothing other than the certainty of his death, probably blown literally to bits by a shell that had burst on the trench where he was working, and observed by too many to make the issue at all doubtful.

'I still cannot dislodge you from my thoughts,' he wrote, 'more than ever now, when you would think there would be so much more to occupy me, like the necessity of surviving. But it all seems so trivial somehow, what goes on here, all so mad, and of no account. The only thing that concerns me, that really matters, is my unforgivable conduct towards you, the real madness that came over me at home last January. I know you said, very sweetly, that you *did* forgive me, but I can't see how, or that you could really mean it, when I can never forgive myself. I can only repeat that it *was* madness, and that my action was against anything I've ever believed in. And still that's no excuse, is it? I will never forget, or forgive, until my dying day, whenever that may be. I want you to know that, and to believe it, my dear Iris.'

Whenever that may be. It had been only a day or two later. Had he known?

She had tried hard not to blush when she met the battalion commander, who himself had taken over only since the early days of the Somme, when his predecessor had been killed. 'He was a Signals Officer. Worked more with the Corps wallahs. Didn't see a lot of him. But a damned fine fellow. Good officer. He was up front doing his job when he bought it. First damned day of the battle. Bad business!' He shook his head. 'We've lost a lot of chaps since then. Hell of a lot. Mess has thinned out a bit. I'll take you over there in a bit. You can meet some of the chaps. Chat to them if you like. They'd like that, I'm sure.'

And now, here she was, struck dumb at coming so suddenly face to face with a world so far away from her present existence it seemed totally unreal. The figure was staring at her with a slowly dawning curiosity, while the battalion commander was introducing her. She pulled herself together, stepped forward, held out her leather gloved hand quickly.

'It's Daniel Wright, isn't it? I'm Iris Mayfield. Remember? We met at your brother's wedding.'

The others looked shocked more than anything at Dan's being singled out. He explained laughingly when, after a lengthy time of polite social chat and falsely chummy and affectionate claims of friendship with Lionel from his comrades in arms, he succeeded in getting her out of the mess for a walk along the muddy lane past the jag-toothed ruins of the village on either side.

'I've only just been made up. Field commission. Second lieutenant. Some of them back there are still reeling from shock. They had to do something, though. We've hardly anyone under the rank of major left. I can't thank you enough. The kudos I'll get from this visit will set me up enormously. Some of them might even talk to me at dinner.'

He seemed so cheerfully unfazed by it all that Iris could only marvel.

'You know of course that Jack's enlisted?' she said, feeling strange at the way he took her arm as they strolled, another courtesy which seemed to her to come from another world.

He nodded, gave a sardonic grunt. 'More fool he! He should've waited till the last possible minute. Then maybe beyond. If he had any real sense he'd have done a runner. Holed up somewhere until this lot's all over.'

She gave a startled sideways glance at him. He gave no sign that he was joking. She was shocked, felt the beginnings of her former patriotic outrage stirring, then glanced about her at the sombre scene of ruin, became aware for the first time of that low, ceaseless growl over the horizon. She thought of all that had happened, the scenes she had witnessed since her arrival two months ago, and shrugged silently.

'I'd 've got up sooner if I could,' she said. 'But we've been kept pretty busy. This is the first chance I've had. They've given me today and tomorrow off.'

Dan nodded. 'The whole thing's bogged down.' He waved his arm wildly about him. 'Christ knows how many lost! And for what?' His voice was raised, harsh, and, for the first time, showing something of the terrible pressure under which he was operating. As if ashamed of allowing some emotion to show through, he pulled himself up, gave an apologetic bark of laughter. 'But you're a fine sight for sore eyes, Miss Mayfield. That you are!'

'Please!' She hugged his arm with both her hands. 'Iris!'

'Very well. Iris it is!' He laughed again, patted her gloved hand as it lay in the crook of his elbow. He glanced directly at her. 'Were you fond of Mr Strang? Sweet on him?'

She could feel the colour mounting, her violet eyes opened wider, giving him a startled, almost pleading look.

'Yes. I was ... fond of him. Not – we weren't sweethearts, or anything like that.' The blush intensified, and she hated herself for the feeling of evasion which came over her. 'But he used to write to me – a lot. We were good friends.'

163

He nodded. 'I saw him, you know. That day. Just before he bought it. He came along our trench, a few minutes before the first wave went over.' He told her what the corporal had said about him, about him never wearing his steel helmet. Dan flung his cigarette away, immediately fumbled for the packet in his breast pocket. 'And he was right, too. Didn't make a scrap of difference. It doesn't when your number's up.'

She stopped walking, clung to his arm. She could feel her heart thudding, her chest straining against her clothing.

'Is there somewhere we could go? Can you get some time off?' Her voice was faint, her stomach was churning unpleasantly. She stared at him, feeling oddly trapped, driven by a weird compulsion. All at once, she saw May's face floating in her mind's eye, the clear, pure beauty of it.

His eyes were staring into hers, holding her. A great deal seemed to pass unspoken between the two still figures.

'If you wait a while I can fix things. Get the rest of the day off. There's a place in Amiens. Some of the chaps have told me about it. You can get a room. Have a meal there.'

It was nearly dark when they arrived in the battered town of Amiens, having hitched a lift on a Service Corps wagon. An hour later, they were sharing a meal of *ragoût de veau* – at least the blowzy French *mere* assured them it was veal – in an anonymous little bedroom of what Iris suspected was little if any better than a brothel.

'You're all right,' Dan told her, with that air of bravado he had adopted which she did not mind at all. 'It's for officers only. Good job I got my commission, eh? Just in the nick of time.'

She drank the red wine glass for glass with him, though it did not make her drunk, or add to her desperate courage. She was glad he made no effort to court her, or behave with false gallantry.

'I may be an officer but I'm no gentleman,' he said, grinning defiantly at her. 'I can't even sit a horse. Are you sure this is what you want? I won't ask why. I'm not such a chump as to question my luck. You're a fine looking girl, Iris Mayfield, and way above my social circles. I say again. Are you sure this is what you want?'

She stood, moved over to the single bed. The room was cold, and she had kept on her jacket, which she now unbuttoned, and draped carefully over the rounded back of the wooden chair beside the bed. She removed the green tie, unfastened her khaki shirt and slipped it off. He was still sitting at the table, his long legs stretched out, at ease.

'I'm ready. Quite ready. With Lionel . . . we almost made love—' her voice caught, she went on quickly, unsteadily, 'Properly, I mean. I wanted it. I—'

He stood up so quickly the chair almost toppled over behind him.

'Right-oh!' he said roughly. 'Let's not get bogged down in words, eh? It's nice to know we both want it.'

In spite of all her best intentions, the most powerful emotion she felt was one of intense embarrassment. She turned away from him, slipped off her skirt, then hastily drew off her stockings and her knickers, leaving on the rest of her underclothing, including the concealing petticoat as she pulled down the covers and climbed into the icy sheets. She huddled on her side, her knees bent, facing away from him, hearing him undressing, shaking with dread, and fighting desperately to prevent the tears from starting.

He was naked when he climbed in beside her. His hands eased up her silk shift, cupped the contours of her legs and flanks.

'Aren't you going to undress properly?' he asked, smiling tenderly, leaning over her, easing the embroidered hem of the slip further up her hip. His hands began to stroke the smooth surface of her legs, her inner thigh, and he bent close, kissed her gently on her lips, felt their grim tightness beneath his.

His fingers started to make love, tracing lightly the shape of her hidden body, the crevices, the springy hair, and he kissed again, more demonstratively, passionately, trying to open her mouth.

'Please!' she gasped, her eyes huge and wild under him. 'Can we just do it? Quickly? I want you—'

She twisted round onto her back, fighting inelegantly to raise her legs under the clinging bedclothes and to encircle him with her thighs. She even reached down between them and with painful inexpertness clutched at his penis. All at once he knew the full weight of her fear and even her revulsion for the act they were almost committing. For an instant, he was choked with livid rage. What did this sick, rich bitch think she was playing at? Did she get her thrill by offering herself to a stranger like this? Then he dismissed his shocked thoughts. What did he know about anything in this maddened world he had lived in these past two years? His thick desire took over and he thrust himself on top of her.

He saw her turn away, saw the angle of her jaw, heard the intense hiss of her pain, felt the clenching repugnance of her whole body. He forced his entrance, rutted furiously. It was over in less than a minute.

She could not keep back the tears, she cried quietly when he levered himself off her as soon as he was able, and clambered out of the bed. She turned away from him again, on her side. He made no effort to hide himself as he cleaned his body, pulled on his clothes. He was sore himself. It was clear she had been a virgin, and he felt a dispassionate kind of pity for the hunched shape snuffling softly under the blankets. He did not understand her, her sick mind, but he guessed it was something to do with the dead man. A quick spasm of self-disgust ran through him. He had the conviction that, like so many girls of her class and background, she would never make a man happy in bed, nor know the supreme happiness of sexual release herself. He smiled sardonically. No doubt she felt she had just made a noble sacrifice. Yet another to the great god of war. What matter if the altar were a creaky iron bed in the upstairs room of an officers-only brothel?

May held out her arms to him as he approached the bed, and Jack paused for just an instant, trying to capture the sight of her, beckoning from the pillows, fixing it with such sweet pain into his consciousness. As he had just now when he stood gazing over the

166

side of the cot, in the flickering dimness of the night light, watching the sleeping face of John. He would be two on Christmas Day,
only three weeks away, and now had the unappreciated luxury of a
room all to himself, the small front bedroom over the porch which
Sophia had formerly used as a sewing room. At six months, Edward
still shared his parents' room, and was sleeping, somewhat snuf-
flingly due to a seasonal cold, in his crib in the corner.

It had seemed hard that their embarkation should come so near
to Christmas, though it was not unexpected. The week's leave had
sped over, despite all their efforts to make time expand by counting
every precious minute together. Yesterday, they had gone to have
the studio portrait taken, all four of them, Jack in his uniform, and
May in her best, dark blue gown, both solemn and unsmiling as
befitted the dignity of the occasion, the bonneted and swaddled
Edward apple-cheeked and dribbling, John smocked and legging-
ed, kicking his heels against the wooden bench until he was transfixed by the hooded shape in front of him.

Jack had to leave early in the morning. He had tried all day to
persuade May not to accompany him to the station. 'You know
what it'll be like. All the lads there. Chaos!' But she was adamant.
Just as she had been about the plans she had divulged for the new
year. 'I'm going to do war work,' she said, quietly determined, and
ready for his arguments. 'If you are off doing your bit, then I can do
mine. I'm going to get a job in Armstrong's. The munitions works.'

She had met Nelly Dunn several times when she was visiting her
mam. The blonde hair was startlingly ginger now at the front, and
her face was even more curiously tanned looking. But she was as
raucously cheerful as ever. 'Sure, kidder. Ah'll get ye in if that's
what ye want.' She winked. 'Harry Turnbull owes me more than a
few favours. And he'll pay 'em, too.' In answer to May's query, she
said, 'Oh, aye. Ah still write to Arty now an' then. Poor old Arty. He
was wounded, ye know. Aye. In the arm. Didn't get sent home,
though, poor beggar. Still, kept him out of the line for ages, thank
God. He's back there now, though, God help him. Your Jack'll
probably meet up with him again when he gets ower there. That'll

be a laugh, eh? Listen! You give us a shout if ye want takin' on at the works.'

'Mam'll look after the bairns,' May told Jack stubbornly. 'They'll be all right, don't worry. It'll give me something new to think about. And I can feel I'm doing my bit, too, like I said.' She looked at him challengingly, waiting for him to say more. He almost did, wanting to point out to her that her role as a mother of two young boys was as fulfilling and as noble a task as any she could wish. But then she knew that. And how could he say that to her, when he was about to go off, to leave them all?

They had made love twice during the five nights they had spent together. Jack had used a rubber sheath, and afterwards was appalled to find May shaking with silent weeping afterwards. 'It's awful. I hate it,' she sobbed at last, when he had held her and asked what was wrong. 'I'd rather we didn't do it than that.'

'We don't have to do it. Remember when you were carrying John? And after?' She blushed fiercely, partly for shame at the vividly recalled pleasure he had brought her. But this last night together, she wanted him more desperately than she had ever wanted him. They slept hardly at all, made love again before the cold dawn of the December day.

'I don't care if I *am* pregnant again,' she whispered, clinging to him. 'I hope I am!'

He smiled in the darkness, rubbed his lips gently against the wisps of hair he could feel at her temple.

'Tiny seeds of love. Remember the song?' Her arms fastened about his neck, she strained to him, and let the well of her grief flow out unrestricted, and he wept, too, their bodies shaking as they clung together in their aching love.

At the station, amid the jostling crowds, she was brave all over again. They kissed before he clambered aboard, weighed down by his pack, which he stowed before he fought his way back to a precious corner of window, where he could just reach her cheek for a last quick kiss as the whistles shrieked and they jerked into motion. She moved with the crowd, keeping pace with him.

'Remember your promise!' she cried out. 'Remember!'
They were pulling away, he was leaving her behind.
'I will, love. I will.'

Thirty-six hours later, just north of Albert, Art Mackay started back to awareness as he heard the distant, dismal clanking of buffers. Another train-load of fodder for the guns he could hear pounding away, even over the music and the drunken singing and shouting that drifted into the shabby room from all around. He blinked down at the rolling bottle, with the dark dregs of wine slopping in it, the broken shards of crockery, the scattered bits of food staining the dirty floor boards.

He realized he was crying, the tears trickling down to the stubble at the sides of his downturned mouth, lodging in his untidy moustache. He scratched at his crotch. Damned lice again. Least bit of warmth and they were off again, eating away at you. He had a sudden urge to strip off again, to remove all his clothes, to head off naked, in spite of the freezing darkness of the winter night. Season of goodwill to all men.

He stared down at the crumpled body of the woman spread out among the debris on the floor The black skirt was caught up, showing the back of a plump leg, with a great circular patch of white where a hole exposed her skin. Her black hair was frizzy, and none too clean, he had noted. It had smelt of grease and tobacco, and countless men who had had her before him. He hadn't meant to hit her so hard. It was just that when he had seen that wad of money in the drawer, his own hard earned francs being added to it, it had seemed so obvious. In a flash, it had come to him.

He had known all along that he couldn't go back up the line on Monday, wondered all day, while they had been drinking, even while he had been shagging with the whore, what he could do about it. Then he saw the money. That's what he needed, that lot would take him well away from all this madness. It all seemed so clear that the fuddled buzzing which had sounded in his brain all day had stopped at once. And if Yvette or whatever her name was had only

handed over the poxy money without all that screaming fuss, she'd
have been all right.

Wearily, he lifted himself to his feet, bent, and dragged her over
to the dishevelled bed. He.put his arms under hers and hauled her
up, toppling her over on her front on the dirty covers. She was still
breathing. A funny, snorting sound, it was true, and the back of her
head was sticky with blood, but she was breathing.

He shook his head sadly, stuffed the money into the pocket of his
filthy coat, shouldered his pack, and let himself quietly out, into
the cold darkness. Reeling figures called out, snatches of song
drifted to him. He began to sing softly to himself, while the tears
rolled steadily down his cheeks.

Goodbye, Piccadilly; Farewell, Leicester Square . . .

He began to move more quickly, picking up the marching rhythm,
heading westward, away from the dim flickers in the sky, the
constant rumble. Away from the war.

SEVENTEEN

THE NEW TYNESIDE contingent arrived in time for the start of the severest winter of the war. They detrained at Bethune, and marched ten miles and more to a tented camp which had been hastily laid out and was far from completion, as they found out early next morning, when, after a cold breakfast sadly similar to the cold supper they had eaten the night before, they had to begin digging latrines in the iron hard ground.

'Regimental cooks'll have something sorted by tonight. If ye're lucky,' their sergeant told them. He glanced sourly at Jack's single stripe. 'Come on, lad! Get your lot to put some beef in it, otherwise you won't be havin' a shit till after Christmas.'

Geordie Blacker spat on his hands, wielded the pick handle with fluid grace.

'Don't come puttin' on ganger's airs wi' us,' he warned Jack. 'Ye only got the stripe cos ye talk so posh.'

'Well, you'd best show us how it's done then, Geordie, eh? Nobody swings a pick like an old pit yacker.'

'Hadaway!' But the ropy sinews stood out on the scarred arms and pitted neck, and their detail was the first to finish their section of the long trench.

They were surprised that they had not been sent to the established network of training camps around Etaples, where places like the 'bull-ring' had gained a legendary notoriety. They could hear the dull grumble of the guns quite clearly from their new quarters, and the sound sobered even the most reckless. The first time they saw an infantry detachment coming back down the line for a relief period, they stared with frank curiosity, and called out encouragingly. The look in the weary eyes said far more than the cursory remarks flung back at them.

'Christ! The' look a bloody shambles, eh?' Geordie said contemptuously, eyeing their filth-encrusted uniforms, the careless trail of weapons and equipment, the scrape of boots on the roadway. Again, Jack felt that inner boil of rage, as he clenched his jaw to keep the angry reply from springing out.

On Christmas Day, Jack stayed in the camp, ignoring the pleas and taunts of his comrades to accompany them into the village after their lunch of potatoes and stew. 'Aw, leave the miserable sod,' Geordie advised, slicking down his hair in front of the tiny mirror fixed to the central tent pole. 'He's too good to mix wi' the likes of us.' When they had gone, and he had the tent to himself, Jack slipped off his boots, pulled on his greatcoat and climbed under the blankets. He took out his small pile of photographs, and the letter from May, and let himself wallow in his loneliness and love. He tried to picture the celebrations. 'You're special,' he whispered to his oldest son's serious picture. 'Two year old today. Same birthday as Jesus.'

They went up into the line for the first time early in the new year. The bitter cold had eased, which had resulted in a thin snowfall. As they got near the trenches, they swung off the muddy roadway, onto a narrower track whose centre was slatted with uneven boards, many of which were missing. If you stepped off this central gangway, you were liable to sink into the icy ooze up to the knees. They passed a field-gun battery, the weapons pulled by mules, who had been led off the track to allow the marching columns to pass more easily. Already, the gun carriages were deeply embedded, the steaming, wild-eyed animals floundering in the blackness up to their quarters, while the crews held the tossing heads and cursed as they struggled to extricate themselves and the beasts.

They had waited for darkness to fall before they made the final stage to the take-over point, and the first of the communicating trenches. There was a series of soft whooshes, like breathy sighs, followed by thuds away to their left, getting louder and nearer.

'Get down!' a voice yelled, up ahead, and they squatted on their hunkers, chins on chests, trying to take comfort from the helmets pressing on their heads. The last explosion was near enough to make them flinch. They felt the ground tremble, and one or two light spatters of earth raining down on them. 'At the double!' the voice shouted, and they were up, slipping and sliding on the greasy planks, suddenly wanting desperately the shelter of those dug-outs they had been dreading.

'Happens every night at this time,' the corporal meeting them told them, with the grin of one who would soon be heading the other way. 'Fritz ain't daft, see? He knows we move everythin' as soon as it gets dark.'

The front line looked comfortingly solid, with walls and redoubts, lined high with sandbags, a wooden step nearly two foot high running the length of the front wall, and every so often a little enclave, with a periscope for an observation post. They had passed the troops they were relieving further back, and they were quickly detailed off into the various dug-outs, propped up with timbers – I wonder if they're Iris Mayfield's dad's? Jack asked himself – and corrugated metal sheets.

You went down two wooden steps, through the narrow entrance hung with sacking, to an earth floor already awash, the slippery duckboards practically disappeared under the liquid mud. The beds themselves were shallow holes scooped out of the earth, again lined with sandbags and propped by short timbers, like shelves in some ancient tomb. Some had scraps of sacking hanging over them, in a pitiful attempt at privacy. Others hadn't bothered. There was a scurry of rustling black shapes when one of the men lit the lantern, several of which skipped over Jack's foot. He shuddered.

'Rats!' the voice of the NCO said at his shoulder. 'Some of 'em as big as cats. There's plenty for 'em to feed on here, see?'

Five minutes later, Jack's heart was thumping as he climbed onto

the parapet for his first spell of lookout duty. The sky was periodi-
cally lit by star shells, which hung and illuminated the surreal
scene in front of him. The odd, splintered tree trunk, shorn of all
branches, stuck up blackly out of a sea of undulating hollows,
hillocks, all man-made from the ceaseless pounding of shells, and
looking like a dead world under the cold, flickering light. There
seemed to be no pattern to the crazy entanglement of the barbed
wire, its angled iron posts leaning drunkenly, while the wire itself
sagged and dipped, and was thickly festooned with what seemed in
the dark to be pale streamers, remnants of the guidelines of previous attacks to shepherd men through, and other, dark, fluttering
rags, which turned out, next day, to be remnants of clothing, or of
the men themselves.

The first casualty came that first morning, just as they were
brewing up for breakfast, and waiting for the duty cook from their
dug-out to come back with the fanny full of hot food from the mess
kitchens. He was a cocky youngster, Arnold Cresswell, who looked
scarcely old enough to be out of school, despite his claim to be a
worldly wise twenty-year-old. His billet was next door to Jack's,
and he was bare headed, his greatcoat, with collar turned up,
draped over his shirt and braces.

He called a greeting, and picked his way along the few yards of
trench between the dug-outs, where water the colour of pale tea had
collected, lapping over the duckboards.

'Where's wor grub?' He grinned. 'Let's 'ave a look, eh? See what
Fritz is up to?'

They had been warned about showing themselves over the top
for even a second. 'Always sharp shooters about,' the sergeants had
told them, over and over, both at home and since they had arrived
in France. It was typical of Cresswell's youthful bravado, a touch of
school yard show-off. He leapt up on the firing step, turned round
with a grin at his companions. 'Let's say good mornin' to Fritz, eh?'
He raised his head over the parapet, melodramatically shading his
eyes with his right hand.

'Get down, ye daft bugger!' someone said, not really concerned.

174

There was a soft sort of slapping sound, nothing like the crack of a rifle, and Cresswell was whipped round, flung back against the rear wall, folded like a home-made guy. Jack had his back to him. The first thing he saw was a glistening, bright red gash of blood, like a carelessly tossed splash of paint across the sandbags to his right. Cresswell had fallen on his left side, down in the mud and water. His eye was shut, he looked like he was in a drunken sleep, but the shallow puddle his head was resting in was turning black, and when they turned him over, the left side of his head was half missing, a flattened mess of inhumanity beneath the sodden, lank hair. Jack thought at once of the coastguard lying near the steps of the station at Whitby. Beside him, someone started to retch dryly.

There was a chorus of good-natured jeers when Dan walked into the mess. His best uniform had been pressed, his belt polished, his lieutenant's pips sparkled. He collected the bulky envelope stuffed with mail for him to post when he reached England.

'Lucky sod.' 'Don't bring back a dose of Blighty clap.'

'Listen, you buggers. It's two years and more since I was back in Blighty. Don't forget I was a poor bloody Tommy! We didn't go swanning off on home leave every five minutes, like you lot.'

Again, there was a rumble of amiable derision. Someone sawed an imaginary violin. He could joke quite easily now about his rise from the ranks. It was remarkable how the majority of his fellow officers had so quickly accepted the notion. Although, he reflected, perhaps not. Faces disappeared and were replaced so rapidly, after two and a half years of this madness.

'Here's that address I promised,' someone said, holding out a scrap of paper. 'Delightful girl. Guaranteed to please.'

'Don't bother!' another called. 'I bet he's fixed it so that he can shack up with that popsie of a nurse he bedded. Irresistible Iris, wasn't it?'

Dan gave his usual enigmatic smile whenever Iris's name cropped up. He had told them nothing. They knew that he had travelled into Amiens with her, and that he had returned the following day, that was all. He said nothing, but denied nothing, either. He had to admit that his status, as well as his reputation, had increased tenfold after her visit. The irony was that he had heard nothing from her since, not a single line. For all he knew, she could be back in Blighty herself by now. He grinned crookedly at the thought of running into her back home some time during the next three weeks.

It hadn't been long before Christmas when they had had their strange night together. Only a matter of three and a half months ago, yet already it seemed to belong to his distant past. All part of the unreality that gripped him. In a matter of twenty-four hours, he would be back in civilized surroundings; a night on the town, a bed at the Officers' Club, then back home. His parents, the two nephews he had never seen. He could not believe it. The only reality was up that bitter, muddy road, to the rumble of the guns, the explosions, the night attacks, the filth, and the icy, relentless sleet that made a mockery of the approaching spring.

'You picked the right time to be going,' B Company commander observed. 'We've got those executions coming up. Chaps court-martialled in Arras. Bad business. One of them's from D Company. The old man's quite worried. You know HQ are insisting we deal with them ourselves? Seems to think it'll boost morale. Clean up our own mess and all that sort of thing. The colonel's going to get the squads from the new battalion. Keep it in the regiment, but at least they won't know anything about it. Chaps involved and all that.'

Dan grunted. 'Funny old world, eh? We invite 'em out here to kill Germans, and the first job we give them is to shoot their own kind.' He knew that wasn't strictly true. The replacements had already done their spell in the trenches. He had been keen to follow their progress, for Jack was one of them. They had been stationed to the north, up near the Ypres section of the Front. Dan had managed to get a note off to his brother, and was planning to get up to see him when this chance of leave had come up, with the sudden-ness with which such things happened. He had dashed off yet another hasty note, telling him of his good luck, and promising to meet up as soon as he could on his return. 'I'll give a kiss to May and the boys for you,' he wrote. 'They must all be very proud of you.'

Art Mackay sat with the mess tin of hot stew balanced on his knee. Its rich aroma wafted up to him, and made his gorge rise. If he forced a few mouthfuls down, he would either bring it all straight back up, or be sat on that foul smelling pail in the corner for hours. What was the point of eating? They were going to take him out and shoot him in the morning. Once again, he felt the wetness on his cheeks, and he heard himself making that plaintive little moaning sound. He still couldn't believe they would do it. Or at least, part of him couldn't accept the awful reality of it. One more agonizing, freezing, sleepless night to endure, then they were going to lead him out under the morning sky, blindfold him, and kill him like a sick animal.

His teeth started chattering, he could feel the cold striking right through him, his bones were aching. He was wearing his greatcoat, and his battle dress-blouse underneath, and had wrapped the grey blanket round himself as tightly as he could. This place looked as if it had been an old stable, or store room. More like a medieval dungeon than anything else, with the great, uneven, stone floor, the rough brick walls. The only openings, apart from the great wooden double door, were high up near the timbered roof. Birds swooped in and out, pigeons chirruped out of sight. The guns were nothing more than the faintest of thunder rumbles.

He had little idea of where he was. He had been in a daze ever since the trial. He had been moved twice since then. Or was it three times? He remembered vividly the stifled exclamation of disgust from the military policeman at his side, when the sentence had been read out, and the warm flow and strong stench of urine had come involuntarily. He had wanted to shout, scream out, but he was dumb, could scarcely make his legs move when they hustled him away, their hands brutal on his arms.

That poxy whore hadn't even died, she was none the worse,

except for a scar on the back of her head and the loss of her bankroll. They wouldn't top the most hardened criminal for that back home. Though that red-faced walrus of a brigadier had made a point of telling him that that wasn't the crime for which they would kill him. Desertion. Cowardice.

How could they accuse him of that? Two years of it, he'd had. The lot. Bombardments, night patrols. The big pushes. Over the top, whistles blowing, fellers cut down, blown to bits all round you. He remembered the trench they'd run into, during one of the first of the assaults. The boot – it had looked so good, practically brand new, that he was glancing about for its companion before he realized that the trailing mess hanging from it was the ribboned remains of a limb, that the foot was still neatly inside it.

Then this last lot. Bloody Wipers again! Up over the top, a stroll, they said, and led them on at walking pace into a storm of machine-gun fire that cut them to pieces. He had lain in a shell hole with Frankie Cook screaming and sobbing and holding his guts that were spilling out all down his front, until Art would have cut his throat for him if he hadn't subsided into moaning unconsciousness. He didn't even know when Frankie actually died. But he crawled back when it got dark, and there was hardly any of the company left, and nobody gave a toss about him. He remembered thinking, I could just walk away from this lot. Nobody would know. They never found half of the battalion anyway.

Should've done. Instead, he stayed. Went through the next few months of endless madness, too. Until they'd pulled them out at Christmas. A well-earned rest, the colonel told them. A lot of them resting for good now. Make the most of it, he said. They didn't bother too much with pep talks any more. Even the brass hats had some feelings. Couldn't take the looks they saw in the men's eyes if they tried any of that claptrap.

He'd made the most of it, all right. A different kind of madness, that's all. One drunken moment. Couldn't they understand? He hadn't even made a decent attempt at running for it. Picked up a dozen miles down the road, in one of those *estaminets*. Pissed out of his mind and buying drinks for all and sundry. He'd probably have gone back next day, once he'd sobered up. And they were going to kill him for that?

He wished the padre would come. He'd be here soon enough. Said he would spend time with him. As much time as he wanted. And that he'd be there – at the end, when it happened. He'd be all right, he truly repented. Funny. He'd told himself he wouldn't have any of that sort of thing. He'd never bothered with religion, why should he rush whining to God now? Besides, what sort of God was it that let all this lot go on, day after day, month after month, year after year? Blokes in bits, bones everywhere, all over the battlefields, thousands of 'em. No one would ever know, never even have a grave. Not enough left of some of them to turn up at Judgement Day.

But he'd ended up running all right. Sobbing in the padre's arms, clinging like a drowning man to the lifebelt of an after life. He'd pray, too, tomorrow, when the time came. And it was coming. He must believe it. Each day he had waited, desperately clinging to the idea of a reprieve. That it was all part of the propaganda to frighten the increasingly disillusioned soldiery into obedience. There'd been so many rumours. That the French were on the brink of wholescale mutiny, that they were ready just to walk away from the line, and shoot anybody who tried to stop them.

He'd learnt his lesson now. Why couldn't they believe him? He'd survived this long, maybe he would make it. At least give him the chance to try. There was no way he would be able to dodge the bullet tomorrow. Only one bullet, they reckoned. The rest of the firing party all had blanks. What if the bastard with the real one missed? They never did, though. Not at point-blank range. They pinned a target on your chest. And anyway, there was always the officer standing by, with his pistol, to finish you off.

He wondered if it would be his own blokes. They said it should be. It was always supposed to be men from your own battalion, your own company, even, who made up the firing squad. He wouldn't mind that. Better really, than a bunch of strangers. He hadn't seen any of the lads since they'd picked him up. Only Captain

Thompson, at the court martial. Put in a word for him, told them of his record, his service. Hadn't done a blind bit of good, though. Wasn't a trial, really. They'd made up their mind what they were going to do. Just going through the motions. Make it legal, like.

Thompson had come down to see him afterwards, when they had him in that cellar, in Arras. 'Sorry, Mackay. Did what I could. Take it like a man, eh?'

And he'd just stood there, nodding. 'Yes, sir. No, sir.' Trying not to cry till he'd got out the door. Nobody since then. Not one friendly face. Except this padre. A decent sort, after all. And what harm was there in it? A few prayers. Christ! He needed all the help he could get, didn't he?

It was so cold. Catch his death, he would. He laughed shakily, while the tears continued to roll down his face. Always a bit of a wag, Arty. Suddenly, he thought of the pretty little blonde, Nelly Dunn. Saw her face, screwed up, flung back with laughter at one of his sallies. Bit of all right, she was. Written to him regular, as he had to her. He used to look forward to her letters, bragging to the lads about her.

He remembered Jack Wright's wedding. Bit toffee-nosed, Jack and his girl, Nelly's mate. There'd been that posh lass there, real toff. And Jack's brother, Dan. Best man. And over here now, in A Company. Been made up to an officer. Not surprising, they were that sort. He'd seen him a couple of times, had been going to go up and speak to him, then changed his mind. The lads would think he was a right one, sucking up to an officer. He wished he was around now, though. Anyone would do, anyone to talk to.

He realized he had risen again and was pacing up and down. Where was the padre? It was pitch black again. Time they came and lit the lamp. What time was it now? How long to go? He wondered if it was better that he didn't have a watch, couldn't watch the minutes ticking away.

'Right, lads. Nice little jolly for you lot. Wright, get your squad fell in. Full kit and weapons. Report to Sarnt Bennet in half an hour.

180

You'll be away overnight. Back tomorrow some time.'

'What's the game, sergeant? Where we off?' Geordie Blacker asked suspiciously.

'Never mind, son. You'll find out soon enough.'

Geordie waited until he had gone before he said, 'Ah don't like the sound of this, mind. If it's a jolly, what are we takin' our weapons for, eh?'

'Well, as the sergeant says, we'll be told when they're ready. Ours not to reason. Let's get sorted, lads.' Jack began to lay out his kit. His thoughts were still very far from here. He had got Dan's note yesterday morning. By now, his brother would be back at home, would be with the folks, with May and little John, and Teddy. It didn't do to dwell too much on such things, but it was hard not to. This little diversion would help, whatever it was. At least they couldn't be going back into the line.

There were two other groups of five men, who assembled outside the temporary battalion HQ. An open-top double-decked bus was waiting to transport them. 'Keep your capes handy!' Geordie grumbled, as they climbed aboard. 'It'll no doubt be pissin' down as soon as we get started.' But, for once, his forecast was inaccurate, and although a fresh wind was blowing, they enjoyed sitting at lordly ease above the crowded road, and the war-scarred countryside, while the two officers accompanying them had the lower deck to themselves.

There was far more motorized traffic on these churned up roads than there had formerly been. Staff cars, motor cycles, as well as the strung out convoys of lorries and converted buses such as theirs. They recognized the ruined buildings on the fringes of Bethune, and soon afterwards they were pulling into the large tented camp where they had spent their brief training period after arriving in France.

'What's going on? You heard anything?' Jack asked his opposite number in one of the other platoons.

The man shook his head. 'They're keeping bloody quiet about it, I tell you. I don't like the smell of it!'

181

They ate a solid lunch in one of the big mess tents, then clambered aboard again to head further south. After a short while, one of the five man squads debussed at a junction, where a corporal was waiting for them. 'See you chaps tomorrow!' the lieutenant called out cheerfully, before signalling to the driver to carry on.

Jack's squad continued until late afternoon before they reached their destination. They had passed the broad highway leading to Arras some time ago. The noise of the guns was louder, individual detonations quite distinct. 'We're a damned sight nearer the front line,' someone said uneasily. They got stiffly down. Young Second Lt Gill was with them. A sergeant was waiting to lead them off. They glanced round curiously. This looked like a typical behind the lines R and R camp. A farmhouse with a few holes in the roof had been set up as an HQ, and the cottages of a hamlet were being used as billets. They were taken straight to a muddy cobbled farm yard, with an impressive row of outbuildings surrounding it on three sides.

'Your men can bed down over there, sir,' the sergeant told Gill. 'There's grub laid on. Be along in a while.' There was a brief, meaningful pause before he continued, 'Lieutenant Colonel Redditch's compliments, sir, but he'd appreciate it if you'd keep your lads away from the camp. Best if they don't mingle.'

They were already staring at a wide set of double doors over the yard. They were shut and an armed sentry was standing outside. 'What the fuck's going on?' There were mutters which the red-faced officer pretended not to hear as they filed into the gloomy, bare room which was to be their quarters for the night. There was a pile of palliasses near the door.

'Have to make do with these for tonight, chaps,' Gill said, his clear embarrassment adding to the general air of unease which had settled over them.

Jack cast a warning glance at Geordie, and said, 'Can't you tell us what this is about, sir?' His voice was quiet, polite.

The youngster's eyes flickered, his embarrassment increased. He found it difficult to begin, but he nodded, cleared his throat.

'We've been given an unpleasant task, I'm afraid. But it's got to be done, and they're relying on us to do it properly. You saw the guard out there. There's a prisoner – a deserter. Picked up behind the lines. Running away. He's been sentenced – to execution. That's why we're here.'

There was a collective gasp, of shock and dismay. 'I thought – I mean – we should've been told! I wouldn't—'

'You're not volunteers!' Gill cut in strongly, his face still flushed. 'We're under orders. We've got a job to do, and we'll do it.'

'Why us?' someone murmured.

'These men are part of the regiment. This is the 1st Tynesiders. They've been through a lot. We owe it to them. It's better that they chose men from our battalion. There's other executions. The other squads—'

Geordie Blacker spoke vehemently into the hushed pause.

'Serve the fuckers right, I say!' He glared round belligerently.

The young officer did not reprimand him. If anything, he looked grateful for the forcefully expressed sentiment.

'Yes, well. You heard the corporal. There'll be some grub up. I'll pop along later. We've got to go through the drill. It's essential we do everything right and proper. Then I suggest you get bedded down. We'll have to be up before dawn.'

'For God's sake, man! You'll have a blank!' Lieutenant Gill was staring wild eyed at him.

Jack looked back at him, his face stricken. 'He's my mate, sir! I know him! I worked with him! He was . . . at my wedding.'

When he had seen Art led out, with the priest's hand on his shoulder, Jack had felt it was part of some nightmare. The fair head was bent, he was weeping quietly, moving like a sleep-walker. He had never even glanced towards the party lined up, facing the stout post. The padre's voice was strong, carrying to them on the breeze, the familiar words of prayer lifting defiantly. The chalk white face of the prisoner was raised blindly to the dull morning, before it disappeared under the black cloth, and his arms were pinioned at his sides while they tied him to the post.

That was when Jack stepped out of the line, swinging away, while the sergeant stared and Gill came forward frantically.

'Get back in line!' he hissed.

Jack shook his head. The other heads were turning now, uneasily. The sergeant stepped forward, savagely tugged Jack's rifle from his grip.

'You give the command, sir! Let's get it done!'

Jack kept his back to them through Gill's cracked, nervous orders, called out with the voice of a shrill schoolboy. He bowed his head, flinched as though his own body had been struck when the loud reports of the guns went off. Tears coursed down his cheeks.

'Get them out of it!' the sergeant hissed, and someone touched Jack's shoulder. He fell in, not looking at the limp bundle hanging on the post, watching his feet as they marched over the cobbles back to their quarters.

'What a fuckin' hero!' Geordie goaded. 'Christ! I'm not goin' over the top anywhere near you, you cowardly bastard!'

Vaguely, Jack heard Gill's voice somewhere. He leapt forward, smashed his fist with all his force into Geordie's face, catching him on the cheek bone, knocking him back, almost off balance. He welcomed the crushing blow from the iron hard fist in return that sent his head singing, the smashing into his ribs of the other fist, which sent him folding to the dirty floor.

EIGHTEEN

'HELLO, DAN. Better not kiss me. I'm all mucky.' She could feel herself blushing under the coating of grime which darkened her face, was aware of her shabby overcoat and drab clothing underneath it, her dirty, coarse hands.

'Nonsense!' Dan answered, in his old, hearty style, and grabbed May by her arms, pulling her in close. 'I never pass up the chance of kissing a pretty girl. You know me.'

She turned her head, and accepted the quick, circumspect peck on her cheek. She studied him with shy excitement. He was different, not just thinner, though that was the first, most noticeable thing about him. His face looked older, there was something about the eyes, a disturbing wariness, a watchfulness that somehow seemed to keep the world at bay, locking up the secret thoughts behind them.

She was embarrassed at him seeing her in her working clothes, and in her dirt from the long day at the munitions factory, though she had known he would be there when she got in from the long shift. She had thought about getting a quick wash at her mam's, and having a change of clothes there. She had called in as usual to pick the boys up. Dan turned to them, reaching out to ruffle John's dark hair.

'My! Who's this young man? So you're John, are you? Chip off the old block, this one, eh? No doubt that he's a Wright!'

John's brown eyes were fixed solemnly on the uniformed figure.

He took a step closer to his mother's side, reached out blindly for the reassurance of her hand.

'Come on!' May encouraged. 'Don't be shy. Say hello to your Uncle Dan.'

'And this must be Master Teddy, is it?' Teddy, plump, round, his much fairer hair poking out underneath his bonnet, gave his habitual sunny grin, and held out his arms at once. Laughing, Dan bent and lifted him from the high perambulator which May had wheeled into the scullery, where they had gathered to meet her. 'You're a solid lad!'

'Yes. It's his birthday in two weeks, isn't it, pet? You'll be one year old, won't you? Big boy now! He's into everything. Crawls all over the place.'

May moved quickly through into the kitchen. She removed her coat, hung it behind the scullery door, deeply conscious of the grubby pinafore over her thick cardigan and shabby skirt. She was very aware of the contrast she presented with the neat household, the smart, upright form of her mother-in-law, and the resplendent figure in khaki, buttons and buckles gleaming.

'They've had their supper, mam,' she said quickly to Sophia. 'All washed and ready for bed, aren't you, boys?'

'May leaves them with their Grandma Rayner when she's on day shift,' Sophia said neutrally. 'They stay at home if she's on late.'

May noted the use of the word 'grandma' and the phrase 'at home'. It was a supposedly jovial bone of contention, the term for grandmother, for May's mother preferred to be called Nanna. 'Good heavens!' Sophia would exclaim with monotonous frequency. 'What an awful name. That's what they call the dog in Peter Pan, don't they?'

May had been strongly tempted to ask her mother if she could put them all up after Jack had left. But she knew it was not very practical, with three of her brothers and sisters still living at home, and the house being so small. Besides, she knew also that Sophia had made a great effort to accept her into the family since they had moved in with the Wrights, and that her love for her grandchildren was deep and abiding. May tried nobly to discount the fact that the Wrights' house was much larger, and more comfortably appointed, where she now had the lonely but appreciated luxury of her own bedroom, not to mention the bathroom with its impressive if formidable geyser belching out hot water on demand, and an indoor water closet.

It was this haven, and the much anticipated hot bath, that she gratefully made for now.

'I'll go and get cleaned up,' she said. 'I must look a right sight. You lads talk to Uncle Dan. And be good for grandma. You're off to bed when I come down. Right?'

Minutes later, she was bending over the wash basin behind the bolted door of the bathroom, rinsing out the stale sweat and grit from her hair, which had been bundled up in the green mob cap which all the girls wore in the Armstrong's works. She raised her head, wiped the cloudiness from the mirror, and stared critically at her reflection. One thing, this short hair which all working girls had adopted now was a lot easier to manage. It dried in no time, she acknowledged as she towelled vigorously.

She flushed at the sensation her action caused in her jiggling breasts. With a shameful consciousness of physical arousal, she gazed at them, lifting them in her palms, caressing until the nipples peaked. They were small again now. They had gone down quickly when she stopped feeding Teddy, which had been some months ago. He had never been really satisfied with her milk, had come on in leaps and bounds once he began on the artificial food.

She paused before stepping into the tub, glancing down at her body. She was still slim, though a little more rounded than she had been before the children. She had to look quite closely to see the faint, silvery traces of the stretch marks, and there was hardly any fold of skin on her belly now, especially since she had started work. She found herself thinking of Dan. What would he think of her? Her looks? She shivered slightly, shocked at herself, and stepped into the water, sliding down thankfully into its enveloping warmth and fragrance.

187

She lay back, savouring the physical relief, the blessed quiet, and, above all, the privacy. She thought of the crowded changing room at work, full of the intimate smells and sights of a hundred women or more, scrabbling out of clothes or into them, wandering about in all states of undress, staring with frank curiosity or boldness. The shocking coarseness of language and of subject. It had appalled her at first, though she had swiftly become inured to it.

Nelly had been her guide and mentor; it was through Nelly that she had been taken on. It was a topsy-turvy world, she thought privately. All part of the general insanity gripping the world at present. Here they were, girls cutting their hair short, going about uncorseted, showing off their legs under short skirts, dressing up as men to do men's work. The girls at Armstrong's had to wear an overall which was really more like a kind of bathing suit, with baggy, knickerbocker legs, gathered below the knee, which left them showing a generous portion of their black-stockinged calves and ankles above the light slippers they wore on the shop floor.

And the work they did! Hard physical labour that would have been unthinkable a few years ago. She even had to hang like a monkey, clinging to one of the chain hoists for all to see, including the men who were still employed at the works, as it sped down the length of the vast shell-room, over the pointed noses of hundreds of the sinister, upended missiles which could bring instantaneous death to so many. It was ironic that she, who was so bitterly against the wicked senselessness of the killing, should now be part of the effort to contribute to it.

But then, Jack was out there. Perhaps at this very moment, firing a bullet, or crouching in some hole, while those dreadful weapons burst overhead. Her jaw clenched. It had sucked them in, this insatiable monster, as she had known it would; she had felt like some helpless victim, struggling, kicking, doomed to be violated by its implacable evil. She sat up suddenly, and began to wash herself, rubbing savagely at her skin with the flannel until it stung and glowed pinkly.

Later that night, perfumed and with hair softly waved, wearing a high-necked, frilled blouse and one of her smartest skirts, May sat on in the lounge with Dan, after the others had gone to bed.

'Don't be too long, you two,' Sophia warned. 'It's already after eleven, and May has to be up at six.'

May sensed some kind of reprimand in her tone. 'No, we won't, mam,' she answered pleasantly. 'We'll be up in a minute.' She laughed self-consciously. 'At least, I will. Good-night.'

As soon as the door had closed, Dan rose. 'How about one for the ditch?'

She laughed, shook her head. 'Not for me. I'm squiffy with all that wine. We really pushed the boat out tonight.' He nodded, poured out another whisky. She had noticed – they all had, though his parents had managed not to comment – how much he had been drinking all night, though it seemed to make little difference, apart from a healthily glowing face.

'What's it really like, out there?' she asked, when he had sunk down on the sofa opposite her. There was a brief hesitation, while he stared into the red and dying coals, and she knew he was weighing up how much to tell her. Or whether to tell her anything.

'It's a shock, at first,' he conceded. 'Not so much the bombs and the shells and the bullets,' he went on hastily. 'You sort of accept that. Anyway, there's not so much of that as you might think, unless there's a push on or something. It's the unending dreariness of it all, really. The filth, the discomfort.' He shuddered, smiled apologetically at her, then turned his gaze towards the embers again. 'Everything's so blooming dirty. And cold, and—' He shook his head again, as though he couldn't find the words.

'I think it's worse for chaps like us. I mean, that have come from decent homes, are used to a bit of comfort, privacy. It really gets you at first. Rat-infested holes to live in. Never getting a bath or a proper wash for days on end. Sleeping in your clothes, not even changing them. Lice, gut rot.' He pulled himself up, gave a short laugh. 'I'd make a great recruiter, wouldn't I? As I said, for a lot of the chaps from the tenements and such like, it's probably not so bad. Even the grub.'

She knew she was not going to get much more out of him, wasn't sure whether she wanted to. In a determined effort to lighten the atmosphere, she said,

'I've had a letter from Iris Mayfield. She said she ran into you.' She was startled at the look he gave her. His head came up, a hardness entered his face, as though she had said something offensive, to annoy him. Iris must have done something to upset him.

The smile he flashed her was false. 'Oh, she's still out there, is she?' She nodded. 'Yes, she turned up in the mess out of the blue one day. She'd come to visit – because of that young man of hers. He bought it, poor feller. Strang. Lionel Strang.'

'Yes, that's right. Awful. He wasn't exactly her young man. But they were good friends. Quite close.'

'Yes. Well. It happens these days. All the time.' For an instant, she saw behind the hardness of that clenched face, felt a great weight of suffering and pain, and had a sudden, shockingly strong urge to fling herself at him, to gather him in her arms, hold him passionately to her. She thought of them making love, and felt the reaction of her body, felt the heat of shame and excitement rise. Her heart ached sharply for Jack.

She stood. 'I'd better get off to bed. I'm glad you're home, Dan. It's so good to have you back again.' Her voice faltered. She passed close, stopped and put out her hand to rest on his shoulder. She had a feeling that he might seize hold of her, kiss her like a lover, but, instead, he picked up her hand gently, and placed the back of her cool wrist against his warm cheek, rubbed it softly back and forth, like a child with a soothing blanket, before he kissed the back of her hand very lightly.

'Good-night, May. We'll make sure that brother of mine gets back to you safely.'

'So! What have you been up to, young un? Been a bad lad, I hear.' Dan nodded towards the faint mark on the sleeve of Jack's coat, where the stripe had been. 'You'd just been recommended for your second stripe, hadn't you? Bloody idiot.'

Jack shrugged. 'Let the side down, didn't I?' It was his turn now to gesture at the lieutenant's insignia at Dan's shoulders. 'I don't think I'm cut out for higher things. Just one of the lads, me. I'd rather have it that way. You heard all about it?'

Dan nodded again. 'You were really lucky,' he said soberly. 'Just getting done for insubordination. They could have tossed the book at you.'

Jack agreed. He thought again of poor Gill's tortured face, the pallor of the young countenance.

'You're bloody lucky you're not facing a court martial yourself, Wright! Disobeying an order. In time of war. I'm putting you down as going sick for the firing detail. And on a charge of insubordination for scrapping with Blacker. All right?'

'Jesus Christ! He was my mate, sir.'

The young officer shook his head. 'I know,' he said quietly. 'It's a bad business altogether.'

Jack had been astonished at the reaction of the others in the small group. He had expected to be villified, to be abused in the way that Geordie Blacker had turned on him. But the other three were largely sympathetic. They even voiced their approval for what he'd done. 'How the hell can ye turn a gun on yer own mate? Bloody murder!' Oddly enough, Geordie's invective had been muted, too. Jack had the strange feeling that the big ex-miner actually approved of his taking a swing at him.

Jack had been taken by surprise when Sergeant Thorburn had come along the trench, shouting for him. 'Someone to see you, Wright.' And, round the corner, heading for the command post, he had run slap into his brother, smartly turned out and freshly back from his home leave.

They had squatted down in a quiet corner, Jack secretly glad that they were out of the way of his mates, for he was embarrassed by the fact that Dan was an officer.

'You've just got to keep your head down and do whatever you're told to do,' Dan said harshly now. 'The whole bloody thing is so crazy.'

'You remember Arty Mackay, don't you?' Jack answered stubbornly. 'I worked with him at Waller's. He was at the wedding.' Dan shrugged impatiently, and Jack rushed on. 'They wanted me to shoot him, man!' His voice reflected his disbelief. 'To kill him. Just like that.'

'He was a deserter!' Dan returned fiercely. 'You know what that means. He was also a thief, and damned nearly a murderer!'

'Would you have pulled the trigger?' Jack asked intensely.

'You carry out your orders!' Dan hissed. He flung his arm out towards the high parapet, where now and then the crack of a rifle sounded, and the comfortably distant deep reverberations of the bigger guns. 'Christ! We lost a thousand men in an hour last July. Twice that before noon.'

'And Art was there. He came through that,' Jack said accusingly. There was a pause while they stared at each other, as though across a barrier. Then Jack shrugged, the tension slipping visibly from him. He smiled. 'It's good to see you. Thanks for coming, Dan.'

Dan reached out, punched him on the arm. He took out the flat tin, offered Jack a cigarette. Jack's eyebrows raised.

'Du Maurier! Very nice, too!'

Dan's lighter flicked, he lit for both of them.

'May and the kids are fine. Teddy's enormous. He had a great birthday, by the way.' He reached inside his coat, pulled out a thick envelope. 'Here. Your beloved. Hot from the press. Letters from ma and dad, too. And even Cissy. Enough reading there to last you a week.'

Suddenly a mortar crew came hurrying round the angle of the trench, and set up the tripod close to the brothers. 'Oh shit,' Dan groaned. 'People just can't stand a bit of peace and quiet, can they?' They both knew that once the mortar crew lobbed a few of the bombs over towards the enemy lines, they would then move on to some other part of the trench, leaving the unfortunates in whose vicinity they had just operated to reap some unwelcome return for the mayhem they had sown.

'Walk back down the alley with me?' Dan invited. 'I've got to pop into HQ on the way back.' Jack willingly followed him, crouching as they doubled along the shallower trench which ran at right angles to the main earthwork of the front line. 'When did you come into the line?' Dan asked, when they were safely in the rear network.

'A week ago. There's rumours of a push coming up. Know anything?'

Dan shrugged. 'About time,' he mused. 'In the spring a brass hat's fancy lightly turns and all that. Keep your head down, little brother. No heroics, mind.'

Jack shook his head fervently. 'Have no fear.' He tapped his inside pocket. 'Thanks for the mail.' He grinned. 'You're not a bad sort for a bastard officer.' They hugged briefly and Dan turned away, while Jack moved back to the suddenly reawakening violence of the front line.

'Here we go. Thank God. I couldn't've waited much longer.' Geordie spat noisily, gripped his rifle as they waited at the bottom of their trench ladder. Second Lt Gill towered over them on top of the parapet, his revolver waving in his right hand. Whistles shrilled all around them. 'Come on, lads! Give 'em hell!'

Jack stared at the bobbing water-bottle swinging away at Geordie's back, cursed as his muddy boot slipped on the greasy rung of the ladder and gouged him painfully. Then he was up, the cool breeze catching him suddenly, the sense of space, the great expanse of the bright morning sky all about him.

The ground ahead was a featureless mass, bare mounds and hillocks of brown earth and muddy puddles. The shells were still whistling overhead, after five days of non-stop bombardment on the enemy positions. The black smoke of their bursts was like an uneven hedge marking the boundary of the German lines. The smoke was beginning to drift back towards them. They viewed this new 'creeping barrage', whereby the guns kept firing ahead of the troops even as they advanced, with the deepest suspicion. There was a perceptible slowness about the steady march forward, the men automatically started to bunch together, in spite of the constant roars and curses from the NCO's as they moved forward through their own defences.

The pace quickened considerably, however, when the machine guns started chattering, raking them from both flanks. Humped bodies, and crawling, groaning wounded, littered the ground thickly before they were a hundred yards out, evidence of how badly the first wave had fared.

'Bastard bombardment!' someone screamed, sobbing at Jack's left. 'The' still in the front line, firin' away at us.'

Three men just ahead and to Jack's right were scythed down simultaneously. Two dropped like sacks, the third screamed shrilly, writhed kicking on the ground, and Jack doubled up, broke into a fast run to get away from the line of fire.

The nearer they got to the enemy trench, the lighter the returning fire. The wire was flattened, blasted away entirely in places, and they saw the sandbagged redoubt quite clearly. The rounded shapes of helmets could be made out. There were isolated shots aimed at them. Another figure fell at Jack's side, then they were on the lip of the trench, and, for the first time at close range, Jack saw the grey uniformed figures, jamming the deep trench as they scrambled back to the corner, and the escape route

'Wait, lads!' a voice roared, and the long, dark shape of a potato masher grenade was lobbed after them. Jack ducked, flinched away from the brilliant flash and billow of smoke. Two of the Germans were lying on the trench floor, the backs of their tunics shredded, dark blood seeping through.

Geordie leapt with a fearful scream bodily down onto the duckboards, falling heavily against the far wall, then righting himself. Jack saw his rifle raised high, then the long bayonet jabbed at the wriggling figures, drawing fresh cries at each jab, until they lay still. Another wild figure appeared at the opening of a timbered dug-out. His face looked as grey as his uniform, his eyes blazed. They were fixed on Geordie's plunging back, and he lifted his weapon to shoot. The tip of Jack's bayonet almost brushed the mud-stained grey jacket as he fired his rifle, and the German slammed back against the timber upright. The mad eyes turned, transformed now to an expression of amazement, and then a look of ludicrously genteel reproach before the life drained and the body slumped quietly down, to rest against Jack's leg.

NINETEEN

JACK WAS LAUGHING madly with the rest of them. They were gasping, could feel the wet of tears on their sooty faces, their blood singing with the joy of being alive. 'Hey! The buggers live better than we do. Look at this!' Someone had hauled the body away from the dug-out opening. They were surprised at how deep it was. There were eight rough hewn steps leading down into the dimness. Someone produced a flashlight, and they peered cautiously into the startling length of the subterranean room, their weapons at the ready.

The sandbagged walls were neatly constructed. Rows of wooden double-tiered bunks lined the recesses; clothing and equipment hung from the rows of pegs. There were small tables with photographs and other personal items, and a long central table with a bench at either side. Tin mugs and mess tins stood on the wooden surface, scraps of food still in them. Geordie picked one up, sniffed suspiciously, then swore. 'Dirty bastards!'

They climbed out again to the daylight, and Geordie turned back to Jack. His foot prodded the corpse lying face down now in the mud, one thick arm stretched out over its head.

'Are ye not gonna get a souvenir, man? It's yours, is that one. Look. I got a helmet off mine, see?'

All at once, Jack started to shake. He felt the screaming rage mounting inside, his knuckles were white on the rifle. He wanted to smash the butt in the grinning, friendly, oafish face.

'Come on, you layabouts! We're regrouping. You don't think we're stopping here, do yer?' Sergeant Thorburn urged them on, towards the angled intersection where the grenade had burst. 'Two thousand yards in less than an hour,' he crowed. 'Next stop Berlin, me bonny lads!'

The Times crackled irritably before Nicholas Mayfield's immaculate but seamed features appeared round it.

'We're damn well getting bogged down again. This Battle of Arras – after such a splendid start, too. Those Canadians did magnificently at that Vimy Ridge place. Now we're stuck again, for God's sake. That Haig feller even tried to send in cavalry. Can you believe it?' He gave a bark of derisive laughter, then slapped the paper with his fingers. 'Casualty lists a mile long again. We'll have no one left under forty at this rate. How do they expect us to keep industry turning with attrition like this?'

'We're not doing too badly, daddy,' Iris said quietly. 'The women are filling the gap rather well, I think.'

'Hm!' he grunted. He nodded towards the paper, which he had laid down on the white cloth beside him. 'At what price, eh? I see they're talking about giving married women the vote now. That should please *your* lot.'

'Over thirty, daddy,' Iris answered, keeping her voice level. 'And only the wives. What about the rest of us? Don't we have a say? Or do we have to catch our man and wait first?'

'Well, my girl. You won't have to wait so long on the age count, will you? It'll be the other proviso that will scotch you, unless you get a move on.'

Iris smiled with bright challenge. 'Oh, I'll never get the vote in that case. I'm a confirmed old maid. On the shelf already! And as you say there aren't enough chaps to go round, anyway.'

'Come on now,' Mary Mayfield's well-experienced peacemaker's voice interrupted. 'Let's have no squabbling, please! Not on Iris's last week with us. It's been lovely having you back home, dear. The last month has gone by so quickly.'

'That's another thing,' Nicholas cut in, ignoring his wife's warning glance. 'I should've thought you'd more than done your share, with what you've been through. Don't you think it's time someone else had a go?'

She shrugged, coloured a little at the grain of truth which lay behind his words. She had been in quite a bad way when she returned from across the water four weeks ago. Not only physically, though she had lost a lot of weight, and her chest rattled like a consumptive, after enduring the worst winter conditions of the war so far. But it was her nerves which felt stretched almost to breaking point by the time the turn of the year had come. That was probably what accounted for that bizarre episode with May's brother-in-law, though, somehow, she felt there was a twisted logic to it which she couldn't fully grasp.

While she had been caught up in her almost ceaseless work, she had had little time to reflect on the appalling suffering and conditions they had witnessed. Being in actual physical danger was a kind of fearful thrill at first; the constant rumble and punch of the guns, the terrifying excitement of coming under shell fire. But then came the shock of seeing the shattering, immediate effect of savagery; the torn, bleeding bodies, the mangled, and missing, limbs, the dark flow and stench of life-blood, and the tumbled, ragged corpses. The nightmare of it all sank into her subconscious. Only now, with so much time to sit and reflect, and to relive the terror, did its sights come to haunt her.

It was not all nightmare. There were other vivid images, powerful in an entirely different, sweeter way. Ollie Willis's young face, her heartlifting girlish giggle. They shared a vehicle – many of the girls were paired up, which made things a great deal easier. They had served together in London, but their duties now, the arduous task, and the horrors they shared, thrust them together in a far closer and more intimate way than back in England.

Ollie shouldn't have been there at all. She had just turned nineteen, and looked about three years younger. She relied on Iris a good deal, for both practical and moral support, and Iris found herself relishing the protective role she was called upon to adopt more and more as the hectic days passed by.

The rain had set in early in 1916, and already the roads were being reduced to a slippery, muddy morass, choked with pack animals, vehicles, and slithering men. They were making their way back in convoy from the field hospital, when the low, grey masses of cloud opened, and the rain came sheeting down in a heavy grey curtain which made visibility severely limited. Long, black lines of trees, stripped of most of their branches so that they stood out like sombre pillars, lined both sides of the route. These, and the ditches at either side, made detour or escape impossible, and soon the surface was churned into a toffee coloured, oozing cream, feet deep in the craters formed by shell holes.

Iris slithered to a halt. The ambulance ahead was tilted at a weird angle, its front wheels bogged down almost completely in a pool of what looked like milky tea.

'I'll see what's up.' Ollie tugged open her door on the left-hand side of the vehicle and stepped down off the high running board. Iris heard a shrill scream, and scrambled across the hard bench seat of the cab. Ollie was standing staring in comic horror at the ooze which had devoured her lower limbs, lapping coldly over the tops of her gum boots, so that she was floundering, arms waving, unable to drag herself clear.

Iris wriggled over until she was sitting with her feet outside the cab, resting on the running board. She slipped her arms under Ollie's, and, grunting with effort, lifted her bodily clear of the mess. Her slim, black-stockinged feet popped out, leaving the boots still stuck in the mud, and she giggled helplessly as Iris dragged her back onto her knee inside the cab. Kneeling on the seat, still snorting with laughter, Ollie leaned down and rescued the mud-coated boots, not without some difficulty. Her stockinged feet were also liberally caked where the mud had oozed over her boot tops, and she was now smearing filthy marks all over the seat.

'Chuck those disgusting things in the back,' Iris ordered grumpily, nodding at the boots. 'And get those damned stockings off. They're filthy, too.'

'Yes, sir!' Ollie snapped, gurgling with laughter. Iris watched her as she hauled the stained cuffs of the baggy overalls way up above her knees and scrabbled down the gartered stockings, revealing her thin, pale legs as she did so. She stuck out her feet, whose paleness was marred by muddy stains, and kicked them like a child playing in water, waggling her toes. She pulled the elastic garters clear, then tossed the stockings carelessly over her shoulder. 'It's freezing,' she complained, tucking her feet underneath her as she sat.

But Iris was already inelegantly clambering over the board partition at the back of the driving cab into the interior of the ambulance. She delved into the canvas holdall, reappeared, leaning her head and shoulders back into the driver's cab, grinning in triumph.

'Here you are. Get those on. They'll keep your little tootsies warm.' She thrust a pair of thick grey socks at her companion, and Ollie squealed now with pleasure as she pulled them on.

'What would I do without you?'

'Take care of them. They're my best bed socks so don't you lose 'em or I'll beat you black and blue, you hear?'

She never had returned them. And she would do very well without her, Iris guessed, in spite of the tears they had both shed at their farewell.

Her mother's voice jerked her back to the present, and the breakfast table in the sunny room.

'Do you think they *will* send you back to France?' Mary asked worriedly. 'You're not really a hundred percent fit, you know, even now. I'm sure Dr Glen will give you a letter—'

'I'm fine now, mummy. Look at me. Growing like a house end. Anyway, I don't suppose they will send me back just yet. It'll be back to ferrying the boys to hospital from the boat-trains again, I expect. There seems to be no shortage of that sort of work,' she added sombrely.

★

May stared at Nelly's face across the narrow boards of the canteen table. There was a rather fetching oily smear on the side of her nose, and the fair curls corkscrewed down onto her brow from underneath the gathered edges of her cap. Her cheeks pouched as she munched vigorously at her sandwich, but the blue eyes were watery and washed out looking, and there were little puffs of redness beneath the lids.

'Cried me eyes out all night,' she told May virtuously. 'Didn't get a wink of sleep. Poor Arty.'

May experienced again the mixture of guilt, at her relief that it was not Jack they were talking of, and fear at the knowledge that Jack was part of the same regiment, the Fusiliers. And Dan, too, of course, she added with quick penitence. But then Jack's battalion were in another sector of the Front, weren't they? Jack had just written to tell her that he had seen Dan briefly, that they were stationed miles apart and couldn't get to meet up.

'What did it say? Did it give any details?' she asked Nelly reluctantly.

'No. Just that he'd been killed in action, like. His mother wrote us. He had my picture and address in his things. The' got them all back. I was half-way through a letter to him. I was real fond of him, ye know.' The watery eyes looked up challengingly at May.

She nodded sympathetically. 'I'm petrified every time the post comes, or there's a knock at the door,' she admitted.

'Ye'll be all right, kidder,' Nelly said, and put her rough hand on May's wrist as it rested on the table. May smiled gratefully.

But afterwards, as they were crossing the yard, heading back for the shell room, the stocky figure of Harry Turnbull appeared, near the high, double-doored entrance. He had clearly been waiting. His cap was set at a rakish angle, and his white muffler was neatly folded and tucked into the front of his jacket, the mark of distinction which picked him out as a foreman. His thick moustache was chopped off at the ends of the upper lip, the rest of his face clean shaven, but with a faint shadow of stubble. The moustache and the neat sideburns were dark, but flecked with iron grey. His upper teeth were just slightly prominent, and their even white tips showed when he smiled, as he nearly always did, particularly in the company of young women. Handsome enough, in a wolfish sort of way, May acknowledged grudgingly, but she felt that fastidious loathing, the cold hardness deep inside her at the predatory grin, the hand that landed briefly but with clear intent on Nelly's shoulder, detaining her.

Forty if he was a day, May surmised, as she carried on alone in the throng of women pouring back into the shop. Married, with bairns, and making no effort to disguise his association with Nelly, who was the latest but by no means the first, according to the gossip-loving women about May. 'At least this un's single,' one of them had laughed cynically. 'He's not keepin' the home fires burnin' for some poor bloody Tommy ower the water.'

She had quarrelled, bitterly, with Nelly, on more than one occasion. They had gone for several days without speaking, until Nelly's infectious grin and readiness to make up had carried the day. And she had defended herself with her customary vigour, guilty or no. 'You always were a little Miss Goody Twoshoes, May. Some of us want a bit of fun out of life.'

It was soon after the news of Arty Mackay's death that May first noticed a change in Nelly's behaviour. She was always so extrovert, chattering away, yelping with laughter, the focus of attention in any group she was part of. She became quieter, increasingly so, and listless. She was moved from the heavy work in the shell room, put on packing cartridges and fuses, then she was off work for several days. After the third day of absence, May made a point of going round to the neighbouring street from her parents', where the Dunns lived, to inquire after her friend.

She had half expected to find her up in her bed, so she was surprised when Nelly herself answered her knock. Her face looked white, crumpled with woe.

'Come in, kid,' she murmured, moving off the step.

The atmosphere was crackling inside the cluttered front room. Mrs Dunn nodded, muttered a greeting through tight lips. Tension hung in the air, there was a hush over the normally exuberant younger members of the family.

'The's still some tea in the pot,' Nelly's mother said belatedly.

'Er, no thanks, Mrs Dunn,' May answered awkwardly. 'I cannot stay long. My ma's looking after my two. It's a long day for her.'

'Come upstairs,' Nelly said abruptly. 'We can talk up there.'

'Talkin'll do no good!' her mother flung at them. Embarrassed but intrigued, May followed her friend out into the narrow passage and the stairs that led to the bedrooms.

'Why, have ye not noticed?' Nelly snapped bitterly, when they were both in the bedroom, which was almost filled with the high double bed Nelly shared with two of her sisters. 'Ye must be the only bugger who hasn't, I should think. Look at us, man!' she cried, when May continued to stare blankly at her. She put her hands on her waist, thrust out her stomach. 'Or do yer think this weight I'm puttin' on suits us?'

May was still nonplussed. Yes, her face was a little fatter, perhaps, she had always had a fine figure, well-rounded bosom, buxom hips— 'Oh, my God!' May breathed, as realization dawned. 'Oh no!'

'Oh aye,' Nelly echoed grimly. She sat down on the edge of the creaking bed. 'Five month gone and too late to do owt about it, the' reckon.' May was still in shock. They gazed at each other mutely, then suddenly Nelly held out her arms and burst into tears. May rushed to her, hugged her, sitting beside her, stroking at the blonde hair, nuzzling her gently, shushing her like a child.

It was a while before Nelly made an effort to overcome her grief, and May released her, while she dabbed at her eyes with a handkerchief.

'I wanted to tell you. To talk to you. I didn't let on to anybody. Except Harry,' she added bitterly. Her eyes reflected the pain she was going through as she glanced up appealingly at May. 'I know what ye think of me. And I've heard it all, 'specially lately.' She nodded towards the floor, to indicate the family gathered below. 'But I love him, no matter what ye think. I thought he would . . . he said when we first started goin' together . . . he said he would leave his wife one day. That we'd be together, when things settled down again.' She sniffed, her shoulders shook as she raised the handkerchief again.

'He wanted me to get rid of it, of course. When I told him. Time wasn't right, he said. But he talked so sweet, like he really wanted to have our bairn. Ye know?' She looked beseechingly at May, who put out her hand, held onto Nelly's wrist as it lay in her lap. 'I thought – if I did nowt, just let it . . . happen, he'd keep his word. He'd leave her. Take me away somewhere.' She fought against the sobs rising in her throat. The blonde head shook violently.

'But he went mad. The other day, when I told him I was still carryin'. Schemin' little bitch, he called me. Just out to cause trouble, he said. Said I was tryin' to ruin his life, for him and his family. Said if I didn't get rid of it, he'd deny that it was his.' Once more she fought to stifle her weeping, and blew her nose noisily. 'I've got no one, May. Me da says he won't have me around, bringin' disgrace on us. I'll have to go to the workhouse. And ye know what that means. They put you in the asylum. I might never get out again.'

Apart from her compassionate tears, May had little to offer her friend. She tried to speak with Turnbull, and was frightened at the vehemence with which he attacked her.

'You keep your busy little nose out of it! She knows what she should've done. If she's got herself into trouble, it isn't *my* fault. And don't you go spreading any stories about me, either, or you'll rue it. Got that?'

And that was that. Nelly did not return to work at Armstrong's. As spring moved towards summer, and the papers heralded another great British victory at Messines Ridge, and the votes for married women was carried by a large majority in the House of Commons, a solution of sorts was found, whereby Nelly was able to go off to stay discreetly with a cousin of her mother's in a pit village in south

Durham, where she was just another tragic young war widow with no one else to turn to.

There was even hope that Nelly might be able to keep her illegitimate baby, and make a new life for them both, but, by the time it was due in the late autumn, May's own world had changed dramatically and for ever.

PART III – Tomorrow

TWENTY

'I cannot stand much more of this! I'd rather be out—'

'It's all right, Geordie, man! Sit tight, eh?' Jack grabbed at Geordie's arms in the dimness, putting his body between the looming figure and the rectangle of light which marked the dug-out entrance. There was another almighty explosion. Dust and earth showered thickly down, while a choking cloud of brown smoke billowed in through the opening, setting them off coughing and spitting as they crouched in the two inches of water which covered the floor. The cursing went on like a chanted litany.

'Bloody country! Soddin' Belgium! To think we went to war for these bastards. August, and it's never stopped pissin' down.'

The deluge had begun on the very day they went over the top, the last day of July, for what would be the third battle of the salient around Ypres. There was to be no repeat of the initial successes of Arras, in the spring. This time, they bogged down within 500 yards of their own line, forced to hold on grimly to the first of the captured German trenches, which were swiftly flooded by the downpour. The tanks, the fearsome weapon on which so many of the strategists' hopes were pinned, proved virtually useless, trapped, too, in the sea of mud which no-man's-land became. Churned up into a featureless morass by the days of ceaseless bombardment, it had become a pitted, nightmare landscape in which men sank and drowned, and the floundering mules had to be shot through the head to save them from the lingering horror of disappearing under the surface.

As always, the enemy troops, and their guns, which they thought had been silenced by the fierce pre-attack barrage, re-emerged literally only hundreds of yards back, and now had the British front line cowering in their hard won positions, still in sight, when the driving rain permitted, of their old earthworks. Every indication was that things had ground to yet another stalemate. They had received no further orders, other than to hold the line, where they had been pinned now for days on end.

'I don't mind when we're out there!' Geordie bellowed earnestly, staring into Jack's face. 'Ye know me. Up and at 'em! Hand to hand! I don't give a shite. But this.' He glanced round pitiably at the dripping, stinking cavern hewn out of the earth, the huddled shapes pressing them on all sides. 'It's like bein' buried alive, man!'

Jack noted the rising panic in the gruff tone, the wild expression. He tightened his grip, squeezing the iron hard wrist.

'We're all right down here, Geordie,' he said, as calmly as he could. He managed a tight smile. 'Unless we get one right on top of us. And we'll know bugger all about that, eh? See you up top with your harp, bonny lad.'

He was relieved to see the white of Geordie's teeth in a ghastly grin. The wild look faded, was replaced by a shameful acknowledgement. He nodded.

'Aye. Ye're right there, Jack.'

Eventually, somehow they got the guns up in close support once again. There was no enemy counter attack, and they moved forward again, this time with only limited objectives, and with a skilful creeping barrage laid down ahead of them, so that casualties were much lighter. Jack's unit found themselves another precious half-mile or so forward, before they settled in for another lengthy stay.

Geordie Blacker volunteered for a night-raiding party. Jack had the feeling that he was trying to atone for the less than stoic behaviour he had displayed under bombardment. These night reconnaissance raids were usually indeterminate affairs, with the small handful of men, led by an NCO and an officer, crawling out through the wire and slithering through the mess of mud and barbed wire and corpses, hoping to find a wounded enemy with enough life in him to make it worth while dragging him back for questioning, with the object of learning something useful about the opposing force in your sector.

This time, Mr Gill, perhaps to celebrate his promotion to full lieutenant, led the party over the top. Jack was on duty, watched them blacken their faces, then wait for the dying of the star shells to roll swiftly over the lip of the trench. The night was overcast and chill, though the rain had actually stopped before dark. Their shapes quickly disappeared in the murk, then, as Jack peered tensely through the periscope, were shown up again with uncomfortable clarity, lying immobile under the British wire as another shell burst high to the right and lit the scene with its ghostliness. It dropped and died, and darkness covered them again.

Half an hour later, there was a flash, and a crackle of small arms fire, which did not seem to come from the German trenches. The firing grew in volume. Jack and the others on lookout were ordered to loose off a few rounds into the blackness, then a machine gun started up to the right, a German gun answering within seconds. Star shells went up from both sides, and Jack stared at the weird landscape of humps and hollows, and dark shapes and twisted iron.

Minutes later, there was a hoarse cry, and the brief flash of a torch, carefully aimed towards the trench.

'Friend! Gallowgate! Comin' in!' In spite of the password, the sentries gripped their rifles, kept them levelled. Then a shape rose upright, dangerously silhouetted against the skyline. A strangely distorted shape, until they realized he was carrying a body draped round his shoulders. Sobbing for breath, Geordie staggered to the edge of the trench, sank onto his knees, rolling his burden onto the lip in front of him.

Lt Gill was moaning softly, the front of his tunic blood-soaked, a frothy pink liquid spilling from his lips. 'Stretcher bearers!' They hurried him quickly away to the command post. Geordie slumped back, sitting in the slime oozing over the duckboards, his chest heaving.

'Get some tea,' Jack muttered, but Sergeant Thorburn had already appeared, with a tin mug.

'Drink this, son.' Jack could smell the pungent aroma of the rum, which Geordie sipped eagerly.

'Ran slap bang into one of their patrols!' he panted, when he had supped the fiery spirit. 'They saw us first. Mr Gill took it right in the chest! We got at least one of the bastards, though.'

'Well done, lad!' Sergeant Thorburn said, and Geordie beamed at this rare praise. 'You did well bringing him back like that. You might even get a medal for it. Our own bloody hero, eh?'

Geordie was proud and excited. He wouldn't turn in, and kept going over the incident, sitting there drinking tea, and talking in animated whispers to Jack's back as he stood on the parapet. The reliefs came, the sky began to show the first grey paling, before he had calmed down a little.

'I think I'll just go and see if anyone knows how he is,' Geordie said proprietorially.

He was away a long time. Jack had pulled off his boots and crawled into his shelf, lined with planks which served as his bed. He found it hard, as he always did after a night-time sentry spell, to get off to sleep, in spite of his tiredness, so he was still awake when he heard Geordie stumble down into the fetid atmosphere of the dug-out.

'How is he?' Jack whispered.

Geordie turned to face him. Jack couldn't see his features. He was just a bulky black shape. His voice was rough, devoid of emotion.

'Didn't make it. I saw one of the medics. Shot through the lungs. He died before they could get him back to the first-aid post.'

In September, the forward momentum was resumed, with the same painful slowness, and with such heavy casualties that Field Marshal Haig had to plead with the War Cabinet to allow him to continue.

The Fusiliers took part in the bloody struggle for the Menin Road, which was not decided until 26 September, by which time Jack's battalion had suffered fifty per cent casualties – eighty per cent among the officers – and only he and Geordie survived from their original eight-man squad. Then, in early October, the implacable weather interfered again, when more devastating rain fell, to add to the misery, and the suffering.

At dawn on 12 October, Jack was slumped in a forward trench, with the rest of a platoon which had been formed by a hasty amalgamation of survivors, waiting for the whistles to blow yet again so that they could force their exhausted, aching limbs up the ladders and over the top in another attack.

'What we waitin' for now?' Geordie muttered tensely. 'Sun'll be up in a minute. Let's get goin'.'

Shells were still whistling overhead in the direction of the enemy line.

'Proper gents, our officers,' a wag answered. 'They like to give Fritz a sporting chance, doncha know? Waitin' till it's light enough to see us. So's they can get a good shot at us.'

The whistles shrilled to their right, and they heard a series of cheers ring out as the initial wave started off. Jack dug his boot into the crevice of a sandbag, lifted himself from the firing step to take a peep at the landscape. He saw the uneven lines of dark shapes advancing, at a steady walk. The sky had cleared. He could see a small knoll, the jagged remains of a small copse, and a few broken roofs.

That was their objective today. Strictly limited, they said. As usual these days. No more than 1,500 yards or so. One of those villages with a name that nobody could spell, could hardly pronounce. Oh well, he told himself, using his thought as a kind of talisman. Nothing different about this one. Just like all the rest. Let's hope they could get there quickly, without too much bother. Maybe they would have time to settle for a bit. Get some proper meals, a real kip. Maybe even a bath, and a chance to change clothes, to delouse themselves. They seemed to have been living like filthy tramps for weeks.

He thought of May. Wondered if she'd be up yet. He knew she had to rise early when she was on the early shift. He tried to picture her, dirty and greasy, smeared with oil, wearing overalls just like a bloke. It upset him, but he had gallantly refrained from telling her that any more. She was 'doing her bit', that magical, hated phrase, and proud of it, too. He no longer felt that she had taken it on as some kind of defiance, paying him back for having gone off and left her.

It was ages since he had had any mail. Perhaps at this next place they would rest up again. Give the mail a chance to catch up. There would probably be two fat letters waiting for him. She wrote a little every evening, before she settled down to sleep. Posted it off at the end of the week. Just like she did that time after John was born, when he was still down in Whitby, and she was up at her mam's. Yes. Perhaps by lunch-time they'd be billeted down in some new trenches over there. Might be good uns, too. The Germans liked their home comforts. Depends how long they've been in 'em. What was the name of it again? Passion something, sarge had said.

Almost as though on cue, a deluge came down seconds after the whistles blew for them to go over. They were still picking their way through the tangled remains of the wire, and the strange, octopus like spread of twisted iron uprights that marked the perimeter of these new Fritz pill-boxes, all blasted and deserted now, their narrow trenches full of water already. The scene ahead faded behind the grey curtain, the rain hammered, drowning even the noise of the battle, streaming down faces, blinding them, soaking them to the skin, so that they felt like some prehistoric creatures lumbering through the glutinous mire.

The whole ground turned into a dancing liquid mess. Shapes were blurred even yards away, voices bawled unseen.

'Keep going, lads! Steady there! Infantry pace, don't run!'

There was a great upheaval of the liquid mud ahead, the din of the explosion strangely muted, though Jack felt the large drops of brown sludge pattering down on him. He veered round the new,

214

shallow crater, thinking, Christ! That's an eighteen pounder! and resisting the temptation to break into a run. He saw the caped outline of someone in front of him, festooned with equipment, carrying the heavy rifle with the long bayonet attached, glistening in the rain. The rapid stutter came, and the figure smashed down. Machine gun! Jack's brain warned. Turn off at an angle, get out of the line of fire. Then something slammed him in the groin, and he was spun round, down on the ground with a force which knocked the breath from him.

The ground suddenly seemed to cave away, and he was slithering on a flowing mass of muck, then down, into a deluge of icy water that covered his face and his arms before he pushed himself clear. Get up, out of this lot. Then he seemed to fall again, rolling over, and he realized he couldn't move his leg. It was warm, heavy, his left leg wouldn't work. He was in the bottom of a crater, lying in water up to his side. He squirmed awkwardly on his hip, rolled onto his bottom, trying to slide up to the lip of the crater – it was only a few feet deep; this was ridiculous. His leg was absolutely dead, heavy as lead, he couldn't move.

He lay half in the water. Why couldn't he haul himself out? There was nothing wrong with his arms, was there? Except that they wouldn't work, either. There was no strength left at all. Blighty! Ye Gods, a blighty wound! His heart sang for a second, as he felt the cool rain beating on his upturned face, then an awful, clammy wave of nausea hit him, the world spun dizzily round, and thick vomit rose to clog his throat. His breath rattled, wheezed with the enormous effort he had to make to fill his lungs. He couldn't, and the roaring, engulfing giddiness came sweeping up to claim him again, and he knew then, with a huge despair, that the warmth at his groin was arterial blood, his life-blood, pumping away. Sorry, May. Sorry, love, was his last conscious thought before the blackness took him.

He had been dead minutes when the shell dropped onto the crater's edge and tore his unfeeling body apart in a last senseless violation.

*

May felt the anger burning like acid in her when she saw Harry Turnbull making his way through the crowded shop-floor. She refused to acknowledge him, and he didn't speak to her directly, if he could avoid it. She felt the gross injustice of it, that he should still be there at all, though she had to admit he was a lot less cocky now than formerly. He no longer tried his patter on with the girls, and, as far as she could tell, kept his hands to himself, at least in the public domain of the works. It just amazed her that he had the nerve to stay on, to face them all. Some of the girls reckoned that his wife knew all about it, and that he had already volunteered to contribute something towards the upkeep of Nelly's bairn, when it was born. Which would be any day now.

She realized he was approaching her, beckoning her, his mouth moving soundlessly in the din. Oh God! she thought angrily, what does he want with me? Then she suddenly thought, with a clutch of panic, It's Nelly! Something's gone wrong! She moved away from the line of shell cases, edging her way past her fellow workers. She wiped her filthy hands on the rag which hung from the belt of her overalls.

He came close, bent and put his mouth to her ear, so that she could feel the warmth of his breath on her.

'Ye're wanted. In the office.'

She looked at him with anxious enquiry. 'What's the matter?' she shouted, but he shook his head, jerked it towards the high doors at the end of the shed, pointed with outstretched arm.

Why was he looking so solemn, so embarrassed? It *must* be something to do with Nelly! She hurried down the length of the long shop, forcing herself not to break into a run.

Mr Bellis, the shop manager, was standing in the doorway of the office, the light catching his spectacles, glinting on the high brow of his balding head. He ushered her inside.

'Come in, Mrs Wright. Bad news, I'm afraid.' She saw Cissy, dressed in her outdoor things, hat and long coat, and still she thought that something must have happened at home, to her folks, or one of the boys.

Cissy's eyes were red, and she started to cry again as she spoke. 'There's been a telegram. Mam opened it. It's Jack.'

Somehow, May found herself sitting hunched forward on a chair, the pain seeming to spread right through her. She stared at her knees, her oily hands, the fingers with their blackened nails twisted together on her lap. She leaned further forward, moaning softly, her brain trying to function.

'No! No!' she whispered. She glanced up quickly, desperately, her eyes on Cissy. 'Is he wounded? Badly?'

Cissy shook her head, the tears streaming down. She had difficulty speaking. 'Dad rang the office. Told me to come over. There's a cab waiting. A telegram came – at home. Mam opened it.'

'He's dead?' May's gasped words showed her disbelief.

'Missing, it says. Missing in action. I've got a cab waiting.'

'I'll have to change,' May said helplessly, glancing up.

Mr Bellis nodded. 'Yes, you go straight away.' He spoke awkwardly to Cissy. 'P'raps you'd like to go with her? I'm very sorry.'

'Missing. He's only missing. He'll be all right. He'll be alive somewhere.' May clutched at Cissy's arm, seizing it as she had seized on the phrase which kept a desperate glimmer of hope alive. Weeping, arms about each other, the two girls moved off towards the changing rooms.

The telegram was crumpled, where Sophia had crushed it convulsively when the boy had first brought it to the door. 'Presumed killed', was the bleak addendum, which May refused to accept.

'No!' she said earnestly, staring up at her mother-in-law's face like a child wanting reassurance. 'He'll be all right, I know he will! I'd've known if – he—' She shook her head, her voice fading.

The tears seemed to have dried up. She felt strangely light, empty inside, like a husk. But it was true, of course it was true. She would have known, would have felt it, felt something, somehow, if

Jack was dead. When was it supposed to have happened? Yesterday? The day before? Two perfectly ordinary days. How could she not have known? He must be alive somewhere, wounded, maybe. Yes, that was it. The battles must be chaotic. How could they keep track of all those thousands of men? Word would come. It must.

'The boys are out with Clara,' Sophia said. Her own eyes were swollen, her face lined with grief. 'We didn't say anything. We sent them straight out. As soon as the news came.'

May nodded, jumped up quickly.

'I'll just go up and get a quick wash,' she said. 'It's going to be all right! You'll see.' She looked desperately from one face to another, pleading for them to respond to her hope, but Edward and his wife both glanced away, unable to bear that fierce desire against the chill certainty of their own despair.

TWENTY-ONE

MAY'S REFUSAL TO accept Jack's death drove her into an arid state of limbo which added to the sense of loneliness and isolation sealing her off from those closest to her. Even when the official letter of condolence, with the regimental crest on it, came, she resisted its verbiage of 'duty' and 'gallantry' and 'honour', and 'laid down his life'. 'They send them out by the hundred,' she muttered tightly, when Edward gently tried to reason with her.

With her own mother, she was not so restrained. 'Ye gonna have to accept it, pet,' Robina argued sadly, after almost a month, when the bitter victory of Passchendaele was at last complete. The fearful cost was just being brought home by the long lists of casualties. Jack's name was among those who would be honoured in a memorial service to be held at the Wesleyan chapel in Durham Road, which May vehemently declared she would not attend.

'Why? Why should I accept it?' she cried passionately, in answer to her mother 'There's no proof at all. He could be anywhere. Injured. A prisoner.'

'He's not, love,' her mother tried patiently. 'Ye read the letter. He's not a prisoner, they'd know by now. And he's not wounded.'

May's voice rose hysterically. 'How do *you* know? How do any of you know? I know . . . he wouldn't—' the sobs came up, shaking her from within, choking off her words once more. She shook her head angrily. The brown curls flying, she dashed the tears from her face.

Only with the children could she feel close, in contact. John's great brown eyes would fill with sympathy, he would cry quietly with his mammy, not understanding anything except the plain fact of her grief. When she hugged him and whispered about 'daddy', he pictured a smiling man, in a shiny uniform, not realizing that he was recalling his Uncle Dan. 'Daddy come!' he would say, to stop her crying, and she would hug him to her breast until he could hardly breathe.

'Yes, pet! Yes!' she would whisper. But the crying didn't stop. Meanwhile, Teddy, sturdy and steady on his legs now, would cling to his mother's skirts and beam up at her, to encourage her to share his enjoyment of the world.

It was lodged inside her, the grain of doubt in her own faith, like the start of a cancer which she tried to ignore. He promised me, he promised, she kept on telling herself. He wouldn't let me down. Our life can't go on – I can't go on – without him.

She had gone back to Armstrong's after the telegram only to tell them she was quitting immediately, and to arrange to collect her final wages.

'I won't say goodbye to the girls, Mr Bellis,' she told the manager, when he had expressed his sympathy.

'If you change your mind later on, Mrs Wright,' he offered awkwardly, 'we can always find a place for you. You've been a good worker—'

'No, thank you,' May answered firmly. 'I'm finished with all of this. I was wrong. I shouldn't have come in the first place. Jack and me – we should never have let it be a part of us.'

She absorbed herself in the children, spending every minute of their waking hours with them, taking them for walks, preparing their meals, bathing them, refusing to allow anyone to help her in these tasks. They helped to take her mind from the stunning enormity of her loss, and the torment of her struggle against it.

One night she woke sobbing his name, shaking with relief and happiness. She had been dreaming, she knew, for she had seen him, just his head and shoulders, framed in the blackness of the window, looking so forlorn, those sadly expressive eyes of his just gazing at her. He didn't speak at all, just looked at her. It was ridiculous, she knew she was dreaming, because how could he be outside a bedroom window, floating about in the air? It's only a dream, she told herself, though the tears started to come, and she could not stop them.

But then she was waking up, and he was real, he was standing there beside the bed, and she could feel all the strength and warmth of their wonderful love, his blessed presence. She sat up in bed, held out her arms, breathed his name, her body racked with sobs. I'm awake! she said, still sensing the reality of him with her. The bed was warm, she reached out to where she had thought he was.

She swung her legs out of bed, the December air icy on her bare feet and legs. She sat there, on the edge of the bed, her feet on the rug. She knew at that instant. He was dead. He was dead, and he had kept his promise to her.

Teddy stirred, and May fought to stifle her weeping, biting painfully at her knuckle, while she fumbled for her thick wool dressing gown, and made her way quietly out onto the dark landing. She crept downstairs, put on the light in the kitchen. She thought about Jack, the countless times he must have come in and out of here, moved to this pantry door, sat at the table, touched this chair, for he had grown up here, he was part of this house, and so, therefore, was she. She put her head on her folded arms and sobbed heartbrokenly.

Sophia came down to her a little later, and gathered her in her arms.

'Thank God!' the older woman said, holding her. 'Now you can mourn. And let him go.'

'Dan's coming home on leave again. In the next week or two, he hopes. We're waiting for news every day.' May studied her friend's face covertly, saw the dull flush spread over Iris's features, which she tried to cover by suddenly ferreting in her bag for something, and by her animated, too bright tone of voice.

'Oh, is he? That'll be nice for you. You won't have seen him since— for . . .' her voice faded, as May nodded.

'Yes. Will you be able to get up home again? You met him – out there. Didn't you?'

'Yes. Just once.' She was still searching through her things, half turned away. 'Seems so long ago now. Absolutely ages.'

'He's a full lieutenant now. He'll probably get made up to captain.' She paused briefly. 'He's all right, is Dan. He can be a bit of a teaser sometimes,' she offered tentatively.

The violet eyes flickered away from hers again for a second.

'Yes. He was a bit of a card. I remember him at the wedding.' Again Iris felt the words come out before she could stop them, and squirmed at her own indelicacy, but May was nodding, smiling. Iris had in some ways dreaded this reunion. She felt so much pain and compassion for her friend, for she understood how strong her love for Jack was, how vital a part of her world he was. She could not get rid of an underlying sense of guilt, or shame, as she recalled the long ago quarrel, the only serious one she and May had had, that day of the picnic, over Jack's not volunteering for the forces. She was sure May must remember it now, must be stricken with bitterness at it. Iris vowed that one day she would find the courage to apologize, to tell her she had been right all along.

Iris had been too close to the conflict, been terrified by it, but, worse, had seen so much of its awful results. They had transformed her beliefs. Not only the horrors in France, and Flanders, but even closer to home. She had not been allowed to return across the Channel, but, as she had anticipated, she had been posted to London once more, where she was being trained for promotion, when, in August, there had been an air raid on Sheppey. Not by the Zeppelins this time, but by airplanes. There had been many casualties, over a hundred deaths, and a great deal of damage. She had stared at the shattered buildings; houses with their fronts torn off as though by a careless giant, exposing the pitiful privacies of furniture, hanging strips of flowered wallpaper, an ornamental bathtub hanging over a precipice of bricks at a drunken angle. Never had the phrase 'total war' been more apt.

And, like so many others, she had this feeling of helplessness, and impotence to stop the madness which seemed to have been going for ever, and would continue to do so until they ran out of lives to sacrifice. Still the powers that be tried to encourage the madness. She had quarrelled bitterly with her father, then lapsed into a hopeless silence in the face of his pounding argument.

It was even more ironic that the crusader spirit of righteous patriotism had been the one thing they had come closest on throughout her young life. Now she was disgusted by her own folly. He ranted on about the 'sacrifice', he had even used Lionel's name, and Jack's now, to justify the war's continuation. 'Has all that been in vain?' he asked her dramatically. 'Are you saying all that courage and sacrifice has been in vain? That we should give it all up, betray them now?'

Even the popular songs were still reinforcing the insanity. 'Good bye-ee, goodbye-ee,' ran the latest, on everyone's lips this year. 'I'll be tickled to death to go.'

The meeting with May had been poignant, as she had imagined. Yet there was none of the guilt, or bitterness. In fact, there had been no need of words, other than the murmur of names, then the tears of love and union, binding them together more strongly than the arms with which they embraced.

There was only this reticence over Jack's brother between them. Iris wondered if May had noticed, wondered, even more painfully, what her darling girl would think of her if she knew the truth. More than horror. Sheer incredulity, Iris imagined. It hurt her to keep such an important secret from her, yet how could she tell even May? She still could not understand it herself.

She had managed under various pretexts to avoid going to visit May's in-laws, which would add terribly to her inner guilt. Now she answered, as casually as she could,

'I doubt if I'll be able to get up north again so soon. With these air raids going on, it's not just the wounded from over the water that keep us busy.'

May's brown eyes filled with sympathy and concern.

'I know. It must be awful, is it?'

Iris shrugged, steered the conversation to different, but equally delicate topics. She put out a gloved hand, lightly touched May's.

'How are you managing? Financially, I mean? It must be diffi-cult—'

It was May's turn to blush, and to glance momentarily down at the table top. 'Well, I'm still with Jack's folks, of course. And my mam and dad help out when they can. It's not what I want. I want to find rooms on my own – with the boys.' Her lips pursed, and she gave a little nod of her head, acknowledging her own folly. 'I should have kept on with work, I know.' She looked across at Iris, the dark eyes wide with appeal. 'But I couldn't, not after . . . after what happened. I couldn't go on, doing that. Making those bombs and shells.'

'Of course not, my pet,' Iris said quickly. The grip of her hand over May's tightened, she wanted to take her in her arms and hug her to her.

'I'll get a pension,' May continued, making a great effort to brighten. 'Should be twenty shillings or more. With having the two bairns. But it takes a while to sort out.' She did not go into the details of a government who, four months after Jack had died, had not officially acknowledged him as dead, in spite of the official condolences from the war office, and the regimental memorial. 'Perhaps later on, when the boys are a bit older, I can find some work, start earning for myself.'

Iris looked at her carefully.

'I'd like to help out. For the sake of the boys. Just until things get a little easier, the pension and everything.' She saw the colour come sweeping up the young face.

'We're fine, Iris, honest. There's no need—'

'Don't be offended, please.' The hand tightened yet again on May's wrist. Iris spoke quickly, her words tumbling out in her desire not to hurt. 'It's the only way I know how to help. I can't take away the sadness, the loss, for all of you. Nobody can do that. But you're my friend, May. My closest friend. I mean that. I really do. I want to help. I think we know each other well enough now to accept help – *any* help – that we can give. I feel I could come to you for anything. You wouldn't let me down if it was in your power to do something. It's—'

May smiled, caught hold of Iris's hand in hers, and held onto it. Her expression showed how touched she was.

'It's all right. I know. But really – with Jack's folks there, we're managing fine.'

'I could help you to find a place,' Iris persisted. 'I have some money of my own. And I've no use for it. Like I said, you're as close to me as my family.'

May blushed again, with embarrassed pleasure. Her eyes moistened with tenderness.

'You're so good to me. Thank you. I know I can come to you, if need be. Bless you.' The emotion clung thickly to them. May made another effort to lighten the mood. 'But don't be too hasty. You never know, you might meet someone—' she was surprised at the vehemence of Iris's denial, and hastened on. 'You might want to strike out on your own. Things are changing. That's if the war ever finishes.'

They were passing through the fourth winter of war. John had celebrated his third birthday and he had never lived in a time of peace. With the threat of air raids in the cities, the violence was being brought cruelly home. People were starting to talk about the 'home front', while the menace of the submarines had forced a ration scheme to be introduced.

As the taxi cab chugged its slow way behind a tram car over the High Level Bridge, and the girls sat holding hands in the chilly gloom of the rear, May felt again the rising emotion she had been holding at bay ever since they had met. Like Iris, she, too, had been anticipating the reunion with mixed feelings. The last time they had seen each other, Jack had been alive. May's whole life now seemed to be divided into before Jack and after Jack. She had never lost that awareness of her loss, not for one minute of her conscious existence. And probably not during her moments of unconsciousness, for she invariably woke in the early hours to find her face wet with tears, to hear herself whimpering softly.

At least she had accepted that he was gone. The night of the dream, before Christmas, remained the most vivid memory. It would always be with her, would sustain her through real agonies of private grief in the years ahead. She was convinced that somehow he had kept his word to her, that he had come back, his love strong enough even to bridge the gap between life and death. It was an unshakable faith which she would never lose.

And yet the perception of her loss was just as great, was there inside like a physical loss, like the loss of a limb, or a sense. It trapped her as though within a bubble, cutting her off from all around her, even her own family. Except for her sons. They were inside the bubble, they were a part of her and Jack, they would always be bound to her in this special way.

It took her by surprise, the degree of tenderness she felt now for the chestnut haired girl beside her, and the responsive flow which she could feel emanating from Iris. It rose, a warm flood of emotion, a sweet, precious kind of pain, different from the pain she had endured since Jack's death. 'My closest friend,' Iris had said.

'Thank you for today,' May said, and leaned forward, pressing her nose against the fragrance of the crisp red curls at Iris's ear as she kissed her on the cheek. The expressive eyes turned to her, the strong face reddened with pleasure and gratitude, and with a vulnerability, and dependence, too, so at odds with the strong-willed assertiveness she had always associated with her companion that May wanted to crush her to her breast for comfort and reassurance.

Clara came into the living room with the refilled coal scuttle. She dropped some new lumps onto the cheerfully red fire.

'You'd better go, Clara,' Sophia said, glancing up at the ornamental clock on the high mantelshelf. 'We'll dish up ourselves, and

226

clear away. I don't know what's happened to Mr Wright. It's nearly seven o'clock.'

May was upstairs, settling John down for sleep. Teddy was already asleep in his cot in the darkness of her bedroom. John was proud of having his own room, though he liked to have the night-light burning, and he always came in to snuggle in beside May as soon as he woke in the gloom of the winter morning.

'God bless daddy and Uncle Dan. And Uncle Joe,' he remembered to add, for the youngest of the Wrights was now in uniform, too, training as an artilleryman down in the south, glad to be serving, and chafing because he had not yet been posted overseas.

May sat with John until he was asleep, then came downstairs into the quiet of the hall. Clara had her hat and coat on, was about to depart.

'It's all in the oven,' she told May. 'Mr Wright's still not back. Don't let it burn, mind.'

Sophia was trying to read the evening paper. Cissy was out, at some supper or other, being squired by a young fellow from her office who had failed his medical for enlistment in the forces.

'She's never in these days,' Sophia complained. She glanced yet again at the clock. 'We'll have to get the telephone in,' she observed. She had changed her mind lately, and had been reluctant to have a private line put in, claiming its shrilling might well disturb the boys. May knew that it was her dread of its being the instrument of terrible tidings which was responsible for her change of heart.

'Edward could have rung. He should have let us know. Sent word. I don't know what's happened to him. He's never this late.'

It was almost eight o'clock before they heard the front door click. They both met him in the dimly lit hall. 'Where on earth have you been? It's eight—'

'I had to wait. I was hanging on for news. I couldn't leave.' May's heart thumped at the sight of his face. 'It's Dan,' he said.

Sophia stared at him 'What? He's . . . not coming home?'

Edward went to her, put his arms on hers. 'It's all right, love,' he began awkwardly, as she gazed at him in terror. 'He's all right. He's been wounded. They've brought him back. He's in a hospital. Somewhere near Southampton, they said.'

TWENTY-TWO

THEY HAD KNOWN something was 'up' by the intensity of the bombardment, which began in the early hours. Though the British army's sector, on the forty-two mile stretch of the Somme front was seriously undermanned, almost a third of the infantry forces was concentrated in crowded forward positions which had not been strengthened adequately for defence. Dan had just settled down after duty when the sudden barrage of high-explosive shells started raining down from the enemy guns. He spat out the grains from the fine shower of sand which had descended on his face, feeling the quiver of the earth about him, and rolled out, cursing. He was glad he had not bothered to undress, or even take off his boots.

He had just ducked into the first of his company's dug-outs, to make sure everyone was all right, and to warn them to have respirators ready in case of gas attack, when a shell from a 21cm Howitzer landed directly on top of the earthwork. The air vanished, sucked away, and Dan felt a brief, searing blast all along his back as he slammed forward into a void of choking blackness. His brain was working. This is it! it told him, and a great sense of relief engulfed him that at last the waiting and imagining were over. But then he was struggling to breathe, the pressure on his lungs was enormous, and horror assailed him. There was pain again, all down his back and legs, as though they were on fire, then unconsciousness claimed him.

It took several hours of digging and clearing before they could get to him, and the other occupants of the dug-out, by which time it was obvious that a German offensive of some sort was being mounted. They found four bodies before they got to Dan, trapped beneath a pile of blackened timbers. His clothing had been shredded at the back, and his skin was as black as the wood which covered him.

They got him back to the casualty station, where the harassed staff decided it was worth a try, and found a place for him in an ambulance to transport him back to the field hospital. An hour later, the forward positions had been overrun, and the majority of Dan's unit were dead or taken prisoner.

His wounds were severe. For a time, it was feared that he might be paralysed. The nerves of his lower spine had been damaged; he could not move his legs, lay heavily bandaged on his stomach. Then the doctors realized that the trauma of being buried alive had created almost equally grave nervous injury. The headaches and nausea eased, as did his initial deafness, until there was only slight defectiveness in his right ear, but his apathy, and sudden bursts of frantic, sobbing temper persisted.

Once back in England, at the military hospital at Netley, on the shores of Southampton Water, he began a long, painful process of recovery. By the time his parents made the journey down to visit him, he was sitting in a wheelchair, and met them on the terrace, newly shaven, in the blue uniform, with a tartan rug tucked neatly under his armpits, to protect from the stiff April breeze.

'You look fine, son!' Edward said, with bluff over-heartiness.

Sophia was thinking how gaunt his face was, and how wild his gaze. Like a frightened animal, she thought, the tears coming as she bent forward and gently placed her cheek beside his.

'Thank God you're safe!' she whispered, and he reached up, patted her shoulder awkwardly with one hand.

'I'm okay, ma, as the Yanks say!' He smiled brightly at her. His lips compressed, he shook his cropped head violently. 'Damn! Damn! I'm sorry.' He began to shake, then sob, harshly, his head down, and Sophia hugged him tightly, murmuring as she had when he was a small child.

By June, when an Allied counter attack to the spring offensive by the Germans was under way, Dan was up on his feet, dragging himself around on crutches. He was transferred to the hospital in Deptford the day that rationing was extended to include most of the basic necessities. The doctor who examined him was optimistic that great improvement could be made. 'We might not have you playing football again, but we should be able to get you walking fairly comfortably with a stick.'

He spent many long, painful hours on the high massage tables, the male nurses pounding at him, bending back his legs, working at his lower back, or administering the electrolysis treatment which made his body tingle, then afterwards ache until he wanted to curse, which he frequently did, shifting and twisting in a constant but unsuccessful effort to find some relief.

His progress was gradual, but, eventually, as promised, he was able to discard the crutches, and walk with the aid of a specially strengthened stick, with a metal clamp into which he could fit his forearm. He walked with a rolling gait, swinging his hips, but at a respectable if slow pace. By September, he was waiting for the day when they would pronounce him ready to leave the hospital. He was not sure what the future would be like, was not even sure whether he would be able to endure for long the smothering tenderness he would have to face back home with the family, but he had had enough of institutions, and of uniforms.

He had been made up to acting captain after the débacle of the Somme, at the end of November, but now, since he had been repatriated, he had been informed that his promotion could not be substantiated and that he would remain as lieutenant. 'Save them a bit on the pension,' he told one of the nurses, a pretty VAD, bitterly.

He received few visitors. London was too far for the family to visit regularly. His parents had made one trip down, and so had Cissy. Joe, too, had managed to turn up, in his ill-fitting uniform, grinning with embarrassed pleasure.

'I don't have to salute you, do I?' he asked.

'Not if I'm not wearing a cap. Just stand to attention. That'll do.'

'I'm being posted in a fortnight,' Joe said, beaming. 'Just on my twentieth birthday. They can't keep me back any longer.' Dan fought desperately not to lose control as he listened to his brother's enthusiasm. 'It's the field artillery that'll make all the difference.'

Dan grunted. 'Just keep your head down. With Jack gone, and me a cripple, you're the last hope.'

He was surprised one day when he was sitting reading in the glassed-in annexe to the ward to find a nurse approaching.

'Lt Wright. Visitor for you. In the day-room.'

Intrigued, he levered himself up, began the slow walk along the corridor. Surely they would have let him know if it had been one of the family? Must be somebody from the unit. Someone on leave? Another walking wounded?

He saw the tall, elegant figure sitting in the wicker chair. Iris Mayfield was in her uniform, and looking very appetizing, too. He saw the crimson tide flood her features under the neat, short red hair. She smiled timidly, her leather-gloved hand came out tentatively in greeting.

'Dan. I hope you don't mind me dropping in like this, unannounced.'

'Not at all.' He stretched out awkwardly with his left hand, touched her fingers. He could sense the curiosity of the nurse behind him.

'Would you like some tea?' she asked.

'That would be lovely,' he replied. He turned to Iris. 'Please – sit. This is a pleasant surprise!'

The nurse went out. There was a group of dressing-gowned patients playing cards at the far end of the room, out of hearing.

'I should have come before. But we're busy as ever. May told me you'd been moved up here. Said I should visit you. She sends her love. Though you know that, I'm sure.'

'She doesn't know – about us, I mean?'

Once more the colour rushed to her face.

'Of course not! No one does.'

She sounded shocked. He wondered with cynical amusement whether she would have preferred not to have it mentioned, for both of them to pretend it never happened.

'I'm the one who should do the apologizing,' he continued levelly. 'I should have got in touch, somehow. I didn't know—'

'No, no! You were quite right. Best forgotten.' She blushed yet again as he gave a quiet laugh.

'Good God! Was it that bad? I really *should* apologize, shouldn't I? From what I remember, it was quite enjoyable.'

'Please!' she said. He saw the hurt, the plea in her eyes. 'Don't. I can't explain – even to myself. It's . . . it wasn't easy, coming here. It's taken me a long time, to pluck up the courage. If it hadn't been for May on at me all the time—'

'How is she? Is she coping all right?'

She flashed him a quick glance of gratefulness at his changing the subject.

'She's – of course, she's knocked for six by it. You know how she and Jack were—' he nodded, his jaw clenched, almost as though it pained him to have to acknowledge it, 'but she's bearing up marvellously. For the boys. She lives for them now.'

He nodded soberly. 'She's lucky. At least Jack ensured that the line would live on, eh?' He gave a grunt of bitter laughter. 'And how about you?' he asked, raising his voice, his tone hardening to one of taunting banter. 'Have you got a lucky young man in tow yet? Better grab one quick. There aren't too many of 'em left.'

The red spots deepened on her cheeks, she flinched and glanced away, as though he had hurt her.

'No,' she said faintly. 'There isn't anyone. I don't think there will be. Not for me.'

'Nonsense. You mustn't be put off. Not by me, at any rate. It can be a lot better than—'

'Oh, please, don't,' she cried again, staring at him pitifully. The eyes filled with tears. 'Don't make me feel any worse than I do. I know – I wasn't ready for it. Didn't know anything about it.'

'You shouldn't feel bad about it. I don't. I meant what I said. I enjoyed it. It's not every day a pretty young virgin comes along and offers it to you on a plate.'

The nurse came back, carrying the tray.

'Here we are.' She looked at Iris, who was keeping her head down. 'Everything all right?'

'Yes, thanks,' Dan said easily. 'You know how it is. It's been a long time. We're old friends. Bit emotional.'

'Of course. I'll leave you to it.' She nodded at the handbell on the table. 'Ring if you want anything.'

Iris had fumbled in her shoulder-bag for a handkerchief, and now she blew her nose vigorously, wiped at it, making a great effort to conquer her fit of weeping.

'I'd be very grateful if you'd try to forget it ever happened. Like I said, I can't explain. I was feeling very confused. Lost. Guilty, too, over Lionel's death. Perhaps because I wouldn't let—' she was blushing fiercely again, fighting against her choking embarrassment.

'Perhaps we should try again,' he said, so baldly that she let out a little gasp, stared at him in shock. 'They say the first time's always an ordeal – for the woman. It gets better. Who knows?'

She was stung into the truth. In spite of her embarrassment, she looked at him directly, held his gaze.

'It won't happen again,' she answered slowly. 'I am quite certain.' Iris could not help a small sense of satisfaction at her awareness that, for the first time, he looked a little off-balance, and less than imperturbable.

People greeted the news of the armistice at first with stunned disbelief. The rumours started, abounded, then, on the raw, damp evening of Monday, 11 November, May heard the cries of the news boys outside. 'Special Edition!' And there it was, on the front of the *Chronicle*, blazoned in huge capitals. 'END OF THE WAR'.

The normally quiet street was full of excited groups, there was much scurrying back and forth and knocking on doors. Sophia invited her neighbours in for a glass of sherry.

'Go and fetch Dan!' she ordered May excitedly.

Dan was lying propped up on his pillows. He was fully dressed, except for his jacket.

'I guessed,' he said, when she told him the news. Slowly and awkwardly, he swung his legs clear of the bed, sat up to reach for his stick.

'Thank God,' May whispered.

Dan nodded. 'I'll need a minute,' he said thickly, and she moved swiftly, standing over him, her knees pressed against his, and gathered him into her, felt his head pressing hard against the softness of her breast, his arms tight around her waist.

'Just come and have a look at it with me,' Iris pleaded. She had caught hold of May's hands in hers, was holding onto them, pulling at her like a child. 'Please. It's perfect. And such a darling little cottage with it. A room for the boys. A huge garden. It's made for us, I swear it.'

May's head was reeling. Iris's suggestion had taken her by surprise. She had seen relatively little of her since the war's end some six months ago, for Iris had remained in the south. It seemed that the hospitals were almost as crowded as they had been during the hostilities, though this time it was an influenza epidemic of staggering proportions which was keeping them occupied. The poorest sections of the community were the worst hit. Undernourished at the best of times, the rigours of the last year of the war had taken their toll. Together with the damp, insanitary living conditions, they helped the flu to spread with alarming effect, until, in London, over 3,000 people a week were dying.

Much closer to home, little Teddy had come down with it, and for several days May and her family had been sick with anxiety, while the fever took its course. He had celebrated his third birthday in bed, safely on the mend but still pale and pitiably thin, so unlike the sturdy sunny infant they had known.

Because of May's preoccupation with Teddy's health, Iris's plan had come as even more of a shock to her. Out of uniform at last, Iris had come up with an idea for the purchase of a tea-room and gift shop, in the market town of Hexham, in Northumberland, with the three-bedroomed cottage accommodation which accompanied it. She had insisted on May's coming out with her to take coffee in their favourite haunt, on the corner of Grey Street, where they had met so many times before.

'It's the chance of a lifetime,' she enthused now, over the cups and the silver pot. She squeezed May's hands again, refusing to let her go. 'Please say you'll do it. It's a dream of a spot.'

'But . . . but I can't – I mean I've got no money. Only the pension, and—'

'I told you. It's going for a song. So cheap it would be a sin not to snatch it. And anyway, I'd work you to death as manageress. And pay you slave wages into the bargain! Oh God, May. You've got to say yes, darling. The boys would love it.'

That was one of the most powerful arguments in her arsenal, and she played it with full effect. May found herself agreeing, with a quickening of excitement which soon grew to match that of her friend – and partner. Still she tried to put up some resistance, for, as Iris had declared, it did, indeed, seem too good to be true.

'What if – I mean, you might meet someone. Or get fed up with the whole thing. You might not want to bury yourself in the country—'

'Fiddlesticks! And in any case, what if I did swan off? You'd still be there. You'd have to get help. But listen.' She made a great effort to calm down. She sat up straight, fixed May with her steady gaze. 'I won't change my mind. I won't want to go off anywhere – with anyone. And the same applies to you – *you* might want to go some day. You might find someone—'

May's eyes rounded in surprise, she looked deeply shocked, and hurt for a moment.

'You know that won't ever happen,' she answered quietly. Then she smiled, reached out her hand again. 'We'll be like an old married couple, you and me. Two old maids together, eh?'

236

TWENTY-THREE

THE SUMMER SEASON was almost over before the girls were able to complete the move properly, though they *did* open up the tea-shop, and, at May's fierce insistence, kept it running through into the gloomy wet days of November, building up a small, select clientele of local ladies, who spent little, but lingered over their teas and coffees, gossiping luxuriously in the steamy fug of the taste-fully decorated café. They were intrigued by the unusual pairing. The pathetically sweet young widow, with her two delightful little boys, and the handsome young woman who spoke so well, and was so clearly representative of the modern female who might now aspire to almost anything, for, even as they sipped and spoke, wasn't Lady Astor about to take her seat in the House of Commons itself?

The rumours soon spread, were confirmed. Miss Mayfield was the daughter of Nicholas Mayfield, soon to be Sir Nicholas, one of the most influential figures in industrial Tyneside; Mrs Wright the widow of a Tommy, coming from an altogether humbler back-ground, definitely labouring class, from the terraced streets of Gateshead. Such a dear, brave little thing though, they murmured kindly, and speaks so nicely, too. And not afraid of hard work, either. Always on the go. In the shop, out the back, baking. Must be wonderful for Miss Mayfield to have a treasure like that. How long will it last? they wondered. Young rich girl's fad, playing at being a business woman. She'll soon tire of it. Meanwhile, let's enjoy it while we can. It made a pleasant rendezvous, and a pleasant addi-tion to the little town's few genteel watering holes.

Some extra trade was provided, by both the senior Wrights and by Mary Mayfield, who urged their friends to call in when on their weekend drives about the countryside. 'What a novel idea! How absolutely gorgeous!' some friends of Iris's mother exclaimed, smiling round at the decor, and the sight of the two young women in their crisp white aprons. 'My dear, you *do* look the part, you know!' they shrilled with delight.

'They think we're only playing at it, don't they?' May said, almost accusingly, later that night. The boys were fast asleep, and they were sharing their cups of cocoa in the stove-warmed kitchen before going up to bed.

'They can think what they like, eh, lass?' Iris asserted robustly. 'Who gives a bugger?'

The boys loved it. The two of them, inseparable as always, roamed about the town, and along the river banks, an indissoluble unit and thus inured to the initial slow suspicion of their contemporaries, and ready to be accepted by them, or not, as the case may be. And, as a result, were, quite quickly. May and Iris had more time, too, as the year moved towards its end, and the close of a momentous decade.

In many ways, it was a relief for both of them to be away from the pressures of their families. Iris from the constant disapproval, often sensed rather than expressed, of her father, May from the cloying, over-watchful compassion of her own parents and her in-laws. Her own folks had given vent to their feelings in their typical forthright way.

'Be tuppence to talk to yer next,' Robina sniffed.

'Ye divven' want to end up bein' a skivvy for yon Mayfield lass,' her father declared.

But she had made her break long ago, when she had married Jack. They knew how quietly independent she could be, and said no more on the subject.

Sophia was the one who took it hardest. The atmosphere at home was heavy, with loss and tension. Dan's moods, his desire for solitude, hung heavily over the household. He sat in his room for hours, the smell of his tobacco permeating the upper storey, a constant reminder of his brooding presence. He was drinking far more than he should, was liable to fly off the handle if anyone remonstrated with him. Officially, he was back at work with his father, though there were days when he did not go near the office, would disappear over into Newcastle, returning in the evening, his face florid, and head off up to his room with a few curt words.

He had been good with the boys, though, May had to acknowledge. Unless one of his black moods was upon him, he would willingly spend time in their company, take them out for trips to town, or over to the park to play on the swings. With May herself, he was unfailingly polite, with flashes of his old teasing manner, but in a gentler, kinder way. 'I wish you'd have a word with him, about his drinking,' Sophia said to her one day. 'He might listen to you. He thinks a lot about you.'

But May was reluctant, even afraid, to do so. She still had the powerfully disturbing memory of Armistice Day, of clutching him tight to her breast, and feeling the racking sobs tearing through his battered body. She had been given an awful glimpse of the private suffering he must endure, spiritual rather than physical. The knowledge of that moment, never referred to, lay between them.

He had disconcerted her when she first broached the plans for the move to Hexham.

'You and Iris?' He had stared at her, so hard, and with such a strange look on his face, that she had felt herself colouring, without understanding why.

'Yes,' she answered. 'Of course. We get on well together. What's wrong? Why shouldn't we? We'll make a go of it, I know we will—'

Still those eyes, hard, glittering, fixed on her. A twisted smile made his mouth ugly.

'If you're sure it's what you want,' he said finally, and turned abruptly away.

It certainly was what May wanted. They even resisted all family pressures and spent Christmas there, John's fifth birthday, alone with the boys, before locking up on the 27th and heading back to Gateshead for a week. When Iris's car came down the street to pull up outside the Wrights' home, at the end of the break, May was happy to see her. She felt a pang at the upright figure of Sophia, dignified as always, waving goodbye to the boys, who were chattering excitedly in the rear, and seemed as happy as their mother to be heading west out of the city once more.

They got the fires and stove going again, dispelling the damp, unlived-in atmosphere. When they had bedded down the boys, and were sitting in front of the blazing fire in the parlour, Iris said,

'How's Dan these days?'

'Drinking as much as ever. He's putting on weight, but he doesn't look healthy. It's not surprising. It's a shame he can't take more exercise. It must be awful. He still gets a lot of pain, I think. I know he doesn't sleep well, even with the booze.' She saw Iris's downward glance, the lowering of the light-coloured lashes, like a screen. She hesitated, then the harmony she could feel, the peace of being together again over their own fire, in this snug room which they had grown so quickly to love, gave her courage to continue.

'Iris. Why are you and Dan so – I dunno. What happened out in France? There's something. I can feel it, in both of you.'

The eyes flicked up to hers, briefly, with an odd, trapped expression, and an appeal.

'It was nothing. Very silly. It was a difficult time over there. We were both – the war and everything. Right in the middle of it.'

'Did he behave badly?' May pressed determinedly. 'Did he – you know – make advances?'

'My God, no! Nothing like that. We were both – we went out for a meal together, shared a bottle of wine. We both got tight. Said some silly things. It wasn't like ... back home. You've got to remember—'

'You – Iris? You're not sweet on him, are you?'

Iris gave her a startled look. She lifted herself out of the chair, knelt on the rug before May, put her hands on May's knees.

'No, I am not! I'm not sweet on anyone. Only you – and the

240

boys.'

May smiled tenderly. She put her hand over Iris's thin wrists.

'Good. I know I'm a selfish little bitch, but that goes for me, too.' Iris gave an embarrassed little laugh, started to move, and May held on tightly to her. 'No. Wait. I want to tell you: I don't know what I would have done without you. It's true. Even with having the bairns – I never thought I'd be happy, ever again. But I am. Thanks to you.'

In the following summer of 1920, the shop and café, which they had named 'The Teacosy', really came into its own. The start of a new decade coincided with the general feeling of relief, and the full realization, that the four nightmare years of war were over. People could take pleasure in simple enjoyments once more, and a day out in the country at the weekend, made easy by cheap access via the railway along the Tyne valley, was within many folks' reach. May and Iris were rushed off their feet, and were happy to take on two of the young local girls to help out at the height of the season.

'We're in danger of being solvent if this keeps up,' Iris told May. Through a contact of her father's, she had got a small firm of accountants to handle books, and was able to disguise the fact that she did not take out of the profits anything like the amount of initial outlay she had expended. 'You'll be a wealthy woman yet, Mrs Wright,' she teased, while May regarded her suspiciously.

'I don't want to be wealthy,' May insisted. 'We've got a roof over our heads and a full larder. I know how lucky I am.'

That autumn, they read that women were to be admitted to Oxford for degree courses. 'That's what *you* should do,' May said to her friend. 'You don't want to spend the rest of your life stuck behind a counter in a tea shop. Remember the votes for women? You did it, didn't you? There's so much you could do. I'll manage here. We can afford to pay someone—'

'All I did was break a few windows. Well, one, to be precise. And nearly got scragged for my pains. That was about the sum total of

241

my achievements. Listen,' she went on firmly, over May's protest. 'I've told you. This is what I want. Doing what we're doing – together. I couldn't be happier. Now shut up or I'll start thinking you want shot of me!'

In November, to mark the second anniversary of the armistice, the body of an anonymous soldier was brought back from the battlefields of the western front, to be buried with due ceremony in Westminster Abbey. Representatives from the armed forces and other organizations connected with the war were invited to attend, and Iris was chosen as the region's delegate for the Ambulance Corps.

'It's a great honour,' May argued, against Iris's professed reluctance. 'Of course you've got to go. We'll have to dig your uniform out and see if you can still get into it.'

When May received one of the regular letters from her mother-in-law, an idea began to form. 'Dan is off down to London on the 9th,' Sophia wrote, 'to attend this interment ceremony at the Abbey, and some sort of regimental reunion. He seems keen, but I'm worried that it will turn into a monumental drinking spree. He still is no easier in his mind, poor lad.'

Several times, May had invited him out to the cottage. He had called in briefly once, with a friend, another young man, both of them quite tiddly when they arrived by motor car. Dan had appeared full of ebullient life, and May was privately upset that he had not come alone. She had hoped to get him together with Iris, and start to smooth the troubled atmosphere between them. Dan was family, after all. Jack's brother. She still felt ashamed of herself at her initial private bitterness when she heard that he had survived, terribly wounded, it was true, but alive, when Jack had been taken from her.

She felt increasingly sorry for him when he returned home after his lengthy stay in hospital. She sensed that he suffered from guilt himself at having come through, and she could feel his loneliness, his inability to pick up the threads of normal life again. It must be like that for all those who had come back from that horror, they must all be scarred for life in some way, mentally if not physically. With Dan, it was both.

And of course Iris was her dearest, her closest friend. These two people meant so much to her, she wanted to share a sense of communion, of contentment, with both of them. If only they could overcome that awkwardness, whatever it was that had happened between them at that strange meet-up in France, it would be wonderful. She had cherished images of Dan's visiting them regularly at the cottage, staying in the spare room, enjoying happy times with them, and with the boys.

She decided to try to force their hand, laid down a devious scheme, with the best of intentions. She ascertained Iris's travel plans, then wrote a note to Dan, with swift conviction, and hastening to post it before she should lose her nerve.

'Iris is catching the 9.45 from Newcastle on Monday. Why don't you meet her and travel down with her? I haven't said anything. It would have to be a surprise. I don't know what happened between you two but it's time it was all forgotten or forgiven. It was a bad time for everybody. People behaved in a funny way, nobody could think straight. Surely you two can sort yourselves out, start afresh? It would make me so happy. You're the two people I care about most, except for the boys. Do what you can, eh? For my sake.'

'A bit more grand than our last little love nest,' Iris remarked, with grim humour, looking round at the comfortably appointed hotel bedroom. 'And the booze is decidedly better.'

'And I'm just as drunk,' Dan grinned, raising his glass. His face was flushed, heavy looking. He had flung his dinner jacket off as soon as they had got upstairs, then torn off his black tie and the stiff collar. 'You don't mind?' he had said, and she had shrugged, maintaining the cool, languidly in-control pose she had adopted for most of the time they had spent together.

It had taken her a while to recover from her shock at seeing him suddenly appear in the doorway of the first-class compartment, with that old, mocking grin, and that look that hotly disturbed her, and which seemed to declare his intimate knowledge of her body beneath the elegant clothing. She had soon discovered May's hand in this unexpected reunion, and smouldered with a private rage at her betrayal.

'She wants us to kiss and make up,' Dan mocked. 'We owe it to the dear girl to give it a try.'

They had achieved a degree of honesty during the long rail journey to the capital, sealed in the comfortable intimacy of the compartment, and forced to conduct their conversation in a restrained tone through the presence of two other travellers hidden behind rustling newspapers.

'I've already tried to be honest with you,' Iris said, with that note of pleading. 'It's nothing to do with you as an individual. I liked – like you. You were honest, too. You didn't try – to bully me, talk me into bed—'

'I didn't need to, did I?'

She flashed him that vulnerable, wounded look as her face crimsoned.

'No,' she murmured. 'That's true. I made the first move. I – wanted it to happen.'

'It could have been with anyone?'

'No. That's not true. It was because . . . we were – you were May's – Jack's brother.'

'You didn't fancy me, though? As a partner?'

She shrugged helplessly, again looked at him pleadingly. 'I've tried to tell you. The last time we talked, at the hospital. I was all mixed up. Feeling bad about Lionel. About myself.'

She could feel the heat of her shame all over her body. She had to make an excuse to escape, and fled to the lavatory at the end of the corridor. When she came back, he beamed at her, and began to chat in a casual manner, choosing safe topics to last them all the way to King's Cross.

'Let's have dinner tonight,' he offered as they made their way behind the porter with their bags. She accommodated her long stride to his lumbering gait. 'Then we can tell May we really *did* make the effort. I'm staying at the Kensington. Where are you?'

She managed a laugh. 'We've got a flat. I'd better come to you. The couple who look after us would be horrified at my bringing an unchaperoned guest back. Seven-thirty all right? I don't want a late night.'

She knew he had been drinking already when she arrived, but he carried it well, all through the meal. His eyes had that hard glint when they rose after their coffee.

'Come upstairs. It's far too early to turn in yet. And we owe it to May to do the best we can.'

She could see the challenge he was flinging out to her, and she was determined to meet it.

'All right,' she answered casually. 'I'll join you for a nightcap.'

After making his remark about being drunk, Dan added, 'But you're not, this time. That's the difference. I haven't managed to get you sloshed, alas. Does this mean I won't have my wicked way with you?'

'You never did,' she replied, striving to match his flippant tone. 'What are you doing?' she asked sharply, for he had slipped down the dark braces from his shoulders, and was pulling the white shirt out from his waistband. He tugged at the studs, and the cuff links, placing them on the table beside the bed.

'You were a nurse, weren't you? And there are no secrets between us. Come and do your angel of mercy bit.'

'I wasn't a nurse,' she said angrily. 'And I don't—'

'Sometimes it's sheer hell,' he cut in. 'Even with the booze and the pills. The nurses at the hospital used to rub it, sometimes for minutes on end.' He eased the shirt up, lay down on his stomach across the top of the bed.

She stared, shocked at the mass of livid scars which covered most of his back. It glistened pinkly in the electric light, with a white network of raised tissue like a spider's web. He gave a little laugh.

'That's not the worst of it. Look at this.'

He wriggled, lifting his loins a little, and pushed down his trousers, and underpants, until half his buttocks were exposed. A

245

long vertical furrow ran through the right cheek, a great white gouge which puckered up the flesh in a fishbone of hollowed tissue. He flicked the cloth up again, to cover the wound.

'Not a pretty sight, eh?' He rolled over onto his back, swivelled round, grimacing with pain, to rest his head against the bedhead. His fly buttons were undone, the white shirt-front billowing out at the V of the black material. He bared his teeth in a grin. 'But, believe it or not, I still function – as a man.' He nodded down towards his hidden genitals. 'I didn't think I would. But I soon learnt otherwise.' He chuckled. 'There was a VAD at the London hospital. Plain girl, really, with those little round glasses. But ever so nice. Good family and all that. Now she was an angel of mercy. Talk about comforting the troops. She had healing hands all right. She came along and worked a modern miracle under the blankets one fine night. And I didn't even have to lift a finger, if you'll pardon the expression.'

'Why are you doing this?' she asked softly. 'Why do you detest me so?'

'Detest you? Rubbish. You intrigue me. I don't know what you're about. I'm telling you this because I'd like another chance.'

Her face was pale, quivered with the hurt and insult. She stared down at him disbelievingly.

'How can you behave like this?'

'The age of chivalry is dead. And it's such a waste. You're a very attractive girl, you must know that.'

The pallor was replaced by a flush of anger.

'How dare you? Some of us are – there's more to our life than copulation!'

'I take it then that marriage is out of the question?'

Now her eyes widened with amazement. She almost gasped.

'You're – asking me to marry you?'

'I wouldn't mind. I wouldn't make too many demands on you. Certainly not of the conjugal variety. You'd be a free agent—'

'I've told you. I have no intention of saddling myself to a man, ever.' Her hurt, and her private shame, made her want to hit back, to hurt in return. 'Why don't you ask May to marry you? You're very fond of her. Aren't you?'

He laughed, without malice, a wry smile on his face.

'And do you think she'd say yes, even if I was the most eligible catch in the world?' He shook his head, winced again as he shifted, lay down flat, making himself more comfortable, with obvious difficulty. He pushed the shirt-front back in his pants, fastened up the buttons. 'I couldn't compete with my brother, in bed or out. I don't think there's anyone who ever will. I hope there is, some day. But I doubt it.'

He sighed wearily, folded his hands under his head. 'I'm sorry, Iris. I'm a bitter twisted sort of a chap, aren't I? You've known for a while that I'm no gent. And I *am* as drunk as a tick. Forgive my unforgivable conduct, won't you? Even though I don't deserve it. I really think a lot about you. What you've done for May – it's tremendous. And that's the truth.' He looked over at her, with an entirely different, gentle smile on his face. 'I suppose she'll make out all right, eh? With both of us caring so much about her.'

TWENTY-FOUR

'I'm pleased for you, you daft hap'orth!' May declared passionately.

'I don't want you to feel that I'm deserting you,' Iris said solemnly. 'You'll always be closest to me – of anyone. And if you really don't want me to, I won't marry him.'

May had the weirdest feeling that Iris was almost begging her to talk her out of the engagement. She was sure that, if she objected, Iris would never go ahead with it. It made her uncomfortable. She had never questioned Iris's love and loyalty to her. Theirs had been an exclusive partnership, for the past ten years. It disturbed her now to realize how much she had relied on her friend all that time. Which was why now she embraced the idea of her marriage to Dan, after this planned short engagement, with such an outward show of enthusiasm.

'I couldn't be happier – for both of you,' she said, hugging Iris again. 'I'm just amazed that it's taken the pair of you so long to get round to it. I've seen it coming a mile off.'

There was still a trace of apology in the tall figure's tremulous smile, and shrug.

'Oh, we've been kicking the idea round for a while. We haven't rushed into anything. We're not exactly spring chickens, either of us.'

'You're not exactly over the hill, at forty-one. I'll be forty myself next year, and I'm not writing myself off yet.'

I *am* happy for them, May urged herself fiercely, to reprimand

248

herself for the deep emotion she felt at the thought that the life she
had shared with Iris was drawing to a close. They had been a seemingly indissoluble unit, together with John and Teddy, ever since
the boys could remember. 'Aunt I', they called her. And now John
was sitting for his matric., at the grammar school where his fees as
a day-boy were covered by Grandpa Wright and his Uncle Dan, and
hoping to stay on for his Higher and entrance to university. Teddy
had shown no such inclination towards an academic career. He was
leaving school this summer. But his skill with his hands had long
been apparent, an inherited talent which gave his mother a deep,
private satisfaction.

Some years ago, she had come upon both boys one day in the
bedroom she and Iris shared, sniggering over her portrait, which
was hung on the wall above the bed. It was no longer taken down
and hidden in the drawer when visitors came. When they were
little, the boys had taken scarcely any notice of it – they called it
'the lady with no clothes on'. Now she explained, carefully and
earnestly, how their father had drawn it, lovingly and with great
skill, when they were first married. How proud he was, and she,
too, of it.

John and Teddy had gazed solemnly at it, while May wondered
amazedly if they had never until now recognized her in the picture.
Then they had gone over to the dresser and looked at Jack's photo-
graph. The sensitive face, and serious eyes, of the man who would
be forever young, and forever unknown, to them.

To his Grandad Rayner's huge delight, Teddy had secured a
place as an apprentice in the drawing office at Swan's, and would
lodge with May's parents when he started in September. His grandfather still worked in the neighbouring yard, and would be retiring
next year.

Change looming all around, May thought, and suffered even
more guilt at her secret, sombre reflections, in view of the forced
positive display she was making for Iris. She ticked herself off even
more harshly. Just feeling sorry for yourself, aren't you, you selfish
bitch? It would be the making of Dan, for, otherwise, he would be

drinking himself into an early grave. And yet, she would miss, too, the innocent way he had dovetailed into their relationship these past years, coming out to the cottage so frequently that the spare bedroom had become known to all of them as 'Dan's room'.

When she told the boys of Iris and Dan's forthcoming marriage, Teddy blurted, with his typical bull-in-a-china-shop approach, 'Why didn't *you* marry Uncle Dan?'

She saw John cringe, and flash his brother a venomous look, and felt herself colouring.

'Don't be daft! Who'd take me on with you two lumps? Besides, what do I need another man for, when I've already got two?'

'Aunt I! Come on! Have some more of these potted-meat sandwiches. We've got to get rid of them. Otherwise the hamper's going to be as full as it was when we brought it.' Iris, her cheeks already bulging with fruit-cake, made a muffled noise of protest, shook her head vigorously. The rakish black beret, pulled down at the side of her bobbed hair, quivered at her movement. John turned appealingly. 'Uncle Dan! Come on. Don't let the side down.'

The corpulent frame was stretched out, the legs wide apart. The stout stick, with its peculiar metal arm-rest at the top, lay on the grass beside the checked rug on which Dan was lying. His jowls showed over the dazzling white expanse of his open-necked shirt. He had taken off his striped blazer and folded it under his head as a makeshift pillow, and his panama hat rested on his brow, hiding the upper portion of his face. He lifted his right hand, waved it in acknowledgement.

'Not for me, old son. You can see how fat I'm getting. I feel like a beached whale. Your Aunt I is fattening me up like a sacrifice.'

Iris reached over, slapped at his leg. 'If you swigged a bit less ale you might slim down a bit. How many pints did you have in The County? Don't you let this old reprobate lead you astray, John.'

'Hear hear,' his mother nodded, smiling across at him from the other side of the picnic spread.

God, she looked good still, John told himself proudly. In that pleated skirt and that loose jumper, with her hair shingled like that, she looked as young as she did in some of the photos in the album. When she was a young girl. When his father had done that drawing of her.

Yes. Mam was a looker, all right. He'd seen some of the chaps staring back at the college, that secondary glance of surprised admiration. It made him both proud and embarrassed at the same time. She must have loved his father an awful lot, never to have married again. Someone as pretty as she was must have had loads of chances. He knew that many women of his mother's generation, the war widows, had remarried. But she had never given the slightest sign of wishing to share her life again, with anyone except himself and Teddy, and the rest of the family of course. And Aunt I.

The three adults still seemed to get on together, just as before. Uncle Dan and Aunt I were frequent visitors, much to Teddy's disgust at times, for the boys had enjoyed the luxury of a room each since Aunt I's departure, and Teddy was required to move back in with John whenever they had guests. Mam was as busy as ever with The Teacosy, and got on pretty well on the whole with Mrs Davies, the woman she had taken on to help since Aunt I had gone.

It had been a significant change, all the same, John felt. It was the first time he had been made to realize that things were never permanent, that change was inevitable. And now, here he was, coming up to the end of his freshman's year at Hatfield College, in Durham, and just about the happiest fellow in the world to be so. The cathedral – he could see the rose window from his room, across the narrow cobbled street; the chimes from the tower often kept him awake at night. Palace Green, the river banks, the magnificent view of the 'twin grey towers' from Prebend's Bridge.

Today was the college Founder's Day, which was why his three visitors had turned up, complete with picnic hamper for a lunch along the bank. The May weather had been kind, and the fresh greenery was buzzing with the promise of a good summer. Before that, though, loomed the terrors of first-year exams. This would be one of the last chances everyone would have to relax before the

251

grind set in, at the end of the month. He found himself once more surreptitiously studying his mother. He felt his stomach tighten a little with apprehension.

This evening – in fact, very soon now, when they got back to college – he would have to introduce her to Jenny. Jenny Alsop, a tall girl with dark honey hair, and beauty unsurpassed as far as John was concerned. She was at St Hild's, doing the teacher training course of two years. She was completing her first year, too, and John didn't even like to think about the year after next, the year of his finals, when Jenny would no longer be here. It was too bleak a prospect to dwell on. She insisted she felt the same way about him – though she couldn't, he kept on reminding himself. No one could feel as strongly as he did. He adored her.

Mam would, too, once she got to know her, he was sure. Wasn't he? Why then this sinking feeling in his gut? He had never had a girlfriend, not one. And his female cousins were all younger than he was. Kids, still. It was just that he and mam and Teddy – and Aunt I, by extension – had been so close. Natural enough, when there was no male figure around; no father, except for the photographs, and the hallowed regimental citation framed on the wall, and the name etched with thousands of others on white marble, in a place in Belgium which she and Aunt I had taken the boys to a few years back. The bond between mam and her sons was so strong; he almost felt disloyal now at the burning love he felt for Jenny.

'This fellow, H.G. Wells, is a gloomy so and so,' Iris's strong tones interrupted his reverie. She was glancing at the newspaper, and he remembered fondly how she had always kept them on their toes, encouraging them to take note of what was happening in the world. 'He's still predicting there'll be another war, in ten years' time at the latest.'

'Thank God we've done our bit then, eh?' Dan's voice came from under the hat. 'It's a load of rot, though. Hitler's got too much sense to plunge Germany into another catastrophe. He was in the last lot.' He raised the hat, turned his head towards John. 'You lot won't have anything to do with it, anyway, I suppose. You'll be with our Oxford conchies, won't you?' He was referring to the debate at the Oxford Union the previous year, when the motion was put that 'this house would in no circumstances fight for King and Country.'

'Of course not!' John began vehemently, when May's voice cut through the argument, with palpable emotion.

'Who in his right mind wouldn't be?' she demanded. 'Anybody – anybody who went through the war—' she paused, choked by her passion. She swept an arm about her. 'Just look at us – all three of us—'

Dan's head lifted, he struggled with great difficulty into a sitting position.

'Sorry, May, love,' he said quietly, while John felt a swift rush of warm admiration for his honesty. 'My big mouth again.' He shook his head. He paused, then his voice came back to its normal heartiness. 'No clouds today, eh? Blue skies, pretty lasses. All we ask, eh?'

May joined him in his effort to dispel the sudden despond. She scrambled up, shook out her light skirt.

'Come on. Let's get cleared away, then we'll walk back along the banks. I need to freshen up before the hop tonight. Give your old mummy a hand, number one son. I'll show you I can still show a nifty leg on the dance floor!'

'Hello, Mrs Wright. I'm so pleased to meet you at last.'

At last! May studied the pretty young girl in the green frock. She was trying so hard to be self-possessed, sophisticated. But May was not fooled. She could recognize the pink glow which was sweeping up under the make up. Why the 'at last'? She realized now why John had been so on edge since they had got back to his room in college. He had tried to disguise it. She had been secretly disappointed, hurt even, for she thought it was because he was embarrassed, or maybe even ashamed of his family. Of her and Iris, statuesque since she had turned the forty mark, and of his uncle, with his heavy, flushed drinker's face and jolly manner, and awkward, crippled gait.

But it wasn't that at all. It was because he had been waiting tensely for this little baggage to arrive. Which meant that he must think quite a lot about her, otherwise he wouldn't be so het up. And the young madam's 'at last' was intended to let her know that she had been on the scene some considerable time, and had her hooks firmly into place.

All at once, May remembered Iris's words of four years ago, just before she had married Dan, when the short engagement was in progress. It was one of the few real quarrels they had had. It began as always over trivia. John had gone to the tennis-club dance, had gone on to a party, and stayed until dawn. He had been drinking, and dancing, there had been girls there. She had torn into him next day, ordering him to stay in and work up in his room. 'Christ, May!' Iris had said, when he had left the room. 'The boy's sixteen! He's practically a young man. You've got to loosen the apron strings a little. It's bound to happen one day. Don't spoil things.'

'Oh! So you think I'm too domineering, do you? Turned them both into mammy's darlings, have I?'

'You might well do if you don't ease up on them a bit.'

'Well, it'll be easier from now on,' May retorted, with rare spite-fulness. 'At least they won't have *two* mummies running their lives for them!'

Iris had been hurt, she knew. They had both kissed and made up later. But the chiding words came back to her now, as she faced this slim, smiling figure, and saw the poorly concealed admiration for her shining in John's eyes. And then she remembered, with poignant vividness, a much earlier scene, in Jack's home for the first time, when she had faced a smilingly hostile Sophia and the dislike and distrust of the older woman had hit May like a brick.

She swallowed hard. 'Yes. Pleased to meet you. What a lovely dress that is. You look very nice.'

The pink deepened, the smile grew broader. She saw the vulner-ability in the blue eyes, the dawning relief.

'Thank you.'

She squeezed the girl's hand firmly.

'It's a warm night. Let's take our drinks out on the terrace, shall we?'

They moved out, the blaring noise of the band in the hall fading. There was a smell of Sweet William and Stock. The flagstoned area of the garden was crowded with dim figures, the conversation muted and peaceful after the noise of the dance hall. Suddenly, there was a strong burst of singing, men's deep baritone voices singing in unison. People turned, in smiling curiosity.

'That's the JCR lot, in the bar,' John explained apologetically.

His mother was standing, her face lifted up towards the sound, a rapt expression on her face.

'What – why are they singing that song?'

He looked at her in some surprise. 'I thought you knew, mam. That's the college song.'

She turned to Dan. 'Listen!' she said.

He stopped, turned his head towards the lighted windows where the sound came from.

'Need to get it on my good side,' he laughed. He heard the words clearly then.

> If I could plant one tiny seed of love,
> In the garden of your heart,
> Would it grow to be a great big seed some day,
> Or would it die and fade away?

May had moved away a yard or two, into the shadow. She stood very still, her back turned to the group, and John looked at her uncertainly. Iris, sensing something, moved over to her at once.

'Are you all right, love?' Iris asked tenderly.

Then Dan came, swinging over to them. He propped his stick awkwardly against his hip, and put both heavy arms up, rested his hands strongly on the backs of their shoulders, standing between them.

'You've done a grand job, lass,' he murmured to May. 'He'd have been proud of you.'

May turned to him, smiling. Her eyes shone. 'I'm sure he is,' she answered.

There were other young men's voices raised in song on that May night. They were students, too, and their deep, unified tone sent shivers of emotion tingling through the spines of all who heard them. Their songs were not of sentimental love, but of a resurgent, nostalgic national pride, of former glory days, soon to come again. The torches lit up the night sky in Nuremberg, 700 miles and more from the college hop. The flames flickered on the red and white banners, stamped with the black spidery symbol which would, again, let loose the mad carnage of war around the world.